# GABBIE S. DURAN

Copyright © 2013 by Gabbie S. Duran
Cover art by ©Sarah Hansen at Okay Creations
Editing done by Stephanie Lott

Printed in the United States of America
First Edition: October 2013
Second Edition: January 2014
Library of Congress Cataloging-in-Publication Data

**www.facebook.com/authorgabbiesduran**

Duran, Gabbie S.
   Unspoken Memories (Unspoken Series) – 2nd Ed
   ISBN-13: 978-0692211892 ISBN-10: 0692211896

   1.   Unspoken Memories—Fiction
   2.   Fiction—Romance
   3.   Fiction—Contemporary Romance

*This book is dedicated to all the runners,*
*family, and friends effected by*
*the tragic event that occurred on April, 15<sup>th</sup> 2013.*
*They might have tried to stop us,*
*but as runners we unite as one. We never give up,*
*we keep moving forward, and we keep running on.*

# Chapter 1

I CAN HEAR voices, two to be exact, a man and a woman. They're speaking quietly, but loudly enough that I can clearly make out their conversation. I can't open my eyes, no matter how hard I try, and they feel heavy, so I keep them closed.

"I can't leave her, she's our money ticket!" he says in a very stressed tone.

"How much good is she to you now? She's in a coma! We don't know if she's ever going to wake up." This comes from the woman, and from the way she says it, I know she isn't happy.

"Well, it doesn't matter, I need a little more time to try to figure out how to access the rest of the funds. The longer she's in this coma, the more time is on my side, and the more money we get."

Okay, this is where the conversation is getting really interesting to me. At this point I'm trying hard to open my eyes, but I keep getting pulled somewhere else, back into the darkness. My gut feeling is telling me keep my eyes closed and keep listening, so that's what I'm trying to do, I'm fighting the pull that wants to take me away.

"Well, I'm tired of being your fuck buddy, I want more!" she demands of him in a very loud whisper.

Fuck buddy? Why is she being a fuck buddy, and whose? But by the way she tells him this, I have a feeling that she's been his fuck buddy for a while.

"Look, when we started this you knew to never expect more, but if she's going to be a vegetable for a while, I'm thinking things are going to change very soon."

This doesn't sound good. I start to freak out, especially since I feel like a vegetable right now. No matter how hard I'm trying, I can't move a muscle. I wonder, are they speaking about me?

The room suddenly grows quiet, and I start to hear footsteps fading in the distance. I believe they're leaving, because I hear the opening and closing of a door.

I give it a couple of seconds, but the room is still silent. I can finally relax. Then all of a sudden, the darkness begins to take over again.

I FEEL MYSELF slowly waking up again and I let out a light moan. I can feel the grumble of it traveling down my chest, and it aches. I feel so groggy and weak. I don't want to wake up, but my body is not allowing me to fall back asleep and I try to slowly open my eyes. It's hard at first, but after a couple of blinks, I'm successful at bringing them to a slit. My body is aching as I try to lift my arm. It feels like weights are holding it down, but I'm able to move my hand,

I think.

What is that sound? It's a constant beeping, coming from the side of my head, and it's speeding up as I move in that direction. I try to lift my arm to get to it, with little success because there's something tugging at it. When I look down, I see an I.V. attached to my arm, why would I have an I.V.? I attempt to completely open my eyes. I see an older lady who is wearing nurse's scrubs walking towards me. She must have done something, because the loud beeping is finally gone. It was making my head hurt, so I'm grateful she finally made the thing shut up.

"Good, you're awake," I hear her say next to me.

I feel her warm hand grab onto my wrist while she looks down at a watch she is wearing. I'm still confused. I have no idea where I am.

I manage to move my head a little and take in my surroundings. It looks like I'm in a hospital room. It's white, and almost empty, with only a couple of chairs in each corner. There's a flat screen on the wall directly in front of me, with a clock to its side, stating it's almost six. Underneath the clock there's a white board with writing on it. I guess my nurse's name is Karen, since that's the name on the board.

"How are you feeling Ms. Adams?" Karen says, still focusing on her watch.

I lie there wondering why I'm even here, and how did I get here? Wait, what did she call me? Is it my name? It doesn't sound familiar.

I have no clue where in the world I am and I don't like it.

"Where am I?" I ask Karen, wondering why I would be in a hospital room.

She looks up from her watch, with a blank face.

"You're at Washington Memorial Hospital, Ms. Adams." Then she goes back to looking at her watch.

I'm still confused, why is she calling *me* that name? "Who's Ms. Adams?" I ask her, confused.

She lightly snaps her head up again to look down at me, and draws in her eyebrows. Her smile has disappeared and goes directly to a frown. "Why, you are, of course," she informs me.

She places my wrist down back on the bed, patting it lightly. "I'll just page your neurologist and we'll go from there, okay?" she says as she turns and walks out of the room, leaving me there still baffled by the whole situation.

A couple of minutes later, another lady walks into the room. I'm assuming she is my doctor because she's wearing a white coat. She looks Indian and young. But as she's walking in she has a smile on her face and it gives me a bit of hope.

A bit.

"Ms. Adams, I'm Dr. Kumar, your neurologist. How are you feeling, dear?" she enthusiastically asks me, while swiftly grabbing my chart, opening it, and beginning to review it.

Knowing the truth will never hurt, I say bluntly, "I feel like shit and I really have to pee."

This makes her laugh, as she pulls out what looks like a pen from her coat pocket, walks to the side of my bed and leans above me. I realize it's a flashlight as she starts flashing it back and forth between my eyes, making me flinch. It burns my eyes and if my arms didn't feel so weak, I would have swatted that darn thing out of her hand.

Trust me, I try, but I quickly give up the notion. Once she's done shining the death light at me she replaces it in her

4

coat pocket and walks to the end of my bed to pick the chart back up and starts scribbling notes into it. I lay here staring at her.

As she's still scribbling, the nurse walks in again with a new I.V. bag and busies herself with changing it while the doctor asks me, "Ms. Adams, would you be more comfortable if I have Karen here remove your catheter so you can go to the bathroom yourself?" She is still staring down at the chart making notes.

I nod my head in agreement, but can't help asking again, "Who is Ms. Adams? You both keep calling me that name?"

The doctor quickly snaps her head up, while the nurse stops fiddling with the bag and they both stare at me in shock.

The doctor immediately looks at the nurse. "Call her fiancé, and order a CAT scan STAT." Then she looks down at me and says, "We'll just order some more tests to make sure there isn't any swelling remaining and go from there, okay?" She finishes with a smile.

Still very confused about what is going on, I nod my head in acceptance and hope that I'll remember something in a couple of minutes. Right now the only thing I keep thinking about is the conversation I heard earlier. Or I think it was earlier. I really have no idea when it took place. It almost feels like it only happened a couple of minutes ago and I'm really anxious to find out who was in my room. But more than anything I still have to pee.

My thoughts must have taken me away for a couple of minutes because the nurse has managed to remove my catheter and with a lot of assistance, I'm able to sit up on the bed. At first my body is wobbly and unbalanced, but after a few minutes I find the strength I am searching for and make my merry way along, holding onto the nurse for dear life. The metal stand holding the I.V. bag follows me the whole way.

It's hard to walk when you have something attached to your arm following you around. After the first tug at my arm, I want to yank the thing out myself. However, the nurse keeps saying I have to leave it in, since it is providing me with the fluids to increase my health.

That is the only reason it stays in.

After some major maneuvering, again with the nurse's help, I'm finally able to relieve myself in the attached bathroom. I can't go at first, knowing she is standing there staring at me. But even after asking her for some privacy, she only moves to the doorframe of the bathroom.

Finishing up what I needed to do, and washing my hands, I take a moment to stand in front of the mirror and stare at my reflection. Other than needing to take a brush to my hair, I look perfectly fine.

Or at least I think I do for someone who is in the hospital.

Actually, I don't recognize myself at all. You would think that I would at least recognize my reflection, but it doesn't come to me. So I stand there staring at myself and take in my features.

My hair is blonde, very long, and my eyes are a very bright green. I'm also tall. I remember being at least half a foot taller than the nurse, towering over her a bit. Another noticeable thing is that I'm very skinny. Don't I ever eat?

When I hear the nurse knock on the bathroom door making sure that I'm still okay, it distracts me from my thoughts, also reminding me that we have to go get my CAT scan done right away. I exit the bathroom and allow her to lead me to the bed, laying me back down.

An hour later, after being put through a cocoon-like machine, as I'm being wheeled toward my room, I see a man rushing in my direction. He's practically running when he walks and he looks exhausted. I don't know who this man is, but by the way he's looking straight at me and still walking in my direction, he knows me.

He looks to be in his mid-thirties and he's wearing an expensive looking suit. He's lean, and tall, but not too tall. He has disheveled black hair, as if he's been running his hands through it. He has stress lines around his face, but at this moment his face is lit up and he's happy to see me.

"Oh honey, you're finally awake, I've been so worried about you," he says as he reaches me, giving me a kiss on my forehead. I'm really confused about who he is because I don't recognize him. But when my mind takes in his voice, realizing that it sounds very familiar, I panic.

If I were still hooked up to the monitor at this moment I'm pretty sure it would be making the crazy noises from earlier, because my heart rate is going crazy. First it feels like it had stopped, and now it's accelerating because I'm freaking out.

This is the voice, the male voice I heard the last time I heard anything, but he's alone this time. I immediately start looking around, thinking about the other mystery voice, the one that belongs to the woman, expecting to hear it any minute. But I don't.

He follows, as the nurse continues to push me back into my room and once we're all in the room, he starts attacking the doctor and nurse with different questions. There are so many, it's even confusing to me. Although the most important one is how much longer I'm going to be here now that I've woken up. That particular question is the one I care about the most, because I'm pretty sure when I leave here I don't want it to be with this guy. The uncomfortable feeling I'm getting from him is not making me feel good.

I keep staring at the guy, hoping that I would recognize him somehow, but I can't. He seems worried about me, so obviously he must be someone important. However, I think about the ominous conversation that took place that included his voice.

Wanting to know who he is, I demand, "Who are you?" I say out loud, looking directly at him.

He snaps his head to look at me and he's disoriented, like I just asked the stupidest question in the world. At this point it sounds pretty stupid to me too, but I really need to know who this stranger is.

He frowns, bringing his lips into a flat line, and finally he says, "I'm Bill, your fiancé."

*Now I'm screwed*, I think. I'm pretty sure that this was the voice I heard with the woman the last time I tried waking up. But, why would my fiancé be someone else's fuck buddy? I don't understand. Right now my life is starting to feel like some kind of soap opera and I'm obviously the starring actress.

They're all still looking at me, as if they're waiting for me to say something.

"Abigail, are you sure you're feeling okay?"

If my throat weren't hurting so much, I would be saying right now: *No you dumb ass, I just woke up, my body feels like shit, and you guys keep calling me a name I don't recognize.*

Another thing to add to the list is that I don't trust them! But I keep my mouth shut knowing this is the best thing to do. However, I ask again, knowing that I still need an answer. "Who's Abigail?"

Ignoring my question, Bill turns to the doctor. "What's wrong with her, why doesn't she know who she is?" he demands, pointing his hand in my direction.

Looking perplexed over the whole situation herself, she answers him, "She seems to have had a bit of a memory loss." The doctor gives him a calming look like this is normal. "She may just need time to recover properly; it can happen with patients in her situation."

Shaking his head, Bill grabs the bridge of his nose with his thumb and forefinger, sighing to himself. He's still quiet, like he's concentrating on what he's going to say next. I think he's still shocked.

I hate that they won't give me any detailed answers.

"What happened to me?" I ask, looking between Bill and the doctor.

Everybody is looking at me, still very uncertain whether to tell me or not.

Bill walks up to my bedside, taking one of my hands into his, and drops his head, looking gently at my face.

He takes a breath and begins, "A friend of ours was having a party at a hotel downtown, and as usual we had a room there so you could get ready. As we were waiting for the elevator to go down to the party, you became impatient, and decided to take the stairs instead. You were wearing some really high heels and lost your footing on one of the steps and hit your head pretty badly on the way down." He pauses like he's concentrating on what to say next, then carries on, "When you arrived at the hospital you had some really bad swelling in your brain, so the doctor here suggested that we put you in an induced coma."

I'm trying to absorb all the information he's just given me, then I look over to the doctor, still really confused about the whole situation.

"How long have I been in a coma?" I whisper, staring at the wall ahead of me, holding back the tears that are fighting to come out.

She looks to Bill first, then directly back at me answering, "It's been a little over four months since the swelling in your brain reduced and we reversed the medication. You didn't wake up right away," she calmly states, as if reassuring me everything is fine.

I look over in Bill's direction and ask again, "Who are you?" I want confirmation.

He's now starting to look irritated by my question, but he responds again. "I'm Bill, your fiancé, baby."

His answer still throws me for loop and I panic a little.

Why would my fiancé want me to stay in a coma? He had looked relieved to see me awake, but I keep replaying the conversation in my head, wanting to doubt it. I know what I heard. It was loud and clear, even if my eyes weren't open.

Another thing that comes to mind, is why does he have someone else as a fuck buddy?

My panic is obvious to Bill, so he says, "We've been together for over a year now. We met at one of your shows over two years ago when I became your agent and we started dating a little while later. It was love at first sight for me." He tries to reassure me with a smile. But I'm not buying it.

I look over at the doctor with a look like, "Please tell me he's kidding." From the way she's looking at me, I know she believes his story. Bill looks up to the doctor and begins asking how soon I'll be able to go home.

While she goes over the lecture about needing my rest before leaving, I block out their bickering at each other.

This is when I start reciting a number in my head, 951-555-2945. It comes to me naturally, like I've called it regularly.

That's weird, why would I be thinking of a phone number at this moment? I'm happy that at least something is coming back to me.

"Bill, what's your number?" I ask, loud enough so they both can hear me.

They both snap their heads in my direction in confusion for asking such a question, but Bill automatically answers. "555-6213, why?"

Mmm, not the answer I was expecting, so I try again, "Is there any other number I would call you at?"

I must have excited the doctor because her face is beaming. "Are you remembering something Abigail? Whatever it is, it might help. What is it you remember?"

Bill looks excited as well, but knowing that it isn't his number, I just fib. "I thought I remembered, but it was only a glimpse of an area code, then it disappeared." I lie to both of them, keeping the number to myself.

"By the way, what is the area code here?"

The doctor is the first to speak up, "206."

That is definitely not the area code I'm remembering. They're both still patiently waiting for me to say something, so I answer with the only excuse that I can think of at the moment. "That's why I asked Bill to recite his number hoping it would spark something, but I was wrong... I'm sorry." I look at them, disappointed.

Seeming just as irritated about the whole situation, Bill turns to the doctor, barks at her to order more tests, wanting to know why I've lost my memory.

The neurologist decides to steer the conversation by saying, "Although she has a bit of a memory loss, she might get it back in time, especially once she goes home and begins to see things more familiar to her. Give her time; she's just woken up," she says before her lips go into a frown of disappointment as well.

"Then how soon can she go home so she can start remembering?" he barks at her, making me flinch from the anger in his tone.

He turns to me and with a nicer voice says, "Baby, your name is Abigail Adams. You're a famous model. Is it ringing a bell?" he questions with desperation.

I shake my head and pick at the imaginary lint on my blankets. The name doesn't ring a bell at all. I want it to, but it doesn't.

Bill notices my lack of response and begins fumbling with his phone like he's looking for something and once he's found it he brings the phone close to my face for me to look into the screen. On it is a photo of myself with a whole bunch of make-up, and I'm half-naked.

"See, that's you at your last photo shoot, it's for *Vogue!*" he says with enthusiasm. "Of course you know who you are, you're legendary since this cover came out." The phone is still in front of my face as if he expects the light bulb to turn on in my head.

When I shake my head at him he only sighs again, clearly disappointed. I think I'm really beginning to irritate him.

He moves to the corner of the room dragging the doctor with him, by the arm, and in hushed tones he begins speaking with her. The nurse walks in at this moment saving me from having to look at both of them, knowing that they are discussing me and leaving me out of the conversation. The nurse entertains herself by fluffing my pillows, in an effort to make me more comfortable, but I know she's really just trying to be nice about the whole situation.

They both stop talking and look over in my direction and he smiles. The only trouble is that his smile is worrying me and I want it to go away. It's the type of smile meant to reassure me that everything is okay, when in reality it's not.

Knowing the situation is not going to get any better until my memory comes back, I bring up the excuse that I'm tired so they will leave me alone. Right now I want to be alone and sleep. My body feels drained, even though I just woke up a couple of hours ago. What I really want is for Bill to leave, so whatever excuse I can give them to make him leave works for me.

They all leave me to get my rest and as I'm left alone with my thoughts. I wonder again if I'm wrong about Bill. I keep trying to convince myself that maybe it was someone else, or maybe I had dreamt the whole conversation. I begin to get drowsy and my eyelids start to feel heavy, dragging me into sleep once again.

*In my dream, I feel happy, and I see this guy who's laughing with me.*

*He's young, early twenties, good looking, and really fit. He's taller than me, enough so that I have to look up at him. He has a narrow looking face, his hair is a dark color, with dark chocolate brown eyes, and thick lashes that are long, curl, and make you jealous that he has them. But what really catches my attention is his smile. He has a smile that just makes you melt inside and it makes you smile with him. He's all sweaty and I note that he looks like he just finished work-*

*ing out. Or has done something that has made him breathe really fast and heavy. His shirt is soaked and he's chugging water from a water bottle like he's dying of thirst. I look at my surroundings and notice that we are in a park, at the end of what I think is a trail, and in the background there are a lot of tall trees. He then throws his arm around my shoulders and says, "Keep up that pace and we're definitely going to PR this race."*

What race and what PR event is he talking about? My dream begins to fade away, and I'm trying really hard to ask him what's going on, or who he is?

Unfortunately, I can't get the words out of my mouth. I want to know his name, but he quickly fades away.

As I open my eyes, I notice it's morning again, with the light coming in through my hospital room window and a new nurse is taking my blood pressure, which is what must have woken me up.

Now that I'm awake, I take the time to focus on trying to bring back some type of memory. When the nurse sees that I'm awake, she informs me that Bill came by early this morning while I was still sleeping and dropped off my stuff.

I turn my head and notice an iPad on the side table and I reach over and grab it. Wanting answers fast, I start to Google my name, "Abigail Adams." Right away all kinds of articles and images come up.

According to the Internet, I'm not a world famous model, but I am in high demand in the states. Thanks to my current fiancé, slash agent and manager, I was on the way to becoming the most highly sought after model in recent history. Before my accident, I had wrapped up an interview and photo shoot with *Vogue* that was going to get me those international shoots I was working towards.

I was born in Seattle, but raised in the foster system. My mother died when I was twelve, leaving me to be raised by the state in different foster homes until I was discovered at the age of eighteen. I had begun with small photo shoots for a local agency that kept me financially above water for a couple of years, until I met Bill, making him my current agent and manager.

On the Internet there were a ton of pictures of me, some from different interviews, photo shoots, or pictures that must have been taken by paparazzi when I was out and about. There were so many, it's almost like I wanted to be constantly photographed or spoken to, which feels a bit disturbing.

After reading a couple of articles and flipping through what seems like thousands of photos, I feel even more confused than when I started. The only thing it's proven to me is that I was a shallow and conceited person who only cared about herself. For some reason this makes me feel like crap.

After sitting in my room for most of the day, I notice that I start to feel jittery and stressed. Eventually, I start twitching my leg, swinging my foot back and forth and feeling trapped like I want to get out and do something. It is driving me crazy.

I blame it on being immobile for so long.

On this second day since I've woken up, the doctor is in my room giving me my routine daily check-up. Bill showed up this morning, but most of the time he's on the phone barking commands at someone about a deal that he's trying to close. He's been coming to visit me as often as he can, but I have a feeling that he'd rather be at his office than with me.

He claims that he is really busy at work, but that he misses me badly and wished that he could spend every waking hour with me, but I doubt it. It takes all of my willpower not to roll my eyes at his response. Even when he kissed me that first day, it didn't feel right. There was no emotion in it on my part. As if to confirm that my body didn't really know him. It had worried me, but I had made it a point to Bill that I just needed time and space, giving him an excuse to stay at a distance.

Before I could even allow him to think things were back to normal, I had to figure out what normal was.

# Chapter 2

"SO EVERYTHING LOOKS okay with your test results, the fact that you're up and moving around shows excellent progress. I'm ordering you not to take it too fast for the next couple of days. Make sure you have the nurses continue to assist you with everything while you're here," Dr. Kumar says, looking very satisfied with my progress.

The memory loss hasn't improved, but what can I do at this point? That's not under my control that I know of.

"Okay. When can I go home?" I ask enthusiastically, hoping once I get home my memory will come back automatically the moment I walk through the door. I know it is wishful thinking, but honestly, the only reason I want to go home is because all I can think about is that phone number and the young guy in my dream. I hoping this number will answer a lot of questions for me.

I tried calling the number from the hospital, but since it was a long distance number, the call wouldn't go through. I also tried googling the number, but I got a dead end there as well. So now I have to learn the art of patience until I can get to a phone that would allow me to make the phone call.

Hanging up the phone, Bill looks my way and says. "Yes Doc, when can she go home? I've already scheduled several exclusive interviews and we need to figure out when those will take place."

Rolling my eyes at his remark, it doesn't surprise me that he'd already be trying to make money out of me. That must have been the deal he was barking about on the phone. I look at him, but he's not even looking at the doctor or me anymore, he's just messing with his phone.

Figures, if I can't make him any money at this moment, I'm not important to him

The doctor gives me the normal sigh and sympathetic look when it involves Bill and tells me I should be able to go home within the next couple of days. As long I take it easy at home.

This excites me and I start thinking of what I need to do when I get home. First thing I plan on doing is hiring a private investigator to help me figure out this whole mystery with Bill. If he were cheating on me, a PI would definitely be able to tell me.

THE TRIP HOME ends up being a circus in itself. Somehow it was leaked that I was being released from the hospital, so there is a crowd of paparazzi outside the hospital as we are leaving. Still, thanks to the hospital security and a private bodyguard, who Bill apparently has on staff, we're finally able to get out of there and back to our apartment safely.

As we enter the elevator in our apartment complex I notice that Bill has to enter a card and code into the panel. The mechanical voice then states, "Penthouse."

I look over at Bill and think, of course, anything less for this guy just wouldn't do.

As the elevator doors open into a foyer, the first thing I notice is that the sitting space is all decorated in black and grey, and it's got a modern feel to it. There is no color in this place at all; even though there is furniture in the room it feels empty of life. Even the pictures on the wall are in black and white, and I notice they're all of me. See, self-absorbed.

"This is the living room," Bill immediately starts giving me a tour, "the dining room, as you can see, is to our left, and the kitchen is further down through that door." He points in the direction of the dining room.

"The bedrooms are down the hallway to the right and my study is through this door over here." From the windows leading out into a balcony, I can see the Space Needle and the view is breathtaking. The sun is beginning to set and the buildings surrounding us are beginning to light up.

"I have to go out tonight for a business meeting. Since you probably want to rest, I won't ask you to come with me."

I nod at him thinking, *I don't care where you go at this point as long as I'm left alone.*

I start to walk down the hallway towards the door at the very end of the hallway. As I walk in I realize this must be the master bedroom. It has a huge king sized bed making it the focal point in the middle of the room. When I turn to the right, I see the entrance to a bathroom and head straight in there. It's large with marble counters and a huge white marble bathtub that could easily fit two people. Across from it is a walk-in shower with different showerheads coming out of the ceilings and walls. Why would anybody need that many showerheads? I look ahead and see two doors next to each other. I continue walking to the door on the right and my breath stops.

I'm walking into the biggest closet I've ever seen, with rows and rows of clothing and shoes. The closet looks like half the size of the bedroom alone.

"You did always complain you never had enough clothes and shoes, but this isn't even half of what you've got waiting in boxes," Bill states behind me.

I turn around looking at him. "Why would I need all these clothes and shoes?" I'm totally confused why this wouldn't be enough.

I'm beginning to think that the look that Bill keeps giving me is the only look he knows how to make, which implies that I'm an idiot.

"You refuse to wear anything twice. You keep a stylist on the books to come and rotate your wardrobe out every couple of weeks. Designers send you their stuff just so you can be seen wearing it."

This isn't making any sense. "So what happens to the stuff that I've already worn, does it go to charity?" I ask him, at a loss for words.

Bill throws his head back and laughs, "You're funny Abigail, but since I don't have to pay for any of it, I really don't care."

Dumbfounded, I say, "Now, that sounds stupid."

Bill gives me that look again and he shakes his head while walking out of the closet.

Feeling very overwhelmed at this point, I leave the closet, following Bill out into the middle of the bathroom. When I reach up to him, I see he is beginning to remove his clothes and he's about to start unbuttoning his pants when I stop him.

"What are you doing?" I ask with hesitation.

He is standing next to the shower doors and looks up at me shocked. "I'm undressing so I can take a shower, what does it look like I'm doing?" Then with a mischievous look, drawing his eyes to a hooded slit. "Do you want to join me?" he asks.

"No thank you, I'll just go look around the apartment and hope that it will trigger my memory."

He places his hands on his hips. "What? You love taking showers with me, especially because you love having sex halfway through." This makes me look away as I begin to blush. I push past him into the bedroom, leaving him chuckling behind me.

He might claim I like having sex in the shower, but right now the last thing I want from him is sex anywhere.

Ignoring him, I begin walking down the hallway, leaving Bill to shower alone. Strangely, the pictures of myself make me feel uncomfortable, so I look away from them, trying really hard to absorb the setting. However, it feels cold and sterile, like nothing is supposed to be touched, or lived on. When I take a seat on the black flat leather sofa it feels very stiff, just like I had imagined it would.

Why would I want to live here? It doesn't feel like me.

Bill enters the living room, dressed once again in a designer suit most likely custom made for him. He walks over in my direction, stops in front of me, with his hands in his pants pockets, and stares at me.

I'm beginning to feel very uncomfortable with him standing there analyzing me, like I'm a child in need of a reprimand. I *hate* that he makes me feel like this.

"Mary left you something to eat in the fridge. Your cell

phone is also on the counter with my number in it if you need me, but only if it's an emergency since I'll be in a business meeting after all."

*Of course, I wouldn't want to bother you,* I think. I'm pretty sure he's planning on meeting with the mystery voice, so no interruptions would be wanted. Or, he really is going on a business meeting, but most likely so he can figure out a way for me to make him more money now that I'm awake.

Then it occurs to me that I don't recognize the name he's mentioned either, the name doesn't sound familiar. "Who's Mary?"

He takes in a deep breath, closing his eyes in frustration. Judging by his reaction, he's obviously mad, but what does he expect? For my memory to just turn on like a light bulb?

Although, at this point even I'm wishing it would.

He lifts his head to look at me. "Mary's our housekeeper. She comes three times a week, but she usually doesn't cook since we eat out most of the time."

He stands there still staring, with his right eyebrow raised. He's making sure I absorb every word he's saying.

Raising my eyebrows right back at him I respond, "Of course," with a nod of my head.

Bill takes his hand out of his pocket and looks down at his watch, checking for the time. "Okay, if you don't need anything else I'll just head out."

Without waiting for a response Bill turns away straight into the elevator, leaving me there in the apartment alone.

I sit there wondering whether I should feel relieved, or saddened, that he's already leaving me. Either way, he's gone for now, and I can now try to figure out who the hell I really am.

I head to the study first thing, but as I try to turn the door-knob I discover that it's locked. Why would it be locked?

Giving up for now, I head to the kitchen counter and pick up my so-called cell phone and begin to scroll through the contacts, but I don't recognize anybody's name.

I enter the number I have been thinking about for the last couple of days, but it doesn't match anybody in my contact list, so I decide to send the person a text with a simple, "What's up?" I'm hoping to get a response.

I wait a couple of minutes, but I don't get one right away, so I figure I should try another number. It's to a private investigator that my doctor recommended.

When I asked her to recommend one, she didn't ask why, but I have a feeling she knew why I would want one. The guy answers right away and after explaining that I need his services, we set up an appointment to meet within half an hour at the coffee shop down the street. Ending the phone call, I grab a banana from the counter and eat it on the way back to the master bedroom.

Knowing that I can't go out looking like myself without being recognized, I head straight into Bill's closet in hopes of finding something that will work. I immediately spot an old Harvard hoodie and grab it, along with a Mariner's baseball cap that has seen better days. I throw the hoodie on and place the cap on top of my head, tucking my long hair into the inside back of the hoodie, and pulling the hoodie lid on over it. Once I'm happy with my disguise, I head out of the building.

## Chapter 3

"SO YOU EXPECT me to find out exactly who you are?"

The private investigator ends up being an older gentleman, in his late forties. He looks more like he should be working in a library, with his wool suit that's probably seen better days, and his gray hair, than working as a PI. Nevertheless, according to the doc, he's the best, and at this point I need the best.

His name is Frank and he's been in this business for over twenty-five years.

"Yes. I mean I know what my name is, and I know what I do. That's easy stuff I could get from Google. However, I need to know all the private stuff, like bank account info, and what the hell happened to my life?"

His lips go flat like he's considering whether I'm pulling his leg or have lost my mind. He takes a sip of his coffee and he stares at me. He's analyzing me, I can tell. So I sit there, drinking my coffee as well and wait for him to give me an answer.

Frank finally replies, "Okay, I'll do it, but it's going to cost you."

"Price doesn't matter, according to Google I'm loaded, so I'm pretty sure I can afford it."

This intrigues him and he slits his eyes, once again analyzing me.

"What I don't understand is why you don't ask this hotshot boyfriend of yours?"

"I don't trust him. I have a feeling he's hiding something from me and since I've conveniently lost my memory I have to go with my gut feeling," I say, shrugging my shoulder.

Frank nods his head once and takes another sip of his coffee.

"I have another request." I pull out the piece of paper that I've kept hidden in my pocket. "I have a number in my head that I keep repeating and it's not matching any of my contacts in my phone, I want all the info for the owner." I hand him the piece of paper so he can study it.

"Well, you don't want much do you?" he says sarcastically. "But it won't be hard."

"Good, how fast can I expect the info? At the rate you're charging me, I should expect something within a couple of days, right?"

The starting rate Frank quoted me in the beginning of our conversation could support a family of four for at least a year. You would think that he'd use some of it to fund his wardrobe. It's a shame he's a man, or I could give him most of mine. I'm desperate at this point, so I would gladly hand over half of my income if he were to request it.

Okay, maybe not that much, but almost as much.

"I should have the info on the number within twenty-four hours, the rest of the requested information within seventy-two. Being that you're a celebrity your info might be tighter to get into."

This doesn't sound good and he sees my apprehension. "I said 'tighter' not impossible. Nothing's impossible for me."

As we've been having this conversation I've been setting up a private email address for myself. The phone I have already has one entered in it, but I don't trust him sending any information to this address in case Bill has access to it, which I'm sure he does. I give Frank my contact information and we depart.

As I'm walking back into my apartment building and towards the elevator, I realize that I don't have one of those card thingies to get back up into my apartment, so I have to do some major sweet talking with the doorman to walk me up. He promises to have a new card for me to pick up tomorrow.

On the way up to my apartment, I'm checking my phone to see if I've received a response from the number that I texted earlier. Realizing that I haven't, I automatically feel disappointed. The phone distracts me as I walk off the elevator at my floor, so I walk right into Bill.

I look up into his face, and he looks pissed as he says, "Where the hell have you been?"

Walking around him I head into the living room. "I went out; I needed to get some air," I say as I start to take off the hoodie and baseball cap and throw it onto the couch.

He sees what I've been wearing and he's astonished. I bet he didn't think I was smart enough to disguise myself with his clothing before going out.

"You're not supposed to leave the building without security, it isn't safe. I told you to stay here, you could have been mobbed," Bill says in a very condescending tone.

I roll my eyes at him, really, a mob? He's just pissed I didn't stay home like the dumbass little girl that he thinks I am at this moment.

"I wasn't mobbed and I really doubt anyone recognized me, since I don't look like her when I'm wearing a hoodie," I say, pointing to the exotic looking picture of me on the wall above the fireplace, as I sit in one of the uncomfortable armchairs in the room.

Looking at the picture, I wonder, where are my clothes and why the hell am I naked and showing my ass off to everyone that's walks into my living room?

That is going to be one of the first ones to come down.

With the look he's giving me I know he's about to start ripping me one, so I quickly stand up. "If you're done lecturing me, I'm going to bed, I'm really tired. Goodnight," I say, clipping off what he was about to say.

My response takes him by total surprise because his eyes go wide and his mouth opens in an O.

I brush past him, moving my legs as fast as they can walk to one of the guest rooms I've chosen for myself, locking the door behind me. I walk over to the bed. Taking off my clothes on the way, I climb into bed, and under the covers. I lay there on my side, staring out the window at the twinkling lights of Seattle. My body feels so exhausted from frustration, and eventually sleep begins to overtake me.

*I'm running outside, along what looks to be a trail made of dirt. There are trees everywhere along the course that I am running. I am surrounded by Mother Nature.*

*The season must be changing to fall or winter because there's a beautiful orange mixed with yellow taking over the leaves of the trees. The air is crisp, with a bit of a chill in the air, and it's taking me to another world completely. One I want to stay in.*

*My body is relaxed as I focus on every breath. I inhale the aromas that Mother Nature is throwing at me. The sound of the wind as I glide through it, mixed in with the birds singing to each other, adds to my footsteps every time they make contact with the ground below me. The pounding of my feet hitting the pavement with every step I take forward, striking them with the vibration of the contact. The swinging of my arms back and forth is matching the tempo of my legs as they stride, one in front of the other. The farther and faster I run, the better my body feels. As if I'm releasing the toxins I've been holding inside my body. Forcing myself to let them go.*

*Even though my breathing is beginning to feel labored, the distance I'm putting behind me is making me happier and happier with each step forward I take. I feel like I want to do this forever, but I'm quickly pulled away from running when I begin to hear ringing in my dream. The sound pulls me from my nirvana, irritating me. The sound stops, then starts up again.*

I slowly wake up and realize it's my phone ringing on the nightstand. Who in their right mind would call me this early? Okay, it's not that early, since I see the sun shining through the windows of the room.

Groggy eyed, I grab the phone and mentally curse it, noticing that the number says "Private." I'm skeptical about answering, but then I remember that Frank has promised to contact me today. If this isn't him, I might just cuss whoever it is on the other end for ruining my perfect dream.

"Hello," I say, still groggy and out of it, as I answer the phone.

"Hey Abigail, it's Frank." Okay, he's safe. "I emailed the info on that number you wanted."

This wakes me up in a heartbeat. I sit straight up and get excited. He promises to keep me updated with the rest of info that I need and ends the call. At this point I don't care about the info I need about me, I want to know more about this number.

I open the email, it's not a huge document, but it has enough information to keep me happy. Including an address and personal info for the owner of the number. As I open the document, I notice the picture that Frank has provided and it's the same guy from my dream. My breath catches, as my heart starts beating rapidly.

I throw back the covers, hop out of bed and get dressed in the clothes I threw off last night. Walking over to the bedroom door, I open it slowly. After making sure the apartment is quiet, I step out, and according to the time on my phone it's 8:42 a.m.

Okay it's more late than early at this point.

The apartment seems pretty empty of Bill since it's silent, so I head to the bathroom and take a quick shower.

After showering, I brush out my hair and put on some light make-up. One thing that I've discovered, and I'm very thankful for, is that I don't need much make-up. My face has a natural beauty to it, and I'm taking full advantage of that today.

I head into my closet, standing there confused and feeling overwhelmed. I pick what looks like simple skinny jeans and a beige cashmere sweater, next comes the shoes, for some reason this is where I feel like I want to start salivating with admiration. I can't find a pair of flats or tennis shoes for the life of me, so I grab a pair of black Prada pumps and put them on.

After taking a quick look in the mirror to make sure my outfit looks good, I'm satisfied with myself and I'm ready to go.

As I was getting ready I multi-tasked and called for a hired car. By the time I get downstairs it is waiting for me. I pick up my new key for my apartment at the front desk, and head out of the building, on my way to Portland.

Chapter
4

ON THE CAR ride to Portland, I take the time to go over the information the private investigator gave me.

The guy's name is Matthew Garcia. He was born and raised in Riverside, CA. His parents died when he was only seven, leaving him to be raised by his sister, a sister who had passed away as well about six months ago with her husband in a car accident. He's currently in his senior year at a private college in Portland, with the assistance of a full ride football scholarship. Instead of living on campus like normal students, he had his own residence off campus, a house. His sister purchased it for him before his sophomore year, and he currently lives with a roommate, another player on the football team.

As we get closer to the city, I give the driver the address and he enters it into his navigation system. At this point I start to get more and more nervous because I have no idea what to expect. My palms are getting sweaty, my stomach is in knots, and my knee starts twitching again. I've noticed it's been doing that a lot lately when I'm anxious or nervous. I still haven't figured out how to make it stop.

We pull up to the house and the driver parks next to the curb in front. The first thing I notice is that it looks like a normal family sized house. I was expecting it to look like a frat house being that they're college kids, but it looks really taken care of.

As the driver opens my door I notify him that I have no idea how long I might be, but to stay close just in case. He nods and informs me he'll be waiting in the car.

As I'm walking up the driveway, there are two cars. One is a Jeep, but what catches my eye is a beautiful, black, classic Dodge Charger. Its glossy paint makes it shine in the sunlight. I think that it is one sexy car.

I walk up to the door and ring the doorbell. My stomach is turning from the nerves and I feel like I'm ready to throw up.

At first, there isn't an answer, so I ring it again. After a minute I start to feel impatient with still no answer, so I start to knock hard on the door.

I finally hear a voice yelling from inside, "Yeah, yeah, hold your horses man. I'm coming!"

The door opens and the first thing that hits me is the smell. Whoever's in there is spending some major time with someone named Mary Jane. I'm almost high just with the first whiff I take.

I'm disappointed when I notice who has answered the door. It's not who I was expecting, which saddens me. It isn't the guy in the picture that Frank sent me, which must mean this must be the roommate, or a friend. He has some running shorts on and a tight white shirt, which stretches over his broad shoulders and muscles.

This guy is huge. He has bulging arms that look like they might be wider than my legs, and probably are. He's a bit shorter than I am but I'm wearing heels after all. By the looks of this guy he must spend some major time in the gym with the weights. His hair is cut really short all over and he's staring at me like he's trying really hard to figure out who I am. Then he shakes his head like he's trying to clear it.

"Is Matthew Garcia here?" I nervously ask.

I'm pretty sure from the smells I'm getting from inside that he is stoned out of his mind.

He is still staring at me, with bugged eyes and his mouth slightly open. Finally a light bulb must have turned on in his head because he finally speaks.

"Dude, you're Abigail fucking Adams."

I roll my eyes. "No, I'm Mother Teresa, I've come to save your soul. Again, is Matthew Garcia here?"

I'm afraid by the way he's staring at me that I'm getting nowhere. But, the now confused look on his face makes me smile for the first time since all this drama has started.

"Dude, are you sure you're real?" Then tilting his head, he says, "This must be some really good shit."

I'm getting really frustrated at this point, I came all this way and right now I'm kind of out of patience from the three hour drive up here. As I'm about to give up, I hear a voice behind the guy staring at me.

"Dude, what the hell are you yelling about out here?" says the voice walking to the door.

When I see who it is, I get excited. It's him! It's really him. I stare at him and even though I know his name already, just seeing him makes my excitement accelerate. Like I really know who he is and I've missed him so much. The next thing I know I'm throwing myself at him and hugging him.

He automatically catches me, but stiffens up as I'm holding him, awkwardly tapping me on the back with his hand and then pushes me away so he can get a clear view of my face. He looks confused, which is understandable when a stranger throws herself at you. I realize what I've just done, and it makes me feel embarrassed; I shouldn't have thrown myself at him like that.

That's when he notices who I am and his jaw drops open. Matthew is holding a joint in his hand, looks down at it, and then hands it over to the first guy. "Here dude, I think this shit is making me trip."

Big muscled guy standing next to us gets all excited and starts hopping back and forth on his feet. "Dude, I'm pretty sure you're not tripping, if you see what I'm seeing." He draws his eyebrows forward in doubt.

"You're seeing her, right?" He doubts again with his eyes. "It's Abigail Adams standing in our front door, right? I'm not tripping?" He gets excited again.

I decide to take over the conversation. "You're Matthew Garcia, right?" I ask, looking back at Matthew, and trying to ignore a gawking muscled guy.

He nods his head and responds, "Just Matt," and holds out his hand for me to shake.

As I'm shaking his hand I say, "Is there any way I could come in? I have something I need to talk to you about," and walk through the front door without waiting for the invitation.

They both look at each other with dazed looks and nod. Matt takes a couple of fast steps to catch up with me and begins to lead me into the house. The first thing I notice is that even though I have heels on, we are matched in height, and he's not as physically big as the first guy.

He's still fit all right, but he's slim and he has enough toned muscle to make you drool. He looks like he should be in an Abercrombie ad.

As he leads me into the living room, he starts guiding me with his hand on my back, and I can feel the warmth in his touch. It sends a thrilling chill through my body and I get excited. Then I quickly remember that this guy is still a total stranger at this point, so I'll just blame my excitement on my nerves.

When we enter the living room, I notice it looks like a typical college bachelor pad. Dirty carpet, stained couches, beer bottles, and cans are everywhere. Including on the coffee table, and counters.

Taking a quick glance at the available seating, I take the only recliner in the living room. It's made of what looks of black leather and I'm praying it's clean enough for me to sit on it.

Facing Matt, I notice he and his friend are both staring at me and they still have confused looks on both of their faces.

I fully take in Matt when he sits down and although I saw him in my dream, seeing him in person is not the same. He's hotter than the picture or my dreams.

He's wearing a shirt similar to the one in my dream, a cutoff and it's emphasizing every muscle on his chest, and arms making him look sexier.

His arms are just as toned as his legs and he's sitting there with his elbows on his knees leaning towards me, which emphasizes a tattoo on his right outer bicep. It's an angel wing, starting at the top of his shoulder, ending with the tip at his elbow.

It's beautiful.

His eyes are light brown and the curl in his long lashes make those eyes pop. As I'm looking straight into his eyes, my body starts to melt from weakness.

How in the world can someone's stare do this? I feel like I can't concentrate from him looking at me with those eyes.

The smell of their friend is still really heavy in the air, so maybe that's what's causing this reaction.

"Can you open up a window or the patio door maybe, please? I need to stay focused for this conversation."

Yes, I'll just blame it on the Mary Jane.

Matt gets up and heads over to the patio door, opening it. Once he's done, he comes back, and sits down on the edge of the couch closest to me once again.

"Umm, not that we're not happy you're here, but, why are you here?" he inquires. He seems pretty calm and under control. Even though I bet he's as baked as the other guy.

The entire car ride here I was thinking about what I would say when I arrived, but now my mind is blank, so I start talking in hopes that it will come back to me.

"Well, you see, I woke up from a coma last week and I seem to have amnesia, I have no clue who I am, other than my name, and that's only because I guess that's really not hard to figure out. But, in reality I don't have any memories at all. The only thing that I could remember when I woke up was a phone number." I'm pretty sure I'm rambling at this point, but I continue, "I hired a private investigator to track the number and he gave me your information," I say, pointing my chin towards Matt.

Although I have my hands folded into each other on my lap, they're starting to get sweaty again from the nerves. The two guys are both still looking like they're trying to absorb the information, this must be a major buzz kill for their high, but I need answers dammit, and at this point they are the only answer to the number in my head.

"So let me get this straight? Other than your name and Matt's number, you have no memories at all?" the big guy asks, trying to figure all this out as well.

"Yes," I whisper, looking down at my hands.

Matt is staring at me with his head cocked to the side.

"But, why my number?" He points his finger at himself. "I've never met you and I'm pretty sure we don't run in the same circle."

"I don't know either, but I kept repeating the number in my head, like it was natural to me. I tried texting you last night but I didn't get a response."

Matt takes his phone from the coffee table and starts searching through it. "Oh, you must be the 206 number. I was kind of busy at the moment with someone," he says with a wicked grin. "It was a pretty crazy night last night. Since I didn't recognize the number I just ignored it. Sorry about that," he says, placing the phone in his pocket of his shorts.

With the look he's just given me I'm pretty sure it was a girl that he was busy with, and I don't blame him. If I knew him well enough I would want to be busy with him myself.

Where the hell are all these thoughts coming from? I have to get myself under control.

I try to distract myself from my carnal thoughts. "It's okay, I pretty much headed over here as soon as I got your information this morning from the PI. I needed to see you, the thing is I've had dreams about you too," I say, looking straight at Matt, while biting my lower lip in embarrassment.

He thoroughly looks confused, his eyebrows arching up in surprise. I know exactly how he feels. The other guy's mouth drops in an O, and then he lightly shakes his head, before taking a sip of his beer. He hands it to Matt and he does the same. I sit there in silence, giving them time to absorb everything I've said.

Trying to distract myself again from the tension beginning to build up inside, I begin to look around the room. I notice on one of the walls is a wall hanger, with a whole bunch of medals hanging from them. I walk over to them and start looking at them. As I'm doing this I get another memory.

*This one is of Matt and me. A crowd of people surrounds us, as a medal is being placed around my neck. I feel ecstatic as I hug him. I'm looking behind him at the big banner that says "Portland Marathon" in big green letters. It's a finish line, and by the year on the banner it was just last year.*

Excited, I turn to face Matt, this must be where we met. Even though I don't remember reading anything on Google that said I was a runner. "We ran the Portland Marathon together last year, that's where we must have met."

He gets up and comes over, standing next me and begins concentrating on the medals with me.

"No, we didn't," he clips out, keeping his eyes on the medals.

"Yes, we did, you're in my memory and we're crossing the finish line together." At least I'm pretty sure we did. "They gave us our medals together and we are hugging."

Matt looks back at me with a fierce glare. His chest is beginning to rise and fall, and he's shaking his head. His eyes turn glassy like he wants to cry, but he's fighting to hold it back. "I didn't run it with you," he insists, staring at me in disbelief, and irritation laces his voice. "I ran it with my sister. It was the last race we ran together."

Oh shit! Then why am I having this vision? It has to mean something, I was pretty sure it was my memory. It felt so real.

"Are you sure? I'm pretty sure I'm right. I clearly see the memory. It was only last year, and I'm pretty sure I was there with you. "Can I be wrong? No, I wasn't asleep when I got this one, so I know it has to be an actual memory. "What about my dream of running with you in the park, that has to be real, right? There's a trail in the background."

This makes Matt angry and he walks away. "Now you're fucking with me. Who's been feeding you her info?"

"What are you talking about, nobody is feeding me info. I told you these are the things that I remember. The *only* things I remember. Besides you, and who is this she you keep referring to?"

Matt shakes his head and runs his hands through his hair. The other guy starts drinking from his beer again. He looks like he wants to put his two cents into the conversation, but he decides to stay quiet. He's trying to absorb everything, and so am I.

"Look, there is no way you would have those memories unless somebody told you about them."

He goes quiet but then his eyes light up, like he's just realized something. I'm soon disappointed when he says, "I get it. She must have done some designer shit for you. That's when she must have mentioned that she ran the marathon. She talked about running to anybody who would listen."

I shake my head in disagreement, wanting him to believe me.

Matt starts pacing the small space in the living room in front of the patio door. What is he talking about, and who would design something for me? I start biting my thumbnail and pacing the room next to him, but in the opposite direction, causing us to pass by each other. That's when the other guy stands up from the couch.

"Dude, you guys need to stop that walking shit, you're making me trip."

I'm irritated again as I look over at him and snap, "Oh, shut it Trey, I'm trying to figure this out!"

He drops his beer and it lands on the floor with a loud thump. Matt's body spins around fast, facing me, and he covers his mouth with a fist.

"Holy shit, she even sounded like her when she said that!" the muscled guy states.

What is he talking about? Then I realized I knew the roommate's name. It had just come to me because he had annoyed me and that line came out so naturally. Well, at least the other guy now has a name. It's Trey.

Trey sits back down on the couch, buries his face in his hands and says, "Holy shit, no fucking way. This is not possible." It comes out more of a mumble.

What's not possible? I swear, these guys need to get a clear head and help me out here. I'm confused as it is, and I came here hoping they would help me out. Only instead of giving me answers, I'm just more confused.

Trey gets up from the couch and goes to the kitchen. He opens the fridge and comes back with three bottles of beer, handing one to Matt, then one to me. I look at him with a confused look and shake my head. "I'm okay. I don't think I like beer anyways."

Matt looks over at me, and chuckles. "Take it; you might end up liking it."

I take the beer from Trey, twist the cap off and take a

sip, keeping my eyes on Matt the whole time. Surprisingly, the moment it hits my tongue, I swallow, and it tastes like heaven. I make a small moaning sound and take a bigger sip.

Matt's mouth goes into a smile and he shakes his head.

"Told you so," he says.

Trey goes and sits back down on the couch and starts to drink his beer, and I return to the recliner. Matt begins to drink from his beer and he's thinking really hard about something.

"How did I know your name all of a sudden?" I ask Trey.

"I'm still trying to figure this shit out myself, but one thing is for sure. I'm really freaked out right now," he says before he starts drinking his beer again.

"Well, that makes two of us," I say, taking another sip of my beer.

With a worried look on his face, Matt speaks, "There's only one person who would snap at Trey like that." I look at him waiting for him to tell me.

"Emily, my sister."

My eyes go wide in surprise. The room starts to spin and I feel really light headed. Matt must have noticed my reaction because he heads straight over to me. "Put your head between your knees, it might help." I do as he says and once the dizzy feeling is gone I lift it back up.

My nerves are getting to me, I start bouncing my knee up and down and Matt looks at it, saying, "Feeling much tension? Maybe you should take up running."

For some reason a run sounds really good right now. Especially after the dream I had last night.

I'm sitting there, realizing that all these memories I've been having, are his sister's. I'm wracking my brain on how or why I would have these memories all of a sudden. It's really freaking me out right now. I turn to look at Matt and I notice he's staring right back at me, studying me.

"So let me get this straight. You wake up with no memory of the model you are, but you keep having these other memories?"

I nod, twisting the beer in my hands, sitting there and I start trying to peel the label off the bottle in an effort to distract myself.

Trey's eyes light up. I could tell he's thought of something.

"Why don't we show her a picture of Em? Maybe she'll recognize her and it might trigger a memory of them working together."

Matt immediately goes over to a wall with several shelves and grabs a photograph.

He comes back and hands it to me. It's one of him and a woman, at what must be Matt's graduation since he's wearing a cap and gown. I take the picture from his hands so I'm able to focus better on the image of the lady, but nothing is coming to me.

Nothing.

Dammit, this is getting more frustrating. I shake my head, handing the photo back to Matt. He grabs it from me, taking it back to its original home on the shelf. As he puts it down, he takes a moment to look at it. His body is tense, without emotion, but his shoulders are slumped.

He turns back at me. "How often do you have these memories?" he asks, drawing his brows down tight.

"I don't know. They just come to me, but they're so real. At first, I thought they were only dreams, since I had the first two while I was sleeping, but the last one was while I was awake. The one I just had."

He walks over in front of the fireplace and starts pacing again. All I can do is sit there and stare at him.

He suddenly leaves the room, going through a door leading into the kitchen. I look at Trey waiting for him to tell me what's going on, but he shrugs his shoulders and takes another drink of his beer.

I stopped myself at the one beer that he gave me because I began to feel lightheaded. With everything going on, I haven't had much of an appetite. So I'd forgotten to eat breakfast, and the alcohol began to hit me hard, and right now I need to be as clear headed as possible.

Another fifteen minutes go by and Matt comes back into the living room with what looks like a planner. He resumes his seat on the couch and starts going through the pages, starting in the middle. I see his eyes moving back and forth with a determined concentration, while slowly flipping through the pages.

"What are you looking for?" I ask curiously.

He shakes his head while keeping it down, but manages to hold up his finger as if telling me to wait. He goes back to scanning the pages. He does this for a while and in the meantime Trey has turned on the flat screen mounted above the fireplace, and is now watching the sports channel. Since I'm not into sports I go back to watching Matt.

My phone begins to ring in my purse that I placed on the floor next to the recliner. I take it out and look at the screen. There is a picture of Bill with his name flashed across the screen. I push the ignore button, because the last thing I need right now is Bill asking where I am and bitching me out again for not taking security with me. It's not my fault he didn't tell me how to get a hold of security.

Another reason I didn't call for a bodyguard was how in the world would I explain my road trip to see a guy from my dream?

I decide to turn off the phone and figure I'll deal with that obstacle when I'm faced with it. This is more important right now. I need to know why I'm having these memories.

Matt has finally reached the last page of the planner he's holding and shuts it. Making an exasperated sigh, he tosses it in front of him onto the coffee table. With his elbows on his knees, he begins rubbing his face with his hands. He rakes his hands over his head, and then brings them down again over his face.

He says into his hands, "I don't get it, how is this fucking possible?" the question comes out more of a mumble due to his hands.

I'm assuming the planner didn't have the answer he was looking for.

I ask him, "What is it you were looking for?"

He takes his head out of his hands, but keeps staring at the floor between his knees. "I was positive that she must have worked with you at some time, but she never mentioned you. But, then again she was not the type of person who would brag about her clients."

Clients, what clients? "What did your sister do for a living?"

He looks at me. "She was an interior designer, and she mostly worked with a lot of high end clients."

So this is why he would think that I would have met her. He must have thought I hired her to work for me, maybe do a design job in my apartment.

I look around the room with shocked eyes, and a raised eyebrow. I'm really confused how, with his sister being a high-end interior designer, this place sure looks like crap. Now that I think about it, why didn't these guys recruit her expertise? But I guess that is boys for you, especially those who are in college.

Trey sees my face and laughs. "Trust me, she would have gone to town if we let her, but she was really cool about giving us our space on the decorations," he says, shrugging his shoulders.

"So let me get this straight, according to that book," I point my chin to the planner sitting on the table in front of Matt, "she never worked with me?"

"Or your dude," he responds, nodding his head.

"But, since I've never met her, how is it that I could have her memories?"

Matt gets a grim look on his face and he stares out into the backyard. I know this must be hard on him, losing his sister, then having some stranger come in and claim to see what she did.

Matt looks at me, and takes a breath. "This might sound stupid, but the way I see it, you are somehow absorbing her crazy memories."

Crazy? She doesn't seem crazy from the memories I'm getting, unless I'm getting the tame ones.

Yay for me, I dryly think.

"How, I don't know. I don't want to know, because all this shit sounds freaking crazy to me as it is. That's the only thing I can think of at the moment." I remain dazed as I'm listening to him.

"I'm still waiting for you to tell me that you're really my sister back from the dead any moment, but seeing that you don't have all her memories, it can't be that," he says, frowning.

He drops his head back into his hands, rubbing his face.

Trey looks just as amazed at what Matt has said as I do. "This shit sounds so crazy to me right now."

I nod my head, not knowing what else to do.

We all sit there in silence for a couple of minutes and it begins to feel really awkward.

Trey finally gets up from the couch and says, "I'm hungry. You guys hungry?" I'm about to shake my head to reply that I'm not, but my empty stomach takes this moment to start to growl, answering his question.

Trey laughs and states he's going to order some pizza.

How he can think of food right now amazes me, but I remember that they were stoned out of their minds when I got here, and then I remember that the driver is still waiting for me. He also must be starving at this point.

"I should let my driver go grab something as well, I'll be right back," I say, standing up.

Matt stands up too, saying, "I'll go with you." He follows me out the door, to the hired car.

I make it down to the curb where the driver is patiently waiting for me in the driver's seat. When he sees me approaching, he immediately steps out and rushes over to me ready to open the door. I shake my head at him and tell the driver to go get his lunch.

At first he seems hesitant to leave, but after reassuring him that I will be at least another hour or so, he gives me his card in case I need him sooner.

As we're walking back up the driveway I notice the black car again and, out of curiosity, ask, "Which one is your car?"

He points his finger to the black Charger.

I can't help myself as my jaw drops. Damn lucky bastard.

I head over to the car and automatically start running my fingers on it, craving to touch it. The feel of the perfectly glossy paint job against my fingers claims it must have been done recently within the last ten years. You can tell he takes really good care of it.

I take a glance inside and notice the interior is clean, with everything chromed to perfection, inside and out. The leather seats are immaculate; the seating looks almost new and redone. He must either have had it restored to its original condition or paid a pretty penny for a car this well taken care of.

I stand there and fantasize what it would feel like to be behind the wheel of this car, driving it. Man, how I wish it was possible.

I look back at Matt, and he's observing me with fascination.

"What?" I ask, looking at him.

He shakes his head and states, "That's one thing you don't have in common with Em. Although I have the car, she hated Eleanor."

What the hell did he just call the car?

"You named your car Eleanor? That's an old lady's name." I look at him horrified.

He laughs. "Eleanor is a vintage name, and being that my car is vintage, it's the perfect name," he declares, happy with himself.

Seeing that I'm not satisfied with his answer, Matt curiously asks, "What would you have named her?"

I think about his question before asking, "So it's a girl?"

"Of course."

I lift my eyes, pondering the question once again and tap my finger to my lips, thinking hard about what he just asked.

"Carly."

Matt now gives me a horrified and disgusted look. "I would never... in my life... name my car, 'Carly'," he says, using his fingers to make air quotations. "It isn't unique enough."

I roll my eyes. "Well, it's better than sounding like an old lady," I say to him.

Thinking about how our conversation started, I ask him, "How can she have hated this car? You're right, it is a classic."

"I first asked her for the car when I turned sixteen. She refused, claiming it wasn't safe enough for me or the environment, but she ended up surprising me and bought it for me anyways." He's looking at the car with a sad expression, his eyes glazing over, and he's blinking like he's fighting back tears.

"She claimed that even though it wasn't the car she wanted for me, it was the one I wanted, and I deserved to have what I wanted, even if it was a car. It was pretty banged up when we bought it, but she said it would give me character if I fixed it up. She also made me get a job to earn the money to restore it. It took me over three years to get it looking like this, but she was so proud of me when I was finally finished."

He's still staring at the car like he's remembering the moment. "But then again I could never disappoint her, because I owed her my life. So I made sure it never happened," he finishes.

"What kind of car did she drive?"

He looks over in my direction and my heart almost melts when he smiles at me with a light chuckle. "A Prius."

This is when I notice he has one sexy smile to go with those killer eyes. Remembering his response from a moment ago, I laugh. I can't imagine driving a Prius. I've got nothing against the whole "green" thing, but that would be the last type of car I would pick for myself.

Probably thinking that our tour down memory lane is done, Matt starts to walk towards the front door and I follow him. As we enter the house he informs me he's going to take a shower, so I decide to wait in the living room with Trey.

As I'm walking back into the house I notice the mess again, and I make myself useful, and start cleaning up all the bottles and cans. For some reason seeing this clutter is driving me nuts.

Trey is watching me and starts to shake his head.

The doorbell rings and he heads to the door. It must be the pizza he ordered earlier. After paying the driver he shuts the door, heads over to the kitchen counter, and places the pizza on the counter. Once I've thrown the last of the bottles away in the recycle bin, Trey hands me a plate with a slice of pizza on it.

He's lightly laughing, "Couldn't help yourself, huh? I should've expected it."

I take a bite of my slice with a confused look on my face wondering why he would expect that of me.

"Em used to always get on our ass about the mess, she always started cleaning up after our shit the minute she was done hugging us. It used to drive her nuts to see the clutter."

I think back to the apartment Bill and I are sharing and realize that everything is clutter free. The closet that held my clothing was neatly organized, and the rest of the place was

49

very orderly.

I know for sure I must have been like this before the whole memory loss so I ignore the comparison that Trey brought up. It must be a coincidence.

Although it does throw me for a loop, because that's exactly how I felt the whole time I was sitting in the living room. I couldn't stand being in the chaos of the mess.

Matt finally emerges from the hallway, looking fresh and clean, and I take the moment to completely take him in.

He's wearing some basketball shorts, with a black t-shirt that is worn tight to his body. Almost like an undershirt. The beautiful winged tattoo on his arm is half covered by the sleeve of his shirt, but the remainder of it is in clear view.

As I'm observing him, my body starts to feel tingly and my head is getting woozy.

What is going on with me? I don't really know this guy and my body is already getting turned on from looking at him. I'm as bad as Bill with the thoughts that are swirling around in my head about what I would really love to do to him at this moment.

All I know is it doesn't involve any clothing at all.

Matt heads straight to the pizza box, grabbing a slice and eating straight from the box.

Good thing I'm already done eating my slice and feeling full because from the guilt I'm starting to feel, I would have lost my appetite.

I know that it's now my cue to get out of there before I try to take action on my X-rated thoughts. "Look, I appreciate the welcome, but I should head back before my fiancé starts to get suspicious about me being gone," I say to them.

Matt and Trey look at each other confusedly and then look at me.

Looking back at me Trey asks, "So, where exactly does he think you are?"

I shrug my shoulder. "Hell if I know, I didn't tell him anything. He called earlier, but I turned my phone off," I tell them.

Matt raises an eyebrow, stopping mid-bite into his slice. His lips go into a deep frown with a somber look on his face. Obviously, he doesn't know what to think of this whole situation, and neither do I. Deciding he's lost his appetite, he tosses the pizza slice on top of the box and leans back against the counter, crossing his arms over his chest.

His deep brown eyes bore into me as he asks, "So what happens now?"

"I don't know," I respond, not knowing what else to say at this point. "I didn't really think this whole thing through. I was hoping that you would be able to give me answers about who I was, but obviously that's not possible," I say, letting out a frustrated breath.

Looking back and forth between the two, I ask nervously, "Look, can I trust you guys with this whole situation? Or am I going to expect tomorrow's headline to label me as a memory stealing psycho who's literally lost her mind?"

Trey is about to say something, but Matt cuts him off. "Of course, your secret is safe with us," he says, challenging Trey to say something different.

Trey closes his gaping mouth and nods his head, while he walks over to me, throwing his arm around my shoulder.

"Supermodel, you got nothing to worry about. As long as you promise not to stay a stranger," he says, squeezing my shoulder at the same time, causing me to wince.

Man, this guy is as strong as he looks and he probably doesn't know how to control it.

I get a big smile on my face from what he's said. Then I look at Matt and he's also smiling with his head cocked to the side, with hooded eyes that are currently bearing deep down to my soul. With the sexy look on his face, I already know Matt is going to be my downfall, I can feel it.

# Chapter 5

AS I'M RIDING in the car on the way back to Seattle I wonder what I'm supposed to do from here on out. This day has been so overwhelming and I still haven't gotten a concrete answer of what's going on in my head.

I do a lot of unnecessary thinking with three hours of road ahead of me. Hating that I didn't get the answers I wanted, or hoped to get, I let the distraction of the landscape outside of my window try to give me something else to focus on, but it isn't helping. I keep thinking back to chocolate brown eyes that stared at me as I drove away.

We finally make it back to Seattle and the sun has already set, lighting up the city with its beautiful twinkling lights illuminating the surrounding buildings.

As the driver pulls up and stops in front of my building I begin to brace myself for what is to come.

I let myself up in the elevator and as I walk through the foyer I see a woman standing inside the living room talking on the phone. As she hears me enter she turns around and says into the phone, "Oh, she's here. Yes, yes thank you for your help."

That voice sounds very familiar.

It happens again, like at the hospital. My heart feels like it's starting to race a hundred miles per hour and I'm desperately trying to get it under control, but I can't. It dawns on me that this is the second voice that I heard in my state of darkness.

She's standing ahead of me, looking upset to see me, and I don't understand why.

She's a beautiful young redhead, with her hair pinned up, and a slim, creamy complexioned body. She's wearing a black pencil skirt, with a black-buttoned blazer jacket, and white dress shirt underneath it. She stands at about average height, but with a pair of red stilettos that give her an extra boost to make her look taller, as she walks to me. She makes a loud clicking sound against the marble floor with every step she takes. Stopping a few feet in front of me, she places her hand on her hip. "Where have you been? Don't you know how worried you've had Bill?" she says in an angry, lecturing tone.

Not wanting her to see my weakness, I stand there with my eyebrows arched in surprise at her. Since I've now pieced together the puzzle that was attaining that part of my memory, I don't care what the hell she says. Even the sound of the way she is lecturing me confirms that she was the other half of the conversation, and I hate it. I had wanted to doubt myself about what I heard, hoping that it *was* just a dream, but reality has a way of kicking you in the ass.

"Why should I care how Bill feels?" I say in a non-condescending tone. Right now I don't give a shit what either of them thinks. I'm more concerned that my suspicions have pretty much been confirmed and I don't know whether to feel relieved or worried.

Her eyes go wide and her mouth falls open. Then she shuts it again, completely surprised by what I've said.

I'm exhausted by the events of the day, so I ignore her reaction and walk towards the kitchen. I can hear her following me as both our heels go tap, tap, tap on the floor.

She's not going to get the damn point to leave me alone. I open the fridge, grabbing a water bottle from inside, opening it, and begin to drink from it. Right now, I'm wishing it were another one of those beers that Trey gave me. I'm pretty sure it would help shut out the world I'm desperately trying to avoid right now.

"What do you mean you don't care? You didn't tell him that you were leaving and he thought something happened to you again, since you didn't answer any of our phone calls."

So she tried calling me too? Now I'm really glad I'd decided to turn off my phone when I did. They both must have been calling me like crazy after that.

I wouldn't have wanted to hear her voice from the other end of a phone call. I don't know how I would've reacted, not that I'm any better at this moment. I look at her and shrug my shoulders emphasizing I still don't care, which I don't. I'm trying to figure out what gives her the right to be in my apartment, besides being Bill's fuck buddy.

At that thought, I hear the ding of the elevator, and Bill's voice booms through the apartment. "Where is she?"

Shit, here comes that damn lecture I was really trying to avoid. First, I had to deal with seeing the fuck buddy, now I'm going to have to deal with Bill's wrath.

Rolling my eyes at his remark, I square my shoulders, and take a deep breath. I'm getting ready for the lecture to come because I'm pretty sure from that tone he's going to give me one.

"We're in here," the redhead yells in his direction.

Placing the water on the counter, I brace my arms against the granite countertop as he walks in, and eyes me with a glare. Like I'm a child about to get reprimanded.

"Where the hell were you!"

Obviously he's pissed, but I expected this.

"I went out to explore the city, I thought maybe if I did the tourist thing it might help trigger my memory," I lie and shrug my shoulders.

"Why didn't you inform me, or take a security guard with you? Do you know how out of my mind I've been today?" He actually looks concerned when he says it.

"I forgot. Since you didn't inform me how to contact a security guard I didn't bother."

The redhead walks up next to me, glaring her hazel eyes at me. "You shouldn't be going out on your own, and it's not safe. What if you were attacked, what if the paparazzi had found you? Don't you even think about the consequences or is stupidity the one thing you were able to recover when you lost your memory?"

What the fuck? She's got some balls to talk to me like that.

Taking another deep breath to calm my raging blood, I ignore her and look at Bill. "Who the fuck is she?" I tilt my head at her, wanting him to shut her up.

"Susan, calm down," Bill commands her, giving me a sympathetic look.

Waving her hand at me, she retorts, "How am I supposed to keep calm, when she's acting like an idiot? She doesn't think what her actions are doing to you. She was better off staying in a coma."

That's when I snap. I don't know what comes over me, but next thing I know I swing my arm back, and bring it forward punching her in the face. As she goes down, I jump on her ready to attack her again, fury running through my veins. I'm stopped when Bill wraps his arms around my waist picking me up like I'm a sack of potatoes. He carries me out of the kitchen, and then tosses me on the couch. While pointing his finger at me, he shouts, "Stay there! I have to go check on Susan."

I gawk at him as he goes back into the kitchen, leaving me in the living room, sitting there wondering what just came over me. I can't believe I punched her!

It did allow me to let out some of the frustration that was building up in me and I feel much better already. Maybe I should do it again and get all of it out.

Then it dawns on me what I really did and I wonder. Is it normal for me to lose my temper? Do I do this often? Man, it really sucks not knowing all this stuff about myself.

I hate that he'd rather be with her right now than with me. That thought fans the flames again, so I get up from the couch and head towards the master bathroom. As I enter I take off my heels, go over to the sink, and begin to run the cold water and I start to apply cold water to my face, letting the coldness calm me down a bit.

Once I'm done, I turn off the faucet and stare at my reflection in the mirror, leaning against the counter with my arms. Who the hell is the girl staring right back me?

In the corner of my eye, I see Bill's reflection in the mirror. He's standing against the doorframe with his arms crossed, and he looks like he doesn't know whether to start lecturing me or to stay quiet.

So I make it easier on both of us, and start. "Who is she?"

"Her name is Susan, she's my personal assistant."

Typical male, screwing his personal assistant, I guess it makes it easier. Obviously she takes her job really seriously; by the way she was pissed at me.

"What the hell came over you, Abigail? Your attitude lately is nothing like you. It's like you're a whole different person." That answers my earlier question about whether this is how I usually act.

"How the hell am I supposed to answer you Bill, I don't even know who I am!" I snarl at him, turning away from him to walk into my closet.

"See what I mean? You've never raised your voice at anybody in your life, let alone punched somebody," he says, following me.

"Well, get over it Bill, because obviously this is the new me."

He's still utterly shocked, not knowing what to say.

"Besides your personal assistant, what is she really to you?"

"What are you talking about?"

"Are you screwing her?" My voice sounds just as pissed as I feel.

Eyebrows drawn and looking stunned at my accusation, he replies, "Susan? Why would you think I'd be having an affair with Susan?"

This is where I'm baffled, what do I say? That I heard them talking about being each other's fuck buddies while I was passed out in a coma? He'd never believe me. Plus this is something I have no proof that I actually heard. For all I know it could have been one of the crazy dreams that I've been having lately.

He's standing there with his arms still crossed, staring at me waiting for me to answer him.

Crap.

Shrugging my shoulders. "I don't know, enlighten me? Don't most hot shots like you usually have affairs with their P.A.s? Besides, the way she was acting, she obviously thinks she has some right to rip me one. There must be something going on."

He's concentrating really hard on how to answer me, so I take his silence and continue on. "What the hell gives her the right to talk to me like that?"

He shakes his head, and sighs. "I know she shouldn't have spoken to you that way, but she was probably just as stressed about today as I was," he says, standing there with his hands in his pockets.

He's still wearing his suit pants, but he's taken off his jacket, leaving on this dress shirt with his tie loosened around his neck. His face looks strained as he studies me.

"She's going to be okay, by the way. She might have a black eye for the next couple of days. Just in case you are wondering."

Call me cruel, but I had forgotten that I had punched her.

"I sent her home and told her to take the next couple of days off."

I start grabbing clothes from the closet to sleep in and grab some extra clothes for tomorrow just in case.

"What are you doing?" he says, staring at me confused while I'm grabbing the clothing.

"What does it look like I'm doing, I'm getting my clothes for bed."

"You know Abigail, I've been trying to be very under-standing and give you your space." He sighs. "But I really miss you and I know we both have needs," he says as he walks over and takes me in his arms. I try to push him away, but he keeps his arms firmly around my waist and starts nuzzling my neck.

It must be all the pent up frustration from the day, or having come down from my adrenaline high, but what he's doing actually turns me on.

It feels good as he takes my earlobe in his mouth and starts sucking on it. The suckling feeling drives me mad and I drop the clothes I had in my hands. I grab onto his arms because my body goes weak and my legs feel like they're going to collapse.

I close my eyes and take in the feelings.

Something in the back of my head says that this is probably not a good idea, but I can't help it. As I'm standing there letting him take control of my body, I'm not thinking of Bill, but of someone else. Someone who is a lot younger and has the most gorgeous eyes that I've ever seen.

Matt.

I keep my eyes closed as he trails kisses down my cheek leading to my mouth, then he kisses me with a soft peck at first like he's hesitant to do so. I still have my eyes closed but inside my eyelids, I'm imagining Matt, as he tastes my soft lips. He then kisses me harder pushing my mouth open with his tongue and he begins to kiss me fierce-ly.

I don't know why I'm letting him, in my mind I know I should stop him, but my body is responding like a starving woman who is about to get her fix as I imagine another man doing this to me.

He brings me closer against his body with his hand on my lower back and with the other hand he starts leading it down to my ass, grabbing it. He begins to squeeze and caress it, making me moan into his mouth.

The sensation is overwhelming and it only gets worse as he starts to lift my shirt over my head and pulls my bra cups down to take my breasts in his hands. He starts kneading them, while pinching my nipples in between his fingers. This shoots a jolt through me and I throw my head back with another moan, giving him access to suck and kiss on my neck.

The crazy thing is that I can't open my eyes, I don't want to, because I know the moment I do I won't see the eyes I want to see.

I feel Bill lower his head and take one nipple into his mouth, after a moment he does the same with the other. I can't help myself when I grab his head for support and keep him there because it feels so good.

I finally allow myself to open my eyes as I feel myself being lowered to the floor and I see the ceiling of the closet above my head. He begins removing my jeans faster than I can process the train of thought and all I do is lift my hips to help him. I know I should stop him at this point, but my body wants this more than my brain comprehends.

Once he's done removing my jeans he comes back up my body, one arm on the side of my head, with the other in my hair holding my head to him as he kisses me again with the same intensity as earlier. We pause just enough so I can take off his tie, then he's back to kissing me. Next I'm taking off his shirt, pulling it apart, causing buttons to go flying in different directions.

He stops kissing me and I let out a whine as he stands

up so he can remove his shoes, socks, and pants, leaving him in black silk boxers. I stare at him with hooded eyes noticing the obvious erection straining towards me.

He lowers himself to the ground again and I reach for his shoulders needing something to hold onto. He lifts me off the ground just enough to get the clasp of the bra at my back and takes it off throwing it to the side and once again goes to suckling my breast. He takes my thong off and as he begins to open my legs wider with his thighs I get enough sense in me to say, "Protection, I'm not doing this without protection."

Confused, he gets up, digs through his pants for his wallet and pulls out a condom. He lowers his boxers and tears open the wrapper with his teeth and begins to put the condom on at a speedy pace. Once he's done he comes back down and pushes inside me, making me gasp as he enters me. The only thing I can do is hold onto him as he begins rocking back and forth, wrapping my legs around his thighs and lift my hips to meet each one of his thrusts.

He begins kissing me again, picking up his speed, thrusting harder against me, making me moan louder, and I have to hold him tighter. The increase builds me up and I let go as my orgasm takes over my body, causing me to squeeze him with my core muscles.

A couple of seconds later Bill throws his head back and he lets out a long grunt while he pumps a couple more times into me, finally finishing him off.

Slowing to a stop he collapses on top of me then rolls off a couple of seconds later.

"Man, I really missed you, and by the way that felt I think you missed me too."

That's when it comes to me. What did I just do? I had

sex with Bill. Bill the guy who, I'm pretty sure, is screwing his personal assistant. I had let my traitorous body take over me and give in to him pretending he was someone else.

As he turns to his side and reaches for me I frantically push him away, stand up, and grab the clothes I dropped on the floor. I rush out of the closet with Bill on my tail. I'm frantic and already regretting what just happened.

"What's wrong with you?" he asks, dumbfounded about why I got up in a hurry.

"That shouldn't have happened," I say, high-tailing it out of the bedroom and into the spare bedroom I used last night.

"What do you mean, that shouldn't have happened? Why not?" he says following me to the room, not caring that he is naked.

At this point, I don't know what excuse to give him, so I stay quiet and shake my head at him.

"Look that can't happen again." I respond, trying not to look at him.

He is standing a few feet in front of me. "Abigail, I don't know what's going on, but I really wish you would talk to me about it."

I don't think he really wants to hear that the only reason I had sex with him was because I was imagining he was someone else.

"Look, I just don't feel comfortable with you yet."

He raises an eyebrow with a mocking look on his face. "That's not what your body just told me," he states.

I'm still gripping the clothing to my naked body, in an effort to cover up as much as I can, but it's not helping. His scrutinizing gaze is still raking my body and I want it to stop.

"It was a mistake and it can't happen again."

"How is having sex with my fiancée a mistake? Abigail, you're never going to get your memory back if you don't go back to doing what you normally did before the accident, and sex was a very normal and regular thing for you."

Now he's trying to play that card?

He's still not leaving and the longer he stands there the more I feel uncomfortable. "Can you go put some clothes on? You're making me uncomfortable standing there like that," I say, waving my hand at him.

"Fine. But I think you should start sleeping in our bed again."

I shake my head, staring at the wall beyond him. "No. I'm staying in here, until things get back to normal. I don't want a repeat of what just happened."

He lets out an angry sigh, turns around, and walks out of my room. As he walks away, he leaves me to stare at his bare ass, and it's not even a sexy one either.

Once he's out the door I quickly walk over to it, shut it, and lock it. I lean against the door, tilting my head back needing to think about what I just did.

I know I shouldn't have had sex with Bill. Especially knowing that he's already screwing someone else, but I couldn't stop myself once it started. Why in the hell did I let that happen?

I'll tell you why. My sexually deprived body was really craving someone else. Someone who I couldn't get out of my damned mind the whole car ride home, and my body took advantage of the first man to throw himself at me. I had to get my shit together and fix things quick, or else Bill would think he could keep taking advantage of me.

# Chapter 6

WHEN I AWOKE the next morning, I encountered Bill in the kitchen, and I immediately tensed up. It was already awkward being around him and after what happened last night, it was even worse. He informs me that he's going to be in meetings for most of the day, but if I needed to leave for any reason I was to take his driver, who also doubled as a bodyguard. Not wanting him to stick around any longer than he needed, I agreed and let him walk out of the apartment. Once he was gone I was able to relax.

An hour later, I was surprised when I received a text from Matt asking if I've had any more memories or dreams of him, sadly I informed him that I had not. The question quickly led to a conversation in which I told him how I was feeling like I was about to go nuts. I just couldn't stop fidgeting. He only found it funny and told me the best thing to do was to go for a run to clear my mind.

I'm glad my predicament was entertaining someone…

Thinking to myself, why not, it wouldn't hurt to try, I

decided to give it a shot. After researching a couple of running stores I found one near my apartment and decided to check it out. Might as well put my new babysitter to good use so I headed out of the door.

Two hours later I was back in my apartment with my new running gear, clothes, and accessories ready for my run. I was so excited just thinking about it, my babysitter not so much. After telling him that I was going with or without him, he knew he had no choice.

After promising not to leave without him, I waited for him while he headed home to change. It gave me time to change my clothing, lace up my new shoes, and throw my hair in a ponytail. By the time he was back, I didn't even give him time to take a breath before we headed into the elevator and down to the lobby.

My apartment building was located fairly close to the water so that's the first place I started walking when I got out of the front doors. I had downloaded some songs as I waited for the babysitter to come back from changing, so I was ready to rock out with my run. With my earphones in my ear, blasting out, "Feel This Moment," I start running.

My body absorbed the beat from the song and immediately took over. It's like it knew exactly what I needed, and took off. With my legs moving down the sidewalk, weaving in and around people, ponytail bobbing back and forth, I felt pressure begin to escape my body with every step I took.

Man, this felt so much better than it did in my dream. I was actually doing it. Every step that I took, with my feet hitting the concrete, I felt so carefree and began to feel all the built up tension leave my body. Forty-five minutes later, I was back, standing in front of my building feeling like the weight of the building I was staring at had been lifted from my shoulders.

When I look over to my right, my babysitter is heaving, chest rising and falling, sucking in air as best as he can. Don't get me wrong, I was just as out of breath and looked almost as bad as he did, but at least I looked forward to doing it again. If you were to ask him, I don't think so. Although, whether he liked it or not, it was going to happen.

Feeling relaxed and satisfied, I took a shower and changed, but almost two hours later my phone rang showing "Private Number" on the screen. I'm hesitant to answer, but do because it could be someone from my past who helps trigger my memories. I'm easily disappointed on that note when I answer.

"Ms. Adams, it's Frank. I got the rest of the info you wanted." He sounds uneasy, even on the phone. "Is there any way we can meet somewhere within the next fifteen minutes?"

"Why can't you email me the info?"

"I think you'd want to hear most of this in person."

"Fine, same place?" I ask.

"I'm already here, waiting."

"I'll be there in five," I respond, grabbing my purse as I'm already heading toward the elevator.

I practically speed walk to the coffee shop, anxious to find out why he needs to see me in person. I arrive in record time, spotting him in a back corner table, almost in the shadows. I sit down, absorbing the smell of the coffee and by the look on his face I know I'm not going to like what he's going to tell me.

"It's not good news, is it?" My voice is almost a whisper and even I can hear the worry in it.

He hands me a thick manila folder and I open it. It has

copies of bank statements, contracts, and several black and white photos. I go straight to the photos and upon seeing them, my heart stops. The photos are of Bill and Susan in different settings. In one of them he is having dinner with her, giving her a very passionate kiss.

He sees which one I'm looking at and says, "That one was taken literally an hour ago, thought you would like to see it."

As I take a closer look at the picture, I realize he is right. It's the same suit I saw him wearing this morning as he was walking out to his *meeting.*

I finally let out the breath I didn't realize I was holding. I had an idea that he was cheating on me, but to see the actual proof of it, was something else. They were both totally screwing me over and I was taking it like the "idiot child" that Susan was claiming I was.

"It gets worse," he says, finally breaking me from the shock that I'm trying to absorb.

"How much worse can it get than my *fiancé, fucking me over literally?"*

"He's also screwing you by embezzling your money. Well, I don't know if most people will see it as embezzling since his name is also on the account. But, being that you've been in a coma for the last four months, I don't know what you would need to spend close to a million dollars on?" he says sarcastically.

I look at him in shock. I feel like my body was just hit by a train, knocking all the air out of me and making me feel like shit.

"How bad is it?"

He points at a contract sitting on the table. "That contract is what's going to screw you over. It pretty much states that he has access to any finances in your name, whether he's on the account or not."

Fuck.

"Where did you get this?" My voice is raspy and still in shock.

Lifting one of his shoulders, with a smirk on his face, he smiles and states, "I told you I was good. It's actually a copy of the one the bank is currently holding."

He looks very proud of himself, which he should be. "Since you're the primary account holder, he's only allowed limited access and withdrawals, but no matter, he has access regardless. The only positive thing about the contract is that it has to be renewed annually, and will expire in three months. Until then you're pretty much screwed."

My head is spinning, I'm forcing myself to breath, and I'm about ready to go crazy on Bill's ass. But I have to force myself to calm down and analyze the situation.

"Since you were in a coma, the bank started getting really suspicious of the amount he was withdrawing, and brought it to his attention. So far he's been a good boy, stating that the large amounts of money are for your personal expenses. Which I find hard to believe."

"So you're saying that I just have to hang in there for three more months. Then make sure I don't sign another one of these contracts, giving him access to my money?"

"And keep from doing anything that will earn you an income in that time as well."

Now this confuses the hell out of me as well. "Why?"

"Being that he's your manager and agent he also has control of the money you get from that as well."

Fuck. I'm screwed either way, what the hell am I supposed to do? Even if I tried getting more money he would easily take it from me anyways.

Frank sees me thinking over my options. "How well do you know this Matthew fellow? What is he to you?" he asks.

I shake my head not knowing what he is to me at this point. "Why do you ask?"

He brings his steepled hands to his lips, cocking an eyebrow with curiosity, shrugging his shoulder. "I only ask because if he's someone you know you can trust, Bill wouldn't be able to touch what's no longer in your account. Especially if it were to say, transfer into this Matthew fellow's account," he says with a grin on his face.

Oh. My. God.

Why didn't I think of that? It's brilliant. The problem is that I didn't know whether I could trust Matt either. Although, at this point I would rather let him have what was left of my money instead of letting Bill and his fuck buddy have another cent.

"I've included his bank account information along with all of your personal account numbers as well. Apparently, you both use the same bank," he says with a smile on his face. "I've also included an account number to which I would like my payment transferred."

He begins to stand up, leaving me to look up at him. "It was a pleasure doing business with you Ms. Adams. If you ever need my services again, I'm always at your disposal," he says before he walks out of the coffee shop, leaving me staring at the wall ahead of me.

After sitting there for a couple of more minutes, I finally gather everything up and exit the coffee shop as well. I have a feeling I am going to have a battle ahead of me and I need to prepare myself for war.

# Chapter 7

"YOU CURRENTLY HAVE 4.3 million dollars in your account at your disposal Ms. Adams, why do you ask?" a young gentleman in his early thirties, dressed in a suit, looking every bit the bank manager that he is, informs me the next morning.

I'm still trying to wrap my head around the whole situation, but I do know one thing for sure, I wasn't letting Bill get another dollar anytime soon.

I'm very sleep deprived, since I didn't get much of it last night. I kept going over everything that had happened. It kept me tossing and turning in my bed, my thoughts going back to Matt.

I look the manager in the eye. "I need two thousand of it in cash for myself."

Then I hand a small piece of paper with Frank's requested amount and account number over to him. "This amount put into that account number." After he takes the first small paper, I hand him another with Matt's account number. "The rest is to be transferred into this account number. Both of which are current accounts here at your facility."

Eyes wide open, he asks, "What do you mean by the rest, ma'am?"

I had a feeling this would happen and was prepared for it.

With a strong stern voice, I say emphatically, "I. Mean. All. Of. What's. Left," indicating just how serious I am.

With a horrified look on his face, unbelieving what he's heard, he protests, "But, that would mean emptying out your account completely, ma'am." His response is just as shocked, as I'm staring him down.

I have a feeling he's going to play this game with me all morning if I let him.

"I know. I'm looking at it as a very generous donation to someone who really needs it. It's only money," I say, trying to sound like I don't care. "I'm pretty sure with my fiancé being my manager, there will be plenty more to fill it up again soon," I say with a sarcastic smile on my face.

He still looks skeptical, but easily gives up.

"Okay," he states with an apprehensive look, and tries to hold himself together as well as he can. "I'll get the documentation for you to sign, authorizing the transfer."

He quickly stands up and heads to his office door. Once he's left his office, I dig into my purse for my phone and I shoot off a text to Matt.

*I need a favor. A*

After a minute, I receive a response.

*What's up? M*

*I'm going to put some money in your account for safe-keeping. A*

*Why my account? M*

*I need someone I could trust, is that you? A*

He doesn't respond immediately, and I'm sitting there thinking maybe this might be a bad idea after all. But, then I hear the ping of a response.

*Of course, Pinkie Promise. M*

That's when I blank out and I'm suddenly pulled into another memory. I'm sitting on a bed in a little boy's room and there is a small child sitting across from me on the bed. It's Matt, his eyes are red and swollen, like he's been crying for a while, and he's looking at me with desperation on his face.

I tell him, "Everything is going to be all right, I'm here now and I'm never leaving you."

He stares into my eyes and says, "Promise?"

My response to him, without a doubt is, "Pinkie Promise." Holding out my pinkie and locking it with his, I hug him with a force promising not to let go.

I hear the ping of my phone again, breaking me from the memory, pulling me back to reality. Why is it that I get these memories like that, randomly? I'm beginning to appreciate when I was dreaming them, at least I didn't spaz out like just did.

*You still there? M*

*Yes. I'm still here, Pinkie Promise. A*

*Do you need my bank info? M*

*No, I already have it. A*

*How the hell did you get it? M*

*The same guy who gave me your address. ;-) A*

As soon as I hit send on the phone, the bank manager walks back into the office with all the paperwork in hand. I place the phone back into my purse as he sits back down across from me in his chair. He places a couple of papers that are in his hand down on top of the mahogany desk in front of us, then slides them across, directly in front of me, handing me a pen to use.

This time I'm not stupid. Before signing I begin to read the fine print, verifying the accounts match the small pieces of paper that he hands back to me. Right now I don't trust many people and the last thing I want is to find out he's working with Bill. Screwing me over once again. Verifying that everything matches, I sign away.

Half an hour later, I've got two grand in cash, Matt is four million dollars richer, and I pray he doesn't screw me over as well.

As I'm walking out of the bank and getting into the car my cell phone rings. Excited that it might be Matt already calling me about the money, I dig into my purse and answer right away, without looking at the screen. But, I'm soon disappointed when I hear another voice at the end of the line.

"Where are you?" Bill's tries to sound calm, but even I can hear the strain coming from his voice.

As the driver is starting to pull away from the curb and into the mass of downtown traffic, I answer, "Oh, out and about."

Knowing what Bill's already going to ask, I notify him. "Yes, I made sure to bring my babysitter with me," I say sarcastically.

I'm looking at the driver as I say it and as expected he's listening. He glares at me through the rear view mirror as his eyebrows rise and I know he doesn't like that I called him my babysitter, but I don't care. That's exactly what he is.

Neither does Bill, apparently. "He's not your babysitter Abigail, he's your bodyguard," he clips out.

I roll my eyes and think, whatever. You know damn well that he's feeding you information. I'm surprised Bill isn't asking why I was at the bank, or maybe the babysitter hasn't informed him yet.

Bill continues, "I have to leave town on a business emergency, one of my other clients is having problems and I have to head to New York to take care of it. Are you going to be okay here by yourself?"

What does he think I am, a baby? I might have lost my memory, but I'm not disabled.

"Of course Bill. It's not like you've been spending much time with me anyways."

"I know; I'm sorry about that, baby. I've been really caught up with work lately, but when I get back, we'll go out to a nice dinner, just you and me. What do you say?"

Apparently, I am a baby to him. The only thing I can think right now, is that I don't want to go anywhere with him, but I don't want to give him any clue that I know about him and Susan. So the only thing I can do is play along.

"Okay, that sounds good," I lie cheerfully for effect.

"Alright. If you need anything at all, call Susan. Her number should be programmed in your phone as well. And Abigail, remember you are not to go anywhere without the bodyguard. You understand?"

Shit, he's really trying to keep me on a leash. Was he always this controlling with me, or was he serious about the public? Since I've hauled my bodyguard with me the last two days, I have yet to see a mob, or anyone, try to approach me. I don't think they even care who I am, so why the beefed up security? This is probably his way of keeping tabs on me.

Then he tops it off by saying, "I've directed him to stay at the apartment in one of the guest rooms while I'm gone, that way you will have him at your disposal, when needed."

Taking in a deep breath, I'm trying to calm the boiling blood that is now rising from what he's said. "Fine, have a safe trip Bill," I clip out to him before I end the call.

Great, I was going to use this opportunity to sneak away back to Portland and spend time with Matt, but I guess that's going to prove to be tricky. I hate knowing that I have to sneak around. Bill expects to go out with his fuck buddy at his convenience while I sit at home acting like the good little fiancée he wants me to be.

We finally arrive back at the apartment and the first thing I do is go straight to my room and lock myself in. I sit on the bed and begin to read the rest of the paperwork that Frank gave me. I discover that the apartment is in Bill's name so I can't exactly kick him out, but it doesn't mean I can't leave. The only problem is where the hell am I supposed to go. I guess I could try to rent a hotel for couple of days until I can figure out what to do from there.

I sit there on my bed as my thoughts begin to wander off as usual, straight to thinking of Matt. As if on cue, the phone rings. I look down at the screen recognizing the number.

"Hello."

"When you said you were putting some money into my account, you didn't say it was going to be millions! What were you thinking? This isn't drug money or anything illegal, is it?" he shouts into the phone, forcing me to remove it from my ear while I flinch.

Rolling my eyes, I clearly state, "It isn't illegal money Matt. It's what my fiancé has left me. He doesn't know I put it into your account," I answer as if it's no big deal.

"Why wouldn't you want him to know you put it into

my account?" he asks, very suspiciously.

"Look the truth is, I found out he's been cheating on me, has been stealing money from me for the last year, and I don't know what to do from here. I needed somewhere safe to keep what was left of my money so he wouldn't take any more of it."

"And you trusted a total stranger with it, instead," Matt says sarcastically, but with a touch of humor as well.

"I really doubt you'd be able to wipe out that much money on beer and pot in a matter of days," I say, rolling my eyes again. "Anyways, you promised I could trust you, so you better not screw me over either," I snap at him.

"*You can trust me.* By the way, that *was* the last of the stash and we don't plan on buying anymore until the season is over. Coach's rules, we have to be clean before and during the season. That's why we decided to light it up one last time. It's not my fault you chose that day to do an impromptu visit."

I shake my head as I take in his statement, giving us both a silent pause on the line.

The silence coming from my end must have made him just as uncomfortable because his voice becomes reassuring as he states, "I'm not going to screw you over, Abigail. I have my own money to spend. I don't need to touch yours. I promise it's safe with me until you touch it," Matt says with a sigh I can clearly hear through the phone.

He continues on, "If you know he's cheating on you, why don't you leave the jerk?"

"I'm working on it. It's not as easy as you think. I have no family that I know of. I still haven't gotten my memory back, and I have nowhere to go." Now I'm sounding pathetic, but I continue. "He's gone for the next couple of days on business anyway, so I'll figure out what to do while he's gone."

We both stay quiet on the phone causing an awkward pause again. I really wish I could see his face right now. It would make me feel so much better.

"Okay. I have to go, but if you need anything, just let me know. Talk to you later, beautiful," he says before he hangs up.

Beautiful? Why in the world would he call me beautiful?

I stare down at the phone, dumbfounded and numb about what he said. The endearment did make me feel better and I sit there on my bed smiling with delight, wishing again that I could at least see him. This whole memory thing might be crazy, but at least I got one positive thing out of it.

# Chapter 8

AS THE DAY wears on, I keep thinking about the situation I am in. I wish that it would get a bit easier to deal with. I need to get out some of my pent up tension, so I decide to go out for a run. After getting dressed and lacing up my running shoes, I head out the door with my babysitter in tow.

Twenty minutes later, as my babysitter and I are pounding the pavement with our shoes, it begins to drizzle. Great, right when I started to hit my nirvana of running, I'm about to get soaked. So we high tail it back to the apartment. I might like running now, but I don't like doing it in the rain.

We make it back just as the rain starts to pour, leaving us a bit soaked as we exit the elevator to my apartment. As we are entering the foyer I hear a noise coming from Bill's study. That's strange. I'd thought he was going on a business trip, who the hell could be in there?

My babysitter goes on high alert, stepping in front of me and begins to walk towards the door, but I follow him.

When we get to the door the sounds are getting louder,

but they're not sounds I would expecting from someone who is working. It sounds more like screams of pleasure.

That's when the hairs on the back of my neck stand up. I step in front of the bodyguard and go straight into the study. I'm surprised when I see Bill pounding into Susan on his desk. I didn't think he'd be brave enough to fuck her in our own apartment.

He must have heard us walk in because he looks straight up as we enter with a look of shock on his face. Of course, you should be shocked, asshole. You just proved what I already knew, but this time I get to see it with my own eyes.

Bill immediately starts pulling away from Susan, leaving her confused, until she turns around and sees me. A smile forms on her face, which doesn't surprise me.

Seeing her, lying on his desk, leaves me frozen in my spot. I can't move. My feet feel like they've been glued to the floor, and I stand there dazed by the whole situation.

"Andre, take Susan home please. Abigail and I need to talk," he says as he's buckling up his pants and walking to me.

Seeing Bill coming straight towards me, I snap out of my paralyzed state, turning around and walking straight out of the study. I hear Bill calling after me, but I ignore him and head to my closet.

"Leave me alone, Bill!" I shout behind my back.

"It's not what you think," he says, finally catching up to me.

I spin around to face him, causing him to stop at the entrance of the bedroom. My chest is heaving from the anger emanating from me.

"Oh, really? You care to explain what I saw then, because I'm pretty sure I just saw you fucking her?" I yell at him.

My arms are at my sides and my hands are forming a fist, ready to hit something. I'm raging inside and the heat in my glare right now is showing him just how pissed I am.

Pathetically, Bill says, "It just happened. I didn't intend for it to, but it did. I'm sorry, it won't happen again. Please Abigail, you have to believe me."

The scary thing is, from the look on his face you would actually think he is telling the truth, but since I know he's lying, I give him a disgusted look.

Who the hell does he think he's talking to? Is this the way he was with me before the coma? Lying to me and deceiving me, making me believe he cared about me? Man, I must have been some naïve person not to figure it out sooner.

I hear my babysitter informing Bill that he's leaving to take Susan home. Bill nods his head in agreement, still staring at me. I turn right back around and keep heading to the closet. I need to get out of here and I need to do it fast.

Once inside the closet, I look around and find a large Louis Vuitton duffel bag. Grabbing it, I start haphazardly yanking clothes off the hangers, tossing them into the bag.

"What are you doing?" Bill asks from the doorway.

"What does it look like I'm doing? I'm leaving."

"Where the hell do you think you're going?"

"I'm not stupid Bill, I know you've been fucking her for a while. I was only in the way of you giving her the attention she's been wanting this whole time."

"What do you expect to do once you leave? You're nothing without me. I made you who you are, Abigail," he claims with a condescending tone. "If you were smart, you'd forget this whole little situation and continue being the good girl that you are."

My temper is rising, but I ignore it, trying to focus on my packing. I don't care what he made me. I don't need it or *this* shit right now.

Finally done packing, I walk out of the closet, clipping Bill on the shoulder on my way out. He spins around and grabs my arm in a firm grip, giving it a jolt of pain.

I look down at his hand and back up at his face with fury. "Let go of my arm Bill," I growl at him.

He brings his face close to mine with a sneer in his eyes. "Or what? You're not going anywhere, Abigail. I own you, and if you know what's best for you, you'll stay. I could easily ruin your career. You'd become a nobody, and trust me, as hard as you worked for it, I could take it all away in a heartbeat."

I'm outraged by what he's said and I end up spitting in his face from my anger. It clearly pisses him off. The next thing I feel is a blow on the side of my face, like I was hit with a brick. My ears begin to ring and I see stars for a moment.

I'm stumbling back from the force, landing with my ass on the floor and I look up to see Bill standing right above me, with rage in his eyes as he begins to wipe his face with the back of his hand.

The monster of aggression that I've been keeping pent up inside of me comes out. Since he's standing closely above me, the first thing I do is bring my foot up and forward between his legs with all of the force that I can muster. I scramble myself up as best as I can, while he's going down to his knees holding his groin, grunting in pain. I bring my fist back and then forward, striking him straight in his nose.

When I hit him, my hand feels like it's going to burst from the force of impact. It physically feels like it hurt me more than it did him, but by the way his head drives back, I know I got him good. He hits the floor with a hard thump, grabbing his now bleeding nose. Even though he's still conscious, he's unable to get up. I grab my bag, which fell on the floor, and head straight for my room.

With a mad rush, I grab my purse and the file that the PI gave me, stuffing it into the purse running to the elevator to enter it, and head down to the lobby. As I'm walking away from the building, I'm shaking from the adrenaline of what just happened.

It finally occurs to me that he was right and I start to panic. I have nowhere to go here in Seattle. The last thing I want right now is to go into hiding from Bill, but it is the safest thing to do, since I had no idea what to do next.

As I continue walking, I see someone exiting a taxi next to me, so I make a rash decision and get into it, informing the driver I need the train station. If I was going to have to hide from Bill, I was going to have to do it somewhere he wouldn't expect me to go.

My face chooses this moment to alert me that it stings from the hit, and I look in the rearview mirror of the taxi and notice that it's starting to swell up and change color on the side of my face. Great, the last thing I need is someone recognizing me with a black eye.

I dig around in my purse and find a pair of big oval glasses, put them on, and pull my hair out of its ponytail to cover the rest up. Even though it's cloudy outside, at least they cover my eyes.

# Chapter 9

I'M ONCE AGAIN standing at the same front door as yesterday, waiting for an answer. I didn't call, because I really didn't want to have to explain why I was on my way here over the phone, in case someone around me was listening. So instead I grabbed a cab from the train station, and headed straight here praying I wouldn't be turned away.

It's dark now, so upon exiting the cab, I took off the sunglasses I was wearing, and now I'm waiting for a savior to open the door. Then he does. Matt is shocked to see me standing there, but the minute I see him I start to shed the tears I've been holding for the past four and a half hours.

He opens his arms without hesitation and I walk straight up to him. He takes me into his arms, and holds me while I bawl my eyes out. I don't know how long we stood there in the doorway, but when I pulled away, I felt so much better.

Matt steps back so we can enter together, closing the door behind us. I was so lost in my world of crying that I didn't even notice the noise coming from inside the house.

I take a peek from the doorway into the living room and notice the large group of people gathered there. I see Trey walking up to us, and the horrified look on his face makes me shed another tear. He's holding a bottled beer in his hand, and his knuckles starts to turn white from the force that he's squeezing it with. He looks rigid and his breathing is now becoming heavy. Just looking at him I'm starting to get a bit frightened again, but Matt reminds me that he's still standing next to me when he pulls me protectively against his body. Trey nods his head, in a silent understanding to Matt, and turns back around towards the living room.

"Alright fuckers, party's over! Everyone out. Now!" Trey yells at the room. The tone in his voice obviously dares anybody to challenge him, but I doubt they will.

I feel Matt tug me towards the hallway leading to the bedrooms and I follow, with my head hung low, thankful that my hair is covering my face. He leads me to the very end of the hallway, and upon entering I already know it's Matt's room. It's the kind of room I imagined him having.

The floor is done in a dark hardwood. The furniture is also dark wood, almost matching the flooring, not masculine, but modern. There is an open door off to the right, which looks to lead to a bathroom. The bed is rumpled with dark coverings, and there are clothes lightly scattered around the room.

Matt leads me over to sit on the bed. "Here, sit down, you look exhausted," he says before he starts picking up the clothing on the floor, in an attempt to tidy the room. I sit there watching him, admiring him, wondering what the hell I'm supposed to do now.

He finally finishes, and stands a couple of feet in front of me. He crosses his arms in front of his chest and his eyes on me, as if waiting for me to say something.

"I walked in on him fucking her," I tell him.

He stays silent, simply staring down at me, expression-less.

Taking a deep breath, I keep going, "So I started pack-ing some clothes, ready to leave, but he didn't take it so well. He stated that I needed him. That he was the one who made me who I was and I was nothing without him, especially since I have no family. He threatened to ruin my career," I say, shaking my head. "At this point I don't really care any-more."

"You don't need him, Abigail."

"I know, but I hate how he's right. I don't have any family, and if he keeps his word about my career, it will be over. What am I supposed to do? I had nowhere to go, I pan-icked, and came here." I bury my face in my hands and begin to sob again.

Matt kneels in front of me, pulling my hands from my face into his. When he looks deeply into my eyes, the sobs stop, just from seeing the comfort in his eyes. He lightly brushes the side of my hair near my injured eye behind my ear, wanting to see more of my face.

He hesitantly touches the tender spot of my eye with his fingertips, making me quickly flinch. Then he gently starts rubbing my chin with his thumb while his eyes stay on mine. I lean my face into his hand, wanting to feel the warmth of it, needing the comfort.

"You were right to come here, and you don't need him for a career. You're a beautiful girl, and could get any job you wanted, if you work hard enough for it." His response makes me smile. "You're not alone anymore. Trey and I are your family now."

The way he says it, I want to believe him, and the look in Matt's eyes seems to indicate sincerity. With everything going on in my life right now, there's nothing I can do but take his word.

I sniffle and nod my head as he pulls me into his body, hugging me, and wrapping his lean arms around my waist. He starts to rub my back and I bury my face in the crook of his neck, taking in the unique scent that is him.

We stay like that for a couple of minutes, and then we hear a knock at the door, pulling us apart to look towards it. Trey walks in, still looking pissed.

"Everyone's gone," he immediately says. "Care to tell me what the fuck happened to your face?" Trey growls at me.

Matt scowls at him. "Leave her alone for now Trey, she's obviously had a rough night," he says to him very sternly.

I stand up now looking back and forth between the two of them, not wanting them to fight. "When I tried leaving, he grabbed my arm so I spit in his face, and he hit me."

"What!" they both say at the same time with fury. I flinch from how loud they say it. But it's Matt who says, "I'm going to kill him!" With Trey saying after him, "Not if I kill that fucker first."

Hearing them say that makes me smile, knowing that I have two guys willing to hurt someone for me. I barely know these two, but they'd be willing to defend my honor in a heartbeat. I tell them what happened, and how I was able to escape Bill. They're both surprised at how I was able to take Bill, but proud of me.

"Damn, supermodel. I'll make sure not to piss you off," Trey says in a mocking tone while taking a sip of his beer.

I silently laugh. Even if he were to piss me off, I'm pretty sure I wouldn't be able to take him out. He's too big. At that moment my stomach starts to rumble very loudly, and it makes us all laugh.

Trey throws his arm around my shoulders, and says to me. "Come on kung-fu supermodel, we need to feed your skinny ass."

It makes me smile while I walk out of the room with him towards the kitchen, Matt following close behind us.

I'm finally able to take in the whole scene and you can tell that there was a party going on in here. I try to ignore the mess as best as I can, since I'm already getting the urge to tidy up, but my stomach is protesting to be fed, which is exactly what I intend to do at this point.

The smell of the pizza hits me when we enter the kitchen and my mouth starts to water as Matt hands me a slice of pizza loaded with all kinds of veggies and meat. As I take a bite, I moan, because this pizza is delicious.

Matt eyes me with a smile. "Good, huh? It's the best pizza in town, but they don't deliver so we only get it when one of us is willing to drive for it."

The boxes on the counter say *Flying Pie Pizza* on them. Shoot, I'll drive from now on just to get this mouth-watering sin.

We eat in silence, standing against the counter in the kitchen and I can tell by the looks on both their faces that they are anxious to start asking questions, but they don't. Which, I'm grateful for. After eating a second slice I feel like my stomach is going to explode, but I am completely satisfied.

Looking back into the living room, I can't take it any longer and finally start to tidy up the place. This time though

Matt helps me. He's quiet the whole time he's helping. I can tell he's thinking really hard, but he still won't say anything.

Once we're done, I go and sit on the couch. Finally feeling like I can relax, I take off my shoes, and curl my feet under my legs. Matt sits on the recliner that I had sat on yesterday, elbows on his knees, staring me.

"What?" I say to him.

He merely smirks. "You took my advice and went for a run."

I look down at my clothes and realize that I still have my running clothes on, including the light jacket that I had worn.

I nod. "You were right, it really did help. At least it helped before the shit hit the fan," I state.

"Are those the only ones you have?" Matt points at my clothes.

Now that I realize it, they are. The new stuff I had bought was in the guest bedroom I was staying in, so I didn't get a chance to pack them in the bag. Good thing I had the shoes on, or else I would have cried all over again.

I nod. "Well then, we'll have to get those washed tonight because we're both going to need a run tomorrow morning."

Trey comes up and sits on the other end of the couch, beer in hand, staring at the flat screen that's tuned to the sports channel. As I'm sitting there, the exhaustion of the day is catching up to me, and my eyes start to grow heavy. Matt notices and stands up, extending his arm and hand to me.

"You look exhausted, let's get you in a bed so you can get your rest," Matt says quietly. "You can crash in my room in the meantime, it's cleaner, and that bed *actually* has sheets on it. I'm taking the extra room until we get this whole situation settled."

I'm so tired right now that I'm not going to argue with him. Grabbing his hand he pulls me up, and walks with me back down the hallway to his room.

"You want to shower?" he says, looking at me with concern.

"That sounds good," I tell him.

Crap, I didn't even think to pack anything to sleep in. I was too focused on clothes to wear. "I forgot to pack something to sleep in."

He heads over to a dresser and grabs a shirt and some boxer briefs, then hands them to me.

"You can wear those for now, tomorrow we can go online for whatever else you need. Remember, I have your money in my account, it's yours to spend however you want."

"Matt," I whisper to him, "I want to say… thank you… for everything. I really didn't mean to impose on you." I pause, taking a deep breath. "I guess I was just scared, and this was the first place I thought of going when I left," I finish, staring down at the floor, feeling embarrassed.

Matt comes over to me, taking me in his arms in a tight embrace. "Look, I don't know what's going on in that beautiful head of yours, but whatever it is, it brought you to me, which makes you mine now, and I always protect what's mine, Abigail."

From the way he says it, the emotion strong with every word, I know he's telling me the truth and I begin to cry. I cry because I know I've finally found someone who cares, someone who I can finally trust, and I don't want to let go.

He pushes us apart so he can look down into my eyes.

"Don't cry, beautiful. We'll figure this out. There has to be a reason why all this is happening, we just have to figure it out. Okay?" He has a calming look, and those damn eyes with long lashes are mesmerizing at this moment, which make you believe anything he says.

I nod my head at him, wiping my nose with the back of my hand. He leaves me, pointing to his bathroom, telling me that the hanging towels are clean.

After showering and dressing in the clothes Matt gave me I climb into bed and fall asleep the instant my head hits the pillow.

I KNOW I'M sleeping, but somehow it feels like I'm wide-awake. I sit up feeling strange and sensing someone else in the room. It's still dark, but since there's a full moon tonight, there is plenty of moonlight shining through the window. It's casting enough light for me to notice the other person I'm sensing sitting at the edge of the bed.

At first, I become frightened, but a feeling of calm takes over my body almost immediately. I don't recognize the person right away, but her face has a familiarity that I've seen before. Then it occurs to me that she is the woman in the picture that Matt showed me yesterday, the one with him at his graduation.

"I see you two are getting along well," she says, smiling.

"Who are you?"

"Abigail, I'm pretty sure you already know the answer to that question."

I know I do, but I'm in denial that I'm sitting here staring at a dead person. I must be going out of my mind. Or maybe this is a side effect of losing my mind completely.

"I can reassure you, you're perfectly fine. I chose you because I thought you needed each other. He's right you know, he will protect you at all costs, so be careful what you ask from him."

Is she talking about Matt?

"Yes, I'm speaking of my brother. It has always been one of his strongest characteristics to protect those he loves. Once he's promised something he makes sure to keep that promise, so I really hope you'll do the same in return."

It takes me a moment to absorb what she's told me and I feel like I should say something in response, but what is there to say?

"I can't explain to you why you're having these memories of mine, but I hope they will help you understand him better. Cherish them as I once cherished making them. Promise me, Abigail. Promise you'll be there for him, just as he's promised to be there for you," she pleads.

I know I really shouldn't make such a commitment, but deep down inside my heart is telling me I should.

"I promise," I almost whisper it to her.

As soon as I'm done promising, she begins to fade away, with a smile on her face, leaving me there alone.

I sit there with the moonlight at the edge of the bed where she was a moment ago, thinking to myself about the conversation that barely took place. What was it supposed to mean? I lie back down and stare up at the ceiling, hoping the darkness will drag me to sleep as it usually does.

I realize, I might not know anything about my past, but I do know that I have a future, and if it involves Matt in my life, then so be it.

# Chapter 10

"HEY BEAUTIFUL, YOU awake yet?"

I hear Matt walking into the room, but I ignore him, refusing to wake up. I'm still tired from not being able to sleep very well after his sister appeared in my sleep. At least I want to believe I was sleeping. I really doubt that if I were to repeat anything from last night to anyone, they wouldn't believe I wasn't dreaming.

Still ignoring the fact that Matt is trying to wake me up, I stay lying on my stomach with my face buried to the side of the pillow. I start to hear the scraping of the dresser drawers opening and closing. A moment later, I hear light footsteps walking towards the closet causing me to crack my eyelids a bit, curious as to what Matt is doing. What I see next makes me catch my breath and open my eyes wide wanting to take in a better view.

He's removing the only stitch of clothing he has on, which happens to be boxer briefs, baring his naked ass in my direction. A fine ass it is.

I start to rake my eyes up and down his body, observing every muscle that is facing me needing to get a better view. His back is rigidly toned, his legs have calves that are obviously built from the running he must do, and his arms are perfectly sculpted.

As he bends over to put on his running shorts, I continue staring. Now there's an ass that would give Adonis a run for his money, perfectly round and lifted to perfection, nary a sign of cellulite in sight.

I see him start to turn his body as he begins to put his shirt on and I automatically shut my eyes, not wanting him to catch me ogling. Hopefully, he won't notice the drool that is probably leaking from my mouth at this very moment.

Suddenly I feel the blanket that was lying on top of my body suddenly disappear, leaving me with a bitter cold to replace the warmth that was once there. As I slightly turn my head to see what has happened, I see Matt silently observing my ass, right before he quickly brings his hand down making contact with it.

If I wasn't awake before, I am now.

"What the fuck!" I yell as I turn my body to face him, shocked and confused. Why the fuck did he just do that?

The sting is rippling through my body, sending an unexpected tingle as I rub my sore bottom with my hand. He didn't slap it hard, but just enough to give my body a message. One I'm still confused about. I don't know whether to be upset or turned on. Right now my body is leaning towards the latter, but I'm not going to announce that to him.

"I thought that'd get you up. Come on, the sooner we leave the sooner we get back to eat a real breakfast," he says, walking back towards the closet to grab some shoes. "I washed the clothes you were wearing last night, they're on the bed," he says before exiting the room, closing the door behind him.

Where the hell is he referring to when he said we're leaving? He didn't mention anything before I went to bed about going anywhere this morning and I'm still confused, trying to make sense of what happened just now.

Why in the world would he be staring at my ass one moment and then slapping it the next? The curious side of me is wondering: does he want me like I've wanted him? If he wanted to touch my ass, all he had to do was ask. I would have been more than happy to let him.

Uhh, there I go again, thinking with my sex-craved mind when it comes to Matt. Okay, I need to get my sore ass up and dressed before he comes in here wanting to do that all over again. Because I guarantee you, this time I would make sure I got more than just a slap on the ass.

"ARE YOU SURE you weren't a runner before this week?" Matt asks me.

We're sitting on the grass in the park, done with our run from this morning. Legs stretched out in front us, crossed at the ankles. With our arms stretched up behind us supporting our bodies. Even though I just put my body through a much faster pace than I normally had before, I feel relaxed and much better than I have for the last couple of days.

Matt is all sweaty and his running shirt is soaked from perspiration, outlining the chiseled washboard muscles lining his stomach. He looks so sexy right now, and all I want to do is run my tongue down his neck to lick the remaining sweat beads. I'm pretty sure he'd taste really salty, but it'd be worth the tangy taste.

"Abigail," I hear Matt say, breaking me from my thoughts.

Remembering that he asked me a question, I have to concentrate to remember what he asked.

"I don't know. I don't think I was a runner in the past. It's really hard to say what I did or didn't do before the accident. The little information I know about myself is what is posted on the Internet, and we both know how accurate that can be," I say sarcastically.

Matt cocks his head to the side, focusing on me intensely. "It's just strange that you were able to keep up with me pretty well towards the end. At first I was thinking that I might have to take it easy on you, but you kept pace, so I decided to speed up. Maybe it's those long legs of yours," he says smiling, looking down the length of my legs.

The heat of his stare as his eyes run down my legs sends a chill through my body, making me shiver.

"Is that good or bad?" I finally say with a chuckle. I find it amusing we're both sitting here obviously checking each other out, but trying to ignore it just the same.

The smile he returns makes my heart skip and makes my body turn to mush. "It's good. Which means I don't have to take it easy on you anymore, and we can get in some good runs."

I'm sitting there, staring at him and my eyes are now focused on his tattoo. It's intriguing and I'm unable to take my eyes off it. "Matt, what made you get an angel's wing?" I ask, still focused on the intricate design on his arm.

He looks down at it, focusing on it for a couple of seconds, then looks up at me. His eyes look glazed and by the way his lashes are rapidly blinking, I know he's now fighting back tears.

"I got it in honor of my sister after she died. I like to think that she's my angel looking down at me and the tattoo is a way of me keeping a piece of her close to me," he says, his voice raspy and almost a whisper.

I feel my chest tighten up and a lump starts to form in my throat as I fight back tears that are threating to flow down my eyes. Matt looks back down to it, he looks just as affected as I feel as he focuses on his bicep.

He takes one last deep breath, and then shakes his head before he stands up, slapping my feet with his hand as he does. "Come on. With a run like that you deserve some pancakes." That distracts me from my solemn thoughts.

"You know, with the way you guys are feeding me, I'm going to blow up like a balloon. I don't think I got this body from eating the way I have the last couple of days."

Walking in the direction of the parked car he looks back at me, with a grin. "Then you'll just have to run more now, won't you?" he states as he keeps walking, leaving me to follow him.

I could think of another activity that would accelerate my heart rate and make me sweat....

I'm relieved when we make it back to the car, since my stomach is starting to growl. As he starts it, I swear every time I get in, I get excited all over again. Just sitting in it while it's running drives me insane. The power of the engine vibrating beneath my body is enough to push me to come right there in the seat.

I don't know whose ride I crave more each day, the owner or the car? It's a tough toss up sometimes. Being that I've ridden in the car already, I would have to say the owner is next in line.

I'm so lost in my fantasy that I almost don't hear Matt when he asks why I had to transfer the money into his account. So I explain the whole story of Bill and the contracts, including what I heard while I was in my coma. As I'm explaining, at first I even think it sounds insane.

"So you simply have to keep from making any money that includes anything to do with your career?"

"I guess so?" I respond, staring at the traffic ahead of me.

Keeping his eyes on the road ahead, he says, "Okay. Three months isn't too long of a wait for you to stay low on your career. With all the shit that's happened to you in the last couple of days, you could look at it as a vacation."

Yeah, one where I might go bored out of my mind unless I can find another form of distraction, quick.

As we're driving, his phone begins to ring. He lifts it up to look at who is calling, then pushes the ignore button just as fast. I was able to get a glance at who was on the screen and there was a picture of a girl.

Crazy as it might sound, I actually feel a little bit jealous. Why? I have no clue. I obviously have no claim on him and I don't know anything when it comes to his personal life. As good looking as he is, I wouldn't be surprised if there *was* a girl in his life. Knowing it's a possibility drives me insane in my seat. I already want to claw the girl's eyes out.

A minute goes by and the phone rings again. He lifts the phone without looking at it this time, and pushes a button on the top, silencing it. It immediately begins to ring again and this must have pissed Matt off because he jerks the car to the side of the road, throwing my body against the door as it comes to a stop.

He quickly answers the call and barks into it, "What do you want? I'm busy right now."

Damn, remind me never to call him repeatedly if he's ignored the first call. Whoever is on the other end of the call obviously doesn't get the clue, and they're lucky they can't see the look on his face. He's scowling at the road ahead of him like he's shooting daggers with his eyes at an imaginary person.

He sits there, listening to whoever is speaking on the other end of the line before saying irritably, "No, not this week, I have a lot going on. I don't have any free time. I'll call you later if I feel like it." He stays quiet a couple of seconds, probably listening to the reply. Then he ends the call. Without bothering to look in my direction, he begins to slowly pull the car back onto the road and I sit there wondering whether to keep to my mouth shut or ask.

Curiosity gets the better of me. "So who was that? Your girlfriend?"

Still staring ahead onto the road, he says, "I don't have a girlfriend, and I definitely don't do relationships. Did that once and learned my lesson for life."

I know I was recently screwed over, which taught me a lesson for life, but not enough to throw dating completely out of the window. Grimacing, I realize I do know exactly how he feels, but that still doesn't explain the phone call, which is the answer I was looking for.

"So if the girl wasn't your girlfriend, then she must be a friend. Why were you so rude to her? Didn't your sister raise you to respect girls?" I throw at him as he focuses on driving.

Sighing deeply, like he's trying to calm himself, he keeps his eyes on the road.

The car pulls up to a red light and when he finally brings the car to a complete stop he turns his body to face me. "My sister did raise me to treat a girl with respect, but being that this one spreads her legs easily, I feel I don't have much respect for her nowadays," he says.

My eyes go wide in shock over what he's said. Whether she spreads her legs easily or not, he doesn't have any right to say it. "That's a fucked up thing to say about a girl. What she chooses to do with her body doesn't define who she is," I irritably say, because only ten minutes ago I was willing to give him my body if he would've asked. So would that have labeled me a slut in his eyes?

Apparently, it would have.

"Look, you're right, I shouldn't judge her, but she can be really annoying sometimes. She gets really needy and it pisses me off," he quietly says, trying to justify his answer.

I roll my eyes for him to see. Is he expecting his response to make the earlier one any better?

The light turns green and he turns to focus on the road once again as he drives the car forward. I'm beginning to discover that I like details, and I want lots of them. So of course, I push the subject, pressing for an answer.

"So if you don't do relationships, how many friends do you have?" I ask, wondering whether I want the real truth to that answer.

A cocky grin spreads on his face. "I have one for every day of the week."

"Who's the slut now?" I respond dryly.

"I wasn't always this way you know," he says in his defense, trying to make his lifestyle seem normal. "I dated a girl all throughout high school. You can actually say we were high school sweethearts. We made plans to go to college together and then get married. You know the whole painted picture of a love story, but life had other plans for us."

As I'm about to ask what the plan was he continues.

"I got a scholarship for here in Portland and hers was to Berkley. It's the college her parents went to, so she was destined to go no matter what. I thought of the pros and cons of the situation and I couldn't refuse a paid scholarship, so we chose to try to have a long distance relationship. It worked for a bit, but eventually party life got to the both of us. We tried really hard to be faithful, but it didn't happen. We both made mistakes, which eventually led to us having a touch and go relationship," he says as he's still focusing on driving through the traffic.

"I don't get it. How would this one relationship screw it up for you, forever?"

He stays quiet for a moment, and then answers, "I guess I thought it would be easier to have friends with benefits than to tie myself down to one girl. In case my ex changed her mind and decided she wanted to get back together."

It occurs to me that he's still in love with her. I can tell by the saddened expression on his face and it's also showing how much it's hurting him to talk about it. She was probably his first love, his first everything, which most high school sweethearts are. Those kinds of girls are always hard to let go.

"Do you still love her?" I bravely ask, almost at a whisper.

He takes a moment to quickly glance at me and answers my question. "Of course."

And there you have it. The answer I desperately didn't want to hear, but have to take because it's reality. It's his reality. The one that I'm going to have to live with if I plan to keep *my* promise. No wonder why he refuses to date anyone. He's still holding out for the happily ever after with Ms. Berkley.

Well, I've learned one lesson from all this. Sometimes the truth really sucks.

# Chapter
## 11

THE NEXT COUPLE of days go by normally, with the exception of Trey not being at the house. He was scheduled to go home back south for the next several weeks, so it was just Matt and I. At first, I had thought it would be very awkward with the two us alone since I had started to develop an attraction for him, but things didn't change. He never made any advances on me. After the whole friends with benefits conversation in the car, I had learned my lesson and forced my sexual attraction to take a vacation along with Trey.

Somehow, Matt got the memo about the vacation my sexual libido was taking, because he had grown comfortable with the *roommate* situation. He'd begun walking around in his boxer briefs when it was convenient for him, torturing the crap out of me.

I had brought up the lack of clothing to him, telling him it made me a little uncomfortable when he did that. He only laughed at me and claimed that according to the photos on the Internet, I should be used to being naked most of the time. So therefore, his boxer briefs shouldn't be offensive to me at all. I was so irritated with his response; I ended up throwing the remote at him.

It had made him laugh harder as he caught it.

He might be intolerable with his boxer briefs, but I guess I could let it slide since he was so good looking in them. It did give me a distraction sometimes.

Another change that took place was the living arrangements. Matt had taken permanent residence in the third bedroom, insisting that I take his old bedroom. When I had refused, demanding that I take the third bedroom, since technically I was the crash roommate, he ignored my request.

He pointed out that a girl needed a bathroom of her own and since the master bedroom already had one, I was to keep the room. I didn't feel too bad when I noticed how disgusting the hallway bathroom looked. How in the world did guys live like that?

Matt had also taken it upon himself to buy me a new phone. I needed one after what happened to my original one. The second night in the house I had sat down with Matt and Trey in the living room to turn on my phone and listen to the voicemails that Bill had placed after I left. They were pretty vulgar. He even went as far as threatening to kill me because of what I did to him. By Matt's reaction he wasn't too happy with Bill's messages and words. He had grabbed the phone from my hand, throwing it against the wall, cracking it to pieces. Which resulted in me needing a new phone.

At first, I was hesitant to take it, claiming that Bill might be able to track me through it. But when Matt informed me the phone was under his name, making it difficult for Bill to find me, I felt a lot more comfortable using it.

It was a shiny new white iPhone that Matt had loaded

with a bunch of cool apps and songs. I was in love with it the minute he handed it to me. I rarely put it down, unless necessary. It had come to the point that it was now a permanent part of my body.

During this time I also discovered how good of a cook Matt was. I was very surprised when he practically whipped up a full course dinner, but he didn't stop there. He also knew how to make an awesome breakfast and lunch if needed.

The first night we ate his full course dinner, he wasn't expecting me to insist we eat at the dining room table. When we were about to walk into the living room to eat as usual I asked, "Why don't you guys ever use the dining table?" Looking over at the table leaning against the wall, I wondered why it looks more like a standing counter top where everything ended up.

He looks over at it, shrugging one shoulder. "I don't know. We've never thought of using it for eating purposes. It gets more usage for beer pong than anything else," he said as he walked completely past it.

Not happy with his answer, I stop and place my plate on the island, then head over to the table and begin clearing the things off. Matt notices and heads back in my direction helping me and within minutes the table is cleared. After a quick wipe down, we are finally able to sit down and have a normal dinner, like normal people.

I would have said like a normal couple, but that was pushing it a little too far when it came to Matt. Knowing that he was willing to change one thing about himself to make me happy gave me some hope. Now if I could only work on changing the one thing I *really* wanted to change about him, but I wasn't going to hold my breath trying.

ONCE I KNEW I had the power to make *some* changes, I took full advantage. The first thing I did was order new couches; the old ones stank like sweat, and had stains. I don't even want to know what they consisted of. With them being guys, I was happy being kept in the dark.

When I told Matt his only response was a raised eyebrow, but he didn't argue. I had to keep in mind that men still lived in the house. So I went with dark brown leather, hoping that it would prevent a reoccurrence of the stains.

I did plan to keep Matt's notorious leather recliner in the equation. Even if it was huge and took up a great deal of space in the room, I couldn't bring myself to get rid of it. Especially since it was the one thing that reminded me of the first day I'd met Matt.

What was hilarious though, was how Matt began to insist that the recliner wasn't going anywhere when the delivery guys showed up the next day with the new sofas. He had thought that I intended on getting rid of the recliner as well.

Knowing how much he loved that thing, I had put up a light argument for the fun of it. Matt was just as hot when angry, as he was any other time. It made me want to laugh. It was hard to stand there staring at him and not tell him the truth, but after a couple of minutes I couldn't hold in my laughter any longer.

Realizing that I was only playing with him the whole time, Matt smiled at me shaking his head and I had thought I'd gotten him good since he didn't really say or do anything to lecture me.

Oh, but I was wrong. What I didn't expect was what happened after Matt had walked the delivery guys out the door.

"Ms. Abigail Adams. That little prank of yours wasn't very nice," he says, stalking towards me from the doorway with the look of a predator on the hunt. The look worried me a bit. I had no idea what he was planning on doing to me, but by the smirk on his face, it was going to be good.

I shrugged my shoulders at him. "You're the one who made assumptions, so I just went along with it," I tell him with the same smirk on my lips.

He starts to come around the large couch that is now in the middle of the living room, and I slowly walk back around in the opposite direction. I know it's not helping my situation to give him a chase, but hell if I am going to give in so easily.

As I come behind the couch with him facing me from the front, he grabs for my wrist, yanking me down over the couch, and making me land right on top of him. I instantly try to pry myself off his body, but he proves how strong he is by wrapping his legs and arms around me. I'm completely trapped against him.

I can feel his lean muscles beneath me and I inhale deeply, taking in the special scent that I now equate with Matt. I can't exactly pinpoint what it is, but every time I breathe it in, it takes me to another world completely. I can't get enough of it.

"Now what do you think your punishment should be, Ms. Adams?" he growls into my ear, sending a shiver to course down to the depths of my toes.

As I take in his question and my imagination gets the better of me, I'm quickly yanked from my impromptu fantasy of my enjoyable punishment when Matt starts tickling me.

My body starts convulsing in laughter with his fingers

quickly moving against my ribs. I didn't know how ticklish I was until now and I don't like it one bit. He keeps it up as my body keeps convulsing with laughter against his body, making me scream, and yell as well. This *was* not the kind of screaming and shouting I had in mind a second ago.

He's still holding me in a firm grip against his body, using only the tips of his fingers to continue to dig lightly into my rib cage. It's pissing me off at this point, making me yell at him in anger in between my bursts of laughter. Matt doesn't give up, but keeps at it, laughing along with me from the enjoyment it's giving him.

As I'm about ready to pee my pants, we roll off the couch from all the wiggling that my body is causing between us and we land on the floor with a light thump, with Matt landing on top of me. The shock of it makes Matt stop his tickling, as he's staring down into my face and my body is now numb from the heat of his stare.

His hand gently pushes the hair that is loosely covering my face out of the way so he can better see me. His face is so angelic as I look into his eyes, returning the heat that is radiating between us. Right as I see him lean his head down, I prepare myself, my body growing excited. When his face is mere inches from my own, his phone goes off, announcing Trey's ringtone.

We both freeze up, but then his body relaxes just as fast. Thinking he's going to ignore it, he surprises me when does the opposite. Bracing his arms on the side of my body, still looking down at me his face grows regretful.

He pushes himself up and off the ground, walking away from me, and into the direction of his singing phone.

Lying there on the ground, I close my eyes, already regretting the loss of his body on top of me. Repeating in my head what just occurred, I'm left confused and wondering why he had that look on this face. I really hate not having answers.

# Chapter 12

THE NEXT MORNING I'm still lazing in bed, playing with my phone, when Matt comes into my room without knocking. Now that I think about it, he does that often. Does he do it on purpose? Sometimes I wonder if he does, in hope that he'll catch me changing?

"Get up and get dressed. You've been cooped up in this house for too long. I'm taking you out for some air," he says, standing at the edge of the bed, looking down at me.

"Where are we going?" I ask skeptically.

"It's a surprise. Hurry up and get ready," he says before he leaves the room again.

Excited that we're actually going to go somewhere, I jump up off the bed and start getting quickly dressed. On the car ride to what appears to be downtown Portland, I keep asking Matt where we're going, but he refuses to say. By the look on his face, he wants it to be a surprise and I'm excited to find out.

My surprise trip lands us at Portland's famous Saturday

Market. It's crowded with people on this bright sunny morning. At first, I'm hesitant since there are a lot of people, but since the day is sunny I am able to wear my sunglasses to conceal my face and with my hair in my normal go-to ponytail, I'm pretty sure I'm unrecognizable.

I *was* actually excited to get to do something normal today, especially since I had begun to keep myself cooped up indoors, so I pushed the fear to the back of my mind, trusting Matt.

We started the day with Matt purchasing what he called an elephant ear. I look down at it, realizing it doesn't resemble its namesake, and it made me laugh. It was delicious though and I shared it with Matt as we walked up and down the aisles of all the booths lining the area. There was so much to look at and choose from; it was amazing what you can find there. I'm surprised I didn't buy one of everything.

By far the best part of the day was when Matt had said he had one more thing he wanted me to taste. He didn't want to tell me what it was, but as we stood in a long line alongside a brick building, I had to wonder if it was even worth it. Forty-five minutes later, I was clued in as to why the line was so long. When I took a bite of what Matt handed me, my mouth felt like it had left earth and gone to chocolate heaven. It was chocolate, mixed with peanut butter, glazed with cameral, and every single bite was just as sinfully delicious as the next. After devouring that bad boy, I already knew I would have to run extra mileage the next day due to the sugar intake, but it was well worth it.

With hours gone and a sugar high to throw me into a diabetic coma, I'm exhausted and relieved that we are finally leaving. As we head to the car I'm feeling happy as ever from our day and take a chance by asking Matt, "Can I drive home?"

"No," he sharply replies without hesitation, without taking a side-glance at me.

I try again. "Oh come on Matt, please," I say, pouting my bottom lip at him.

He suddenly stops walking, curiously looking at me and I get excited thinking he's considering it for a moment. "Keep begging like that and I'll let you drive me, beautiful," he says wickedly, ending with his half smile.

Uhhh! Keeping him off limits is close to impossible sometimes. How in the hell am I supposed to refuse his proposal when he throws shit like that at me? If it wasn't for the fact that I knew messing around with him wouldn't get me anywhere, I might have taken him up on that offer.

Instead, I roll my eyes and stomp away. Behind me I hear him laugh as he catches up to me, and my body is jolted to a stop when he wraps his arms around my waist pulling my body against his.

"Sorry beautiful, I couldn't resist," he whispers lightly into my ear.

The feeling of his body against my own, and the warmth of his breath against my ear force me to close my eyes for a split second. My body is absorbing the feeling as he's physically touching me. The shivers that run through my body as he says it drive me insane.

Dammit, why does my body always react to him this way? I'm supposed to be resisting him, not giving in to his touch. Realizing that being in his arms is not helping to get what I want anyways, I quickly unwrap his arms from my waist, and turn to face him throwing my hands on my hips.

"Why do you keep calling me that?"

"What?"

"Beautiful. Why do you call me that?"

He cocks his head to the side, considering my question. "Why wouldn't I call you beautiful?"

I shake my head, not satisfied. "Why the nickname? You should only give a nickname to someone you're dating or in love with," I say to him, lifting my forefinger up to stop him from speaking so I can continue. "Being that I'm not your girlfriend, and I'm definitely not one of your friends with benefits or someone you love, it doesn't give you the right to label me with a nickname."

His lips go up into a smile and his eyes become hooded with his long lashes dropping low. "Has anyone ever told you how adorable you look when you're mad?" he huskily inquires.

Dammit, with him looking at me like that I lose my focus on what I'm trying to prove. My body already knows its weakness, and he's standing right in front of me. Since I know I'm never going to win with him looking at me like that, I throw my hands up in defeat and turn to start walking back to the car again. I already know I'm a lost cause.

Once we're at the car I get into the passenger seat. Obviously I know I won't be driving, and buckle up. I cross my arms in front of me in irritation over the whole situation, wondering why we even had the conversation in the first place.

The drive home is spent in an awkward silence, but the whole time I keep thinking, *why do I let him get to me like this?*

When we finally reach our street, I notice another car in the driveway parked next to Trey's Jeep. When I look over in Matt's direction wondering if he knows to whom it belongs, my question is answered, just by looking at him. By his body language, he obviously knows. He's gone completely rigid and the paleness of his face starts to worry me. His face just as quickly grows irritated and he looks really pissed. The kind I don't want to mess with at the moment.

Scowling, Matt says, "Fuck. She didn't tell me she was coming over."

He brings the car to an abrupt stop, throwing the car into park. He exits the car, slamming the door behind him, making me flinch. I recover and get out in the same hurry as him. I don't want to miss meeting this mystery girl he is so pissed about. I know I shouldn't be so eager to find out, but then again, I'm a nosey person.

Sue me.

"Who is this *she*?" I ask, as I quickly follow him.

He doesn't look at me as he continues to the front door. "Just a friend that I have come over every now and then."

His tone when he says it doesn't make me feel any better. He's obviously upset about this *friend* being here. He keeps walking ahead of me into the house, leaving me behind. As we walk in, a girl is already walking towards the exit and when she sees Matt she throws herself up at him, wrapping her legs around his waist. "It's about time you're home, I'm horny and I need a good fuck," she says in a whiny voice as she grinds herself on him.

Whoa. The scene that has just taken place in front of me makes me stop in my tracks for a second. I recover myself and keep walking past them straight into the house. So she's *that* kind of friend, I realize.

Ignoring the possible mating session that might take place in the doorway, I brush past them, and head straight for the kitchen.

"Wait, who was that?" I hear the girl exclaim as I'm

taking a water bottle from the fridge, twisting off the cap and taking a drink. I turn my body to face them and lean against the counter, trying to get a better view.

"What are you doing here, Lizzy? You know the rules, you're supposed to call first," he tells her, ignoring her question, prying her body from his, depositing her back onto the ground. He tries to use his body to block the line of sight between the both of us, but it doesn't help.

Lizzy is a short little bleached blonde, with styled wavy hair past her shoulders. She is wearing cut off jean shorts with a white tank top that is clearly a size too small, making her assets very noticeable. She has her hands on her hips and she's obviously not happy I'm here as she's glaring in my direction.

I'm taking another sip from the bottled water, acting as if I'm ignoring them. In reality, I'm being the nosiest person in the room right now.

"You're screwing her now, too?" she says, pointing her finger at me with a furious glare.

I spit out the water I was drinking, with a mortified look on my face, coughing at the same time. Screwing me too? I knew he was screwing a bunch of girls, but how does this chick know he's screwing anyone other than her? Do they all know about each other?

I grab a dishtowel from the side of the sink and start to clean up the mess on the floor. The whole time, I'm trying to keep them in my vision so I can listen in and see the expressions on their faces.

Matt's clearly not happy with her question as he glares down into her face. "No, I'm not screwing her. She's just a friend. She lives here now. So if you have a problem with it Lizzy, there's the door." He tilts his head in the direction of the front door.

This makes both of our mouths drop. Mine because Matt is being a jerk in my defense, and hers because she probably wasn't expecting him to defend me like that.

Lizzy shakes her head and glares back at Matt. "Is this why you haven't returned my phone calls these last couple of days?"

"I shouldn't have to explain why I haven't returned your phone calls. You're not my girlfriend and you knew the rules when we started this thing. If you don't like the rules, then let me repeat myself. There's. The. Door," he growls.

Fuck, what an asshole.

I stand there, confused whether I should be happy he's standing his ground when it comes to me or go comfort the poor girl for his attitude. It only makes me wonder if he'd be just as big of an asshole if he were someone's boyfriend?

"Fuck you Matt," she growls back at him.

"Been there, done that. To tell you the truth, there wouldn't be much to miss," he says to her as she's walking away and out the door.

I can't believe what I've just witnessed. This is a side of Matt I had no clue existed. With me he's this gentle overprotective guy who went out of his way to make me feel safe and secure. What I saw must have been the asshole Matt who clearly needs to be kept away from.

Once I hear the door shut, Matt walks into the kitchen ignoring me, and he starts to take things out of the fridge and cupboards, clearly trying to avoid me.

Throwing the towel into the sink, I go over to the island in the middle of the room and hop right onto it. I bring my legs up onto the counter crossing them, sitting Indian style.

"Does that happen often?" Without giving him a chance

to answer, I continue, "I really hope you're not planning on making her prediction correct by adding me to that list of friends," I say with a bitter tone.

Matt stops what he's doing, turning in my direction. "You really think I'd do that to you?"

I shrug my shoulders at him and stare down at the floor wanting to ignore the surprised expression on his face.

I see Matt walk over and stop in front of me. He places both hands next to mine on the counter, touching them with only his thumbs. When I lift my head to look at him, his eyes are narrowing into mine. "I wouldn't use you the way I use them."

I sigh, but he continues. "You know why I won't commit. I told you that in the car. But they don't know that. When I started seeing them they knew not to expect more because I laid it flat on the table before I even fucked them. Once they get clingy I cut them off, easy as that."

So him telling me about the girl at Berkley was his way of laying the rules on the table for me without having to tell me. I'm the stupid one who thought he'd be different.

Forced to see the truth of the situation I'm in, I nod my head in agreement, holding back the tears that threaten to surface.

"Look, I'm not one to judge, but don't you think it's a little fucked up that you're using them like that?" I query.

Matt pushes himself away from the counter, shrugs his shoulders, and goes back to what he was doing before I interrupted him. "Who says they aren't using me instead?"

Yeah, right. If that's what you want to think to make it all better in your eyes. I have a feeling this could end up being an endless argument, like earlier. So I surrender by telling him, "I'm just laying down the rules, between you and me. As long as you don't expect to add me to that list of friends, we'll be fine."

Matt pauses, looks back at me with a smile then says, "Deal."

# Chapter 13

A COUPLE OF days later, I'm laying on the couch watching a reality show on the entertainment channel, when Matt comes into the living room. He lifts my legs from the couch, sitting himself under them, and then rests them back on his knees.

I look around the room and wonder why he picked that spot when there's a whole other couch, not to mention the recliner, empty for him to sit on?

He looks at me with a casual smile, and starts massaging my calves and ankles. They're a bit sore from our long run yesterday, a run that ended up being a total of ten miles without me realizing it.

Matt had said we were going for a run, so I laced up and followed. Lesson learned, as I was cursing him halfway in, next time I'd ask him how many miles before we even head out of the door and double it in my mind.

Halfway through the run my body began to notice that we were running more that our *usual* five miles. When I questioned Matt how much longer we were going to run, he wouldn't answer, but stated that I could handle it. Repeating, *one foot in front of the other,* I just kept running.

After the second time of him saying it, I wanted to strangle him. The only reason I didn't was that he kept pulling ahead of me, keeping me at an arm's length. I would have given up had we not been running in the direction of the car.

He's still moving his large hands up and down my legs, gently rubbing and massaging them. It's really hard to lie there, trying to ignore the flurry that is running up them, directly to the center of my thighs. I'm using a great deal of effort to focus on watching TV, hoping he doesn't notice how turned on I'm getting right now from the rubbing of his hands. I'm saved a couple of minutes later, when he stops, leaving me already longing for his next touch. I clap my knees together, uselessly trying to calm my turned on body.

I finally look back at him, trying to look bored, and he has a shameless smile on his face. He's not buying my boredom for a minute. He knows exactly what he was trying to achieve when he was giving me my rub down.

"Did you need to tell me something?" I ask, narrowing my eyes at him. "Wait," I say, holding up a finger to stop him. "If it involves a girl, or body parts connecting in places, then I don't want to know after all," I say, scrunching my nose at him.

The last thing I want to hear from those lips are sex stories about other girls, but Matt finds it amusing and throws his head back laughing. When he's done, he looks at me. "Why don't you want to know? You aren't jealous, are you?" he says, wagging his eyebrows.

Focusing on him, I roll my eyes and look back at the

television saying, "Never mind, I don't want to know after all."

"Actually you do, since it involves you," he states.

I yank my head back at him, apprehensive about what he's going to tell me. My face goes into a grimace as I try to think of what he could possibly tell me and he chuckles.

"You know how I'm running that half in two weeks?"

Matt had mentioned during one of our runs last week that he was going to run the Portland Marathon again this year, in memory of his sister. That's why he needed to run long distances every week. He was preparing his body for the race by building endurance and distance. He was running half the distance of a marathon, which would be thirteen miles soon.

I'm still confused how this involves me. "Yeah. What does that have to do with me?" I ask.

"Wellll, I signed us up to run a 10k." He's says it as if I should be ecstatic about what he's just said.

"A what K?"

"A 10K, it's a charity race."

Ok, I'm all for charity, but it still doesn't answer why he recruited me to do it with him? "Okay. When is it?"

"Tomorrow," he says, tossing my legs off as he stands up, walking away. I'm left wondering why I have to actually run the thing. "Couldn't you just have made a donation in my name?" I protest from the couch I'm still laying on.

"Actually, you already did when I registered you, but this kind of donation involves running it as well."

"Why would anyone pay to run, shouldn't it be the other way around?" I say in disgust.

Matt sighs, taking a deep breath. "Look. I've signed you up already. It's not a big deal, it'd be like one of our usual runs," he says before heading into the hallway bathroom forcing me to take in what he's said.

Dammit. Maybe I should follow him into the bathroom, but I already know that even if I did it wouldn't get me any-where. When it comes to arguing with Matt, he is just as stubborn as I am.

THE NEXT MORNING Matt walks into my room yelling "Wakey, wakey, eggs and bakey."

"Since I don't actually smell bacon, I've decided it's not worth getting up," I say into my pillow, turning onto my stomach, yanking the blanket with me to my chin.

Last night I had decided that I wasn't actually going to run this "K" thingy. I wasn't the one training for a big race, so why did I have to keep putting my body through hell? Nope. I was putting my foot down today and sleeping in.

I feel the covers being yanked from the bed, and when my mind has comprehended what has happened, I feel Matt's large hand on my ass. The God-awful sting that comes with it causes me jolt up, a reflex reaction that anyone would have.

Groaning, I immediately grab my pillow and throw it at Matt, hitting him in the chest with it. He throws the pillow right back at me, hitting me on the ass. At least that didn't hurt.

He laughs and says, "Sorry beautiful, I couldn't resist," tilting his head to the side staring at my butt, "it's such a sexy ass."

"Just remember Matthew, payback's a bitch!" I say to him as I get up from the bed and head to the bathroom, rubbing my ass at the same time.

As he exits the room, I hear him shout, "As long as you promise it's something nice." His retort makes me roll my groggy eyes.

An hour later, I have realized that putting my foot down does not work when it comes to Matt. We ate a banana and half a bagel instead of eggs and bacon. Which makes me swear if I don't get eggs, bacon, *and* pancakes after this I just might have to murder this man, no matter how good looking he is.

I didn't realize that Matt had woken me up at 5:30 this morning until I looked at my phone as we got into the car. I could have murdered him for that alone. He claimed we had to pick up our packet before 6:30 because the race started at 7:00. Being that I've never run with Matt before 8:00 in the morning, my body was still trying to wake up. I couldn't keep from yawning.

"I didn't know you could open your mouth that wide. It's giving me ideas," he says as he's driving.

Right now I'm so tired that I don't even have a rebuttal for his perverted mind. Besides glaring at him, which causes him to laugh at me. I give up and sit there trying to stifle my yawns with no success. I already have a feeling this is going to be a *really* long day.

We finally arrive at the race location and make our way into the line for registration pick-up. After a couple of minutes of standing in line, Matt and I finally reach the front of the booth, and I hand the volunteer my ID to receive my packet. She sees the name on my ID, snaps her head up at me, and her eyes go wide.

"OMG, it's Abigail Adams!" she says with excitement, practically jumping out of her seat.

I wince since I'm still half-asleep, but this helps wake me up a little as I begin to yawn again behind my hand.

"I can't believe you're running our race. This is good, I'll make sure they know you're running," she says as she starts looking around like she's looking for someone.

I panic, my body going rigid and Matt notices. "Actually, she was hoping not to bring attention to herself. She's doing this for charity and would really appreciate if you don't mention her name please," he says, trying to save me.

The girl gives Matt a puzzled look. "And you would be?" she says in a snotty voice.

"Her assistant. Now can we have our packets so we can line up?" he demands sternly.

Her shoulders sag in disappointment and she begins to look for our packets. Once she has handed them to us, she moves on to helping the person behind us.

As we're walking away, I'm staring at the bib with my number on it. "See, this is why I should have stayed at home," I say dryly while I cover another dreadful yawn with my hand.

From the corner of my eye I see Matt grin and I really don't want to know why he's smiling like that. I doubt it's because of what I've said. We keep walking in the direction of the start banner and find a spot off to the side.

With Matt's assistance, I get my number on, and we're standing in line with the crowd of people waiting. As I stand with him I start to get my playlist ready for the run, trying to select my favorite ones. Done, I start fumbling with my earphones, and I'm beginning to grow curious about how far this race is. He never did mention it.

"So how many miles exactly is this 10K we're supposed to run?" I inquire, staring at the start banner ahead of us.

"Six miles," I hear him say besides me.

Horrified, I turn to him. I wasn't awake before, but I am now.

"You want me to run six miles?" I exclaim at him. "Are you crazy?" I practically squeal.

I hear someone standing behind me chuckle and right now I'm thinking I should walk off. Ignoring the agitation growing inside of me, I go back to messing with my phone, ignoring Matt as well.

He breaks our silence by saying. "Why don't we make this run a little fun?" with a mocking tone.

I stop fumbling with my phone and turn to look at him with my eyebrows raised. "What did you have in mind?"

He tilts his head up as if thinking, his eyes going directly up to the sky, and then says, "Loser has to cook the winner dinner."

My mouth falls open. "That's not fair! You know I can't cook."

He smiles in victory. "Then you better not lose," he says as he inserts his ear buds into his ears, walking forward as they herd us to the start line to begin the race.

I narrow my eyes at him. Inserting my ear buds into my ears, I realize that I might be screwed. I can't lose this race. Not only for bragging rights, but also because I *really* don't want to have to cook.

The gun finally goes off and the runners slowly start to jog over the start line to the course ahead. Matt begins moving to the outside of the crowd and I try to follow. It proves a bit difficult being that there are quite a few of people huddled together as they run forward, but he manages to find an opening in the small crowd and moves through it. Speeding through them, he leaves me stuck behind a couple running side by side.

I'm shocked that he left me behind like that. He didn't even bother looking back to make sure I was following.

How rude!

Already seeing him advancing in the crowd it pisses me off that I'm stuck here. I move to the left of the couple, find an opening to run through, and take it. I'm able to catch up to Matt by a couple of feet, but once again I get stuck behind another bundle of a crowd.

Don't these people know to move out of the way if they're slow?

I'm practically dancing back and forth as I'm running, trying to find a way to move forward and ahead of them. I finally find another open pocket and squeeze my way forward.

I see Matt again and he must be focused because I see him weaving around people to get through openings and ahead. I keep watching him and I realize what he's doing to make it easier to get ahead. So I follow his lead and finally start to advance. It's not easy, because unless you want to be impolite, you have to keep bobbing back and forth around people to get forward.

Somehow after fifteen minutes of doing this, a majority of the people split off to the left. The remainder of us go running to the right, in the direction of the sign with an arrow that says "10K runners this way."

I see Matt up ahead and I begin to speed up my pace, catching up to him. I'm thinking he's going to run the rest of it with me, but I was wrong. Once he spots me at his side, he gives me a smile, and speeds up again. Realizing that he's mocking me flares my temper.

All right buddy, you want to play these games? It's on.

I start to speed up and pass him, feeling better now that I've given him a taste of his own medicine. But then he catches up to me, and next thing I know; it feels like a normal run with Matt all over again. He always does this to me when we go on our usual runs. He'll let me pull ahead of him a bit, allowing me to catch my breath. Then he'll speed up making me follow him.

I slowly start to feel that we're both running faster and faster. Since there aren't many people left on this part of the course, we are able to weave by them with speed. Then I see a sign that says Mile 4.

Mile 4!

I get so excited because I know it's almost over. I could easily handle two more miles. I can do this, I think to myself.

It continues with Matt and me running side by side for the next mile, and by the time the last mile comes up I keep thinking, not much to go. Then I see a sign that says Mile 6 on the side of the road, but I don't see a finish line anywhere in sight. I thought he said this thing was only 6 miles?

As I run past the sign, confused, I start to slow down thinking maybe we're just supposed to stop. Comprehending that we are not anywhere near done when there are people still running around me, I keep going.

What the heck? I thought this race was only 6 miles. He lied to me, but I keep running. After another minute, I finally hear the crowd and we turn a corner, and I see the finish line up ahead. I pushed my body to the limit before the 6th mile mark thinking that I was done, so I am beat at this point. My body feels like it's ready to collapse and I haven't even finished yet. My legs are burning, wanting to give out. My lungs are screaming for air, and I want to give up.

I can see the crowd roaring at us and I turn my head slightly to look at Matt before he smiles at me. Next thing I know he's speeding up ahead of me, leaving me behind by a couple of feet right before he crosses the finish line. There's no way I can say that it was a close call because I even saw him cross ahead of me.

Fuck! He's beaten me and now I'm stuck cooking dinner for his ass.

All that is going through my mind right now is that I want to strangle the hell out of Matt for signing me up to run this thing. I walk over to the side to get a bottled water that volunteers are handing out to the racers who have finished, relieved that at least I get something out of this. Even if *it* is only water.

I take up a spot to the side, twist off the cap of the water, and take a huge gulp out of it. I see Matt come up to stand in front of me, and he's beaming from ear to ear.

Right now I want to smack that smile off his face.

"By the way beautiful, my favorite dish is enchilada casserole. Try not to burn it; I *would* actually like to enjoy it," he says as he walks with the crowd towards the exit.

The only thing that keeps me from chucking my bottled water at him is that I desperately need it to quench my thirst.

WHEN WE GOT back from the race, I headed straight to my room. I was so tired that I wanted to take a nap without even taking a shower. To say my body was worn out was a bit of an understatement.

I throw myself on the bed, letting my body sink into the mattress. As I am lying there, beat from the morning, I hear

128

Matt walk in.

"Hey beautiful. You okay?" He sounds concerned.

Being upset about this morning I say, "Leave me alone Matt, you're not my favorite person right now."

He chuckles and climbs into bed next to me. I'm already facing in his direction, with my hands tucked under my pillow. He looks at me, while I shoot him with a glare.

With his usual mocking smile, he says, "Don't tell me you're a sore loser?"

"It's not about the losing. It's about you lying. You said it was only six miles. According to the six mile sign that I passed, it was obviously more," I bitterly respond.

He shrugs the one shoulder that isn't lying against the bed. "Okay, technically it was 6.2 miles. I didn't think that .2 miles would be much of a difference to you."

I roll my eyes and turn over, wanting to ignore him completely. I quickly feel him grab my body and pull me against him into a spoon position. He tucks his muscled forearm under my head and I feel his other arm that is wrapped around my ribcage tighten, pulling me closer against his chest. I'm so tired at this point that I lie there and take in his warmth. My mind immediately forgets why I'm even upset at him, and I fall asleep.

When I awaken a couple of hours later, I'm alone again in my bed. He must have left while I was still sleeping, but his smell is still on my sheets. I lay there taking it in, wanting to absorb as much of it as I can. I don't know why he came to lay with me, it's just another thing to add to my list of questions when it comes to Matt.

# Chapter 14

I'M STANDING IN the kitchen the next afternoon reading a recipe on how to make Enchilada Casserole that I got from the Internet. I watched several YouTube videos, but it looked easier to watch someone else make it, than trying it myself. Matt always makes cooking look easy, when in reality it isn't, as I'm now learning.

As much as I'm dreading making this stupid thing, I did lose fair and square. So I have to keep my side of the bet and cook dinner for Matt. At this point I've got sauce all over the stove, counter, and myself. I think I even have some in my hair. Matt had wanted chicken instead of ground beef. Although, I didn't have to cook it since I was able to buy a rotisserie chicken to shred. Another plus to recipes online is that they come with a list of ingredients to buy, because I would have died trying to figure out what to put in this thing.

All of a sudden my mind goes blank.

*Matt is standing over the stove, with a spatula in his hand. He's staring at a pan with eggs in it. Although he looks to be only twelve or thirteen, he has apparently hit puberty already. He's taller than I am and his voice is deep.*

*"Now what do I do?" he asks.*

*I look at him, saying, "You have to let the eggs cook a little, then you begin to stir them around slowly."*

*He goes to try to stir the eggs, but I stop him by placing my hand on his wrist. "Give it a couple of seconds. If not, you're just going to be stirring around liquid."*

*He starts to look impatient and I laugh at him. "Okay, silly. Go ahead and stir away, find out for yourself. These are your eggs, you can cook them anyway you want."*

*He starts stirring with force and it spills over the pan. We hear a sizzle from it hitting the flame, and some of it has fallen on his hand, burning him a bit.*

*"See, that's why you have to let it cook a little, or else that could happen as well," I say, still chuckling.*

*He lets out a groan. "I don't know why I have to learn to cook. Isn't that what women are for?" he says.*

*My lips go into a frown. I cheer up and say, "Let me tell you a secret. If you know how to cook, you'll have girls falling over you."*

*His face brightens up with a smile and he enthusiastically goes back to his task.*

*I stand there smiling at him, beaming with pride.*

"Abigail!" I hear Matt shout my name and it startles me out of the memory.

I look around the kitchen and it's full of smoke. The pan in front of me is bubbling, with tiny geysers of sauce shooting everywhere.

"Oh shit. I'm so sorry," I say, embarrassed about the mess.

Matt starts turning off the stove. He moves pans to cool

on the other burners that are turned off. He reaches for the dishtowel on the sink, and starts cleaning. I reach for another and start helping him, mortified at what happened.

As I bend down to the floor, I stare in disgust at the mess. I'm so disappointed in myself that I start to tear up. I've even managed to screw this up; I can't ever get anything right. The tears start to trickle down my cheeks causing me to sniffle and Matt hears. He bends down to pull me up and pulls my chin up to look at him. "Why are you crying, beautiful?"

I shake my head and duck my eyes as I try to help wipe the counter down.

"Come here," Matt says as he pulls me into a hug. I try to push him away because I really don't want his pity at this moment, but he doesn't let me. He pulls me tighter against his body, holding me tight, rubbing my back with his hand. I finally give up and let him comfort me.

I sniffle again, turning my face into the crook of his neck, and say, "I'm so sorry; I've screwed up the one thing you were looking forward to."

He keeps rubbing his hand up and down my back, making me feel better. "Shhh, don't cry. I hate seeing you cry. It's not that bad. It's the fact that you at least tried that counts."

Not happy with myself, I shake my head. He always knows what to say or do to make me feel better. This is the only side of Matt I know. Not the asshole side of him. He's never shown that to me.

"It's not completely ruined, you just burned the tortilla and the sauce, that's all. You're halfway done anyways," he says into my hair.

I take a deep sigh in defeat.

Finally calm, he kisses my head and lets me go, looking at the counter. "How about I help you finish up? That way I can make sure you don't kill the dish completely, giving us food poisoning," he says chuckling.

His comment hurts my feelings all over again. I can't believe he thinks my cooking would give us food poisoning. I wonder if he's always thought this? If he did, then why in the hell did he tell me to cook for him?

I hit him on the chest with the dishrag I'm holding and growl at him. He laughs harder and just kisses me on the cheek. Taking the dishrag from me, he uses it to finish cleaning up the stove.

While Matt takes over the cooking on the stove, he instructs me on how to do most of the layering and it goes smoothly from there. His instructions seem much easier than trying to read or watch how to make it. Fifteen minutes later, we are done, and he is grabbing plates so he can serve our portions.

Although dinner ends up turning out delicious, it's only because Matt came and saved the day. I know if he hadn't taken over, it would have been a total disaster. We would have been eating take-out right now. I don't know what I would do without him and I really don't want to find out.

## Chapter 15

ANOTHER WEEK GOES by with Matt and I acting normal as can be. We both eventually get into a routine when it comes to running. We go out every other day, but now instead of an easy 3-5 miles, he's pushing me 6-8 miles. I would have thought that I wouldn't be able to hang, but the look of pride from Matt when we're done makes me finish. Plus, him making us pancakes afterwards really helps too.

On the second week, Trey is scheduled to arrive back, so naturally Matt went to the airport to pick him up when his plane landed. I wanted to stay home and catch up with one of the reality shows on TV so I stayed behind.

Hearing Matt and Trey walk through the door, I sit up looking for them and see the confused shock on Trey's face.

"What the fuck happened to the couches?" he says, turning to Matt.

"Abigail didn't like the old ones, so she ordered new ones."

"What was wrong with the old ones? They had history

and mileage on them. Especially with the girls." I'm pretty sure he added the last line just to disgust me.

I scrunch my nose, trying really hard not to picture Matt with a girl on the couch. Now I'm *really* happy I got rid of those suckers. My new couches were *not* going to have any of Matt's mileage with any other girls. Actually I shouldn't say that, the way he claims to whore himself around, only time will tell how soon that would happen.

Trey walks over to the small couch and takes a seat, moving around making himself comfortable. After a couple of seconds he shrugs his shoulders. "They're cool, I guess. Have you guys broken them in yet?" he says, waggling his eyebrows.

My jaw drops in shock, remembering what almost *did* happen when they got delivered.

"No and it isn't going to happen either," Matt snaps at Trey from behind me.

Well, that answers the question about me ever getting a chance with Matt on the couch.

Trey chuckles at his response and changes the subject. "So you guys up for the Brewhouse tonight? I want a good beer and you can't find a good fucking brew back home."

"What's the Brewhouse?" I ask, looking at Matt.

Shocked, Trey looks at Matt then back at me. "He didn't take you to the Brewhouse?"

I shake my head. "The only time I got out was to go for a run or the races. Oh and the Market, that was fun."

He looks back at Matt with his eyes wide open. "Fuck, dude. Aren't you being a little overprotective? When you said you weren't having any parties or anyone over because of her, I didn't know you were also keeping her prisoner."

"I'm not keeping her prisoner, fucker. I'm just keeping

her safe," he says, and then continues. "I also didn't take Abigail out to a lot of public places because I didn't want her to feel overwhelmed. She hasn't complained."

Yeah, I didn't complain because I was scared shitless of going out in fear that Bill would find me. I didn't want to risk it. So being at home was fine with me.

"What the fuck have you guys been doing besides running then?" His brow shoots straight up in curiosity.

"Not what you're thinking," I shoot back at him.

I really hope he can't see the disappointment in my face, wishing that a lot more *had* happened. Maybe I should have walked around the house naked while Trey wasn't home. Give Matt the opportunity to see what he was missing out on. He was obviously showing me what I couldn't have every morning, driving me insane.

"Then now that I'm back you're not keeping her cooped up. We're going to the Brewhouse, and she's coming with us," Trey states as he stands up, walking to the door.

I stand up to follow him and notice Matt dropping his shoulders in defeat. I'm glad, because by the excitement on Trey's face about this place, I really want to go now.

We all piled into Matt's car to make the drive over to this Brewhouse.

On the drive, Trey takes this time to tell me it's a brewery, slash restaurant. It's supposedly the team's favorite hangout, next to the house, of course.

According to Trey, a lot of the guys on the team weren't happy the partying was halted the minute Trey and Matt got a new roommate. Their whole "Bros before hoes" motto got thrown out the window the minute I became a permanent resident. That disappointed a lot of them.

That only made me laugh.

Matt cursed at Trey to keep his mouth shut, making me giggle again. Of course, Trey ignored him and continued on. He informed me that Matt's *special* friends were even more upset, thinking they had competition now, even though they had no idea who the new roommate was. According to Trey, Matt kept reassuring his friends that he wasn't getting any of those special benefits, but they didn't believe him. That remark only made me gawk at Trey. I really hoped he believed us when we said there was nothing going on.

We finally pull into the parking lot and it looks like a typical laid-back brewery. I can't help it; I get excited that I'm finally going to get to see another part of Matt's life. We get out of the car and Trey throws his arm around my neck, leading the way to the entrance.

As we walk in, the hostess automatically recognizes Matt and, without pause, leads us through the restaurant. I notice that even though there are plenty of open tables in the middle, she keeps walking until she comes to practically the back of the building. Once we've reached what looks like a huge wooden bench table in the corner, she sets the menus down and walks away. This table is huge and could easily seat about ten, but it's just the three of us so I'm really confused as to why she would give us this table?

Matt sees my confused face. "It's our usual table. It's unofficially reserved for us," he says with a wink as he climbs into the seated bench.

I take the spot next to him, and Trey climbs in after me. I wonder why we are facing away from the crowd, but my question gets answered when I see the flat screen TVs mounted against the wall. No wonder they like this spot. It's facing three different TVs with several behind us for the other side to easily watch.

I look up to notice that of course the TVs are set to different sports channels, showcasing several different games. Uhhh, boys and their sports, even here I can't escape it. As I'm done rolling my eyes, I notice our waitress show up with two pints of beer already in her hands, lightly slamming them down on the table. She stands to the side of our table, with her hands on her hips.

She stares directly at me as she says, "Is she gonna want anything or is she too prissy for beer and going to stick to water?"

I *was* going to ask for water, but only because I'm really thirsty right now. Not because I'm prissy. I drink beer.

Matt pushes his pint of beer over to me and tells her, "Just bring me another, Carol."

She huffs at him and walks away with her lips pinched. What the hell got into her pants, but my question is quickly answered. "She's just pissed 'cause she's one of Matt's special friends," Trey whispers into my ear.

Now I know exactly what got into her pants and I don't blame her for not being happy. I turn around and look at her wondering what I'm missing compared to all these girls that he's had. She's standing at the bar, speaking to the bartender, but looking in our direction. I'm pretty sure she's shit talking us right now. I know I would.

Or maybe just me, by the daggers her eyes are shooting directly at me.

Matt is staring at the flat screen, but says to me, "Ignore her. She'll get over it. If not, she also knows where the door is."

I can't take it anymore and now I'm irritated. I snap at him, "No wonder you kept me prisoner in the house. Otherwise, I could easily run into one of your friends with benefits."

Trey's loud laughter stops Matt from responding. "She's got you there, man. I'm pretty sure *everywhere* we go she's bound to run into them. *You* do have a friend for everyday of the week, remember?" he says teasingly.

Now I'm reminded of what Matt had said during *that* conversation.

Matt slams him with a glare that could kill, but it only makes Trey laugh again. I laugh along with him, making me feel a little better. Matt ignores us with a groan and Carol shows up with his beer, slamming this one on the table a little harder before walking away.

I laugh at her little attitude, not blaming her. I pick up my beer and take a sip. Half an hour later, a couple more guys show up. One of them is with his girlfriend, making Trey and Matt give the usual introductions. I start to feel a bit uncomfortable not knowing what to expect, but they easily start talking about everyday life, making me feel comfortable again.

Kelly, the girlfriend of Matt and Trey's friend David, ends up being really nice and starts making conversation with me.

Kelly is a hispanic little thing, about 5'3, with dark brown wavy hair, almost down to her waist. She has pretty, light brown almond shaped eyes and a very friendly personality. She becomes an ally with me against the guys and I take notice how much her boyfriend David adores her. He smiles every so often at her and would easily defend her when needed.

It reminds me a lot of how Matt acts with me. The only difference is that they are obviously in a relationship, and we are not. It almost makes me jealous that I didn't have that, but I have to remember what happens to the girls in Matt's life when they want more from him.

"So Abigail, what's it like being a famous supermodel?" Kelly finally asks the dreaded question.

Shrugging my shoulders, I say, "I don't know, I don't remember," before taking a sip of my beer.

The guy on the other side of Kelly looks confused before asking, "What do you mean you don't remember?"

"I had an accident and woke up with amnesia."

"What, really? So you don't remember what's it's like being a supermodel?" Kelly asks.

"I don't remember anything of my past before the day I woke up. It really sucks, but I can't miss something I don't remember." I shrug my shoulders again trying to make it seem normal.

I'm starting to feel really uncomfortable with the conversation, but Matt reaches for my hand underneath the table, giving it a reassuring squeeze. I look over at him and the smile he returns makes me feel better.

"Man, that must really suck," Kelly says looking disappointed.

I agree.

"So how in the world did you and Matt meet?" the guy in front of me asks.

"Actually, the only thing I could remember was Matt's number."

The guy draws his eyebrows down looking confused, and I don't blame him.

As I'm about to attempt to explain the number, Matt jumps in. "My sister worked with Abigail once, and had given her my number in case she couldn't get a hold of her. Abigail was really needy and would call me when my sister didn't answer her phone. My number was one of the first numbers she called hoping to remember something and we started talking."

I don't say anything, because at least his lie is better than my psycho story of how I really got his number. I don't like how he's emphasizing how needy I used to be. I wasn't like that anymore, was I?

"It still doesn't explain how she ends up living with you, dude. Unless there's really something else going on?" the guy says, obviously trying to dig for gossip.

"I caught my fiancé fucking his assistant when I came home, and I really didn't think I needed to stick around after that. Since Matt is technically the only person I knew after my memory loss, he was kind enough to give me a place to stay. *No strings attached,*" I stress the last sentence with a nasty glare for the guy to get it through his head.

"I guess I was lucky she only knew me," Matt says lightly, chuckling at him.

"Hell yeah, you lucky fucker," the guy responds holding his hand up for a high five, which Matt gives.

Kelly rolls her eyes at their action, making me laugh, lightening the mood.

The subject gets dropped when something happens on the TV making everybody groan in disappointment.

Three hours later, with two and a half beers in my stomach, we are finally ready to head out. As I stand up I notice that my head feels woozy and it's hard for me to keep a steady line as I walk. Matt notices after a couple of steps, wraps his arm around my waist for support, and walks me towards the exit. On the way out I see Carol watching us from the corner of my eye and again she is spitting daggers at me.

GABBIE S. DURAN

Once outside, we stay close to the entrance, while the guys keep having their conversation about the upcoming season. Since I'm tired of standing there listening to even more football talk, I try to walk to the car and have to walk slowly since it proves a bit difficult. Next thing I know Matt is standing right in front of me with an amused look on his face. He then picks me up, throwing me over his shoulder, making my head spin even more as he walks off to his car.

Since this is making me sick, being half upside down I just yell at him, "Put me down Matt, I can walk perfectly fine."

"You know you can't. You're such a light-weight. You got drunk off two beers," he says chuckling.

I don't like that. "Hey, you're the one who gave me those beers, and I'm not drunk. Just really tipsy," I retort with a hiccup.

Trey only laughs at me and tells Matt, "At least we know she's a cheap drunk."

I scowl at Trey as best as I can, but I don't know if it really looks like a scowl from this point of view.

As I'm bouncing over Matt's shoulder I watch the view below me, taking in how his jeans are perfectly molded to his ass. Feeling brave, I reach down and tightly grab one of his butt cheeks with my right hand, liking the feel of it.

I suddenly feel him grabbing my ass in return, and I yelp from the pain.

"If you touch, so will I," I hear Matt say as we finally reach the car.

He stands me on my feet, holding me by the shoulders, and looks straight into my eyes. "If you feel like puking you'd better do it now, 'cause if you do it in my car it will be the last time you ride in it. Understood?"

Even though I know he wouldn't hurt me, his tone is frightening me. It also makes me pull my head back away from him with my eyes wide. With the look that he gave me, I'm pretty sure he means it, and I don't plan on crossing that line.

I begin to analyze whether I need to throw up or not, and once I've determined I'm good, I nod my head and get into the back seat of the car. I sit back, leaning my head on the seat, praying that I don't lose my stomach on the way home.

It turns out that even with Matt's speed racer driving, I'm able to hold my cookies just fine. We arrive at the house and I slowly climb out of the car and make my way in, going straight to my room. I throw myself on the bed wanting to fall asleep already. As I'm about to, I hear the door open and with the hall light I see Matt's silhouette make its way in.

"Here take these and drink all of this." I sit up as he hands me two pills and a full glass of water. I swallow both and hand him back the empty glass, tossing myself back onto my pillow. I feel him begin to take my shoes off, and then he reaches for the buttons on my jeans, sending me into high alert. My body goes rigid and my hands stop his, not knowing what he's planning on doing.

"I'm just taking your pants off so you'll be more comfortable. I really doubt you want to sleep in them."

Since my head is still spinning, I close my eyes and lift my hips as he continues to remove my jeans. Once he's done, he starts to pull the blanket from under me, and then brings it back up to cover my body. Still lying there, I feel him give me a kiss on my forehead before saying, "Goodnight beautiful."

I hear his footsteps walk away, and then I hear the

clicking of the door. I'm left to sleep away my tipsiness.

WAKING UP THE next day to the sun shining through my window makes me realize that I really need to get some darker curtains for days when I just want to sleep in. I reach over to the bedside table, looking for my phone, and realize it's not where I usually put it before I go to bed. This wakes me up in a panic. The last thing I need is to lose my phone after just getting it. I scramble off the bed and notice my jeans draped on a chair that is in the corner and I immediately rush to them searching the back pocket where I usually put it, and it's there. Thank god. I've come to love my baby.

I quickly hop into the shower, hoping it will help wake me up. Once I'm done dressing, I head out into the living room and instantly notice that there are several guys sitting around watching TV. They notice me walk in and some of them give me a casual head nod in hello. This is the first time since I've moved in that we've had any guests, so it surprises me to see them here.

I walk straight to the kitchen and pour myself a bowl of cereal. I'm facing the front of the house, looking out of the window, wanting to take in the view. I'm about to take my first bite, when I hear Matt say into my ear, "Good morning beautiful, how you feel?"

I turn around to face him, which makes me bump into his chest. I'm surprised by how close he is and I accidently spill some of the bowl's milk on his chest.

"I'm sorry," I say to him as he's backing away.

He just chuckles, grabs a dishtowel and wipes his shirt. "Don't worry about it," he tells me.

"Why would you ask how I feel? You didn't really expect me to wake up with a hangover from two beers, did you?" I irritably snap at him.

He shrugs his shoulders and walks away, leaving me standing there, eating my cereal. I look over in the direction of all the guys in the living room and although there are only about five or six of them, you can tell how close they are.

They're joking with each other about their summer. What they did or didn't do, and I stand there staring in Matt's direction. I wonder what he usually does for the summer. Did he go home to visit his sister or would he stay here and hang around? It was obvious he wasn't in any big need of money. How he had it was another mystery to me.

With every spoonful that goes into my mouth, I keep staring at him, unable to control myself. Already knowing what he looks like half-naked doesn't help either. The desire running through me right now from looking at him is burning high. It sends a current of electricity coursing through my veins, that I want him to extinguish with his body.

Thinking about last night and wondering what would have happened if I'd pulled Matt into bed with me doesn't help. Would he have stayed and satisfied both our lust? Or is that why he'd walked away? I know I wasn't over the limit drunk, but I had enough alcohol in me to give me the encouragement I needed to follow through with the act.

No, I can't think like that. Tipsy or not, Matt knew exactly how much he could have taken advantage of me and he didn't. Which only proved that he had no intentions of ever doing so. He didn't see me that way, and to be honest, I don't think he ever will.

As if sensing that I'm thinking about him, he looks up in my direction for a split second, and stares right back at me. He flashes me one of his wicked grins.

This is exactly what causes me to have these illicit thoughts, his sexy eyes and wicked grins that leave nothing for the imagination.

Knowing that he's purposely trying to bait me again, I turn my body around and proceed to rinse out my bowl. As soon as I'm done, I feel a presence behind me and my body goes stiff, not knowing who it is. I quickly glance over my shoulder and relax as soon as I see Matt standing behind to me.

"Sorry about the guys. Trey invited them over without telling me, or else I wouldn't have them stay," he says, nodding his head in the direction of the rowdy crowd filling the living room.

I look at him. "It's okay. It's his house too, I'd already said you shouldn't have to change your life because of me, but you keep doing it anyways," I say as I lean against the counter, trying to put as much distance between us as it allows.

By the reaction on his face, I can tell he isn't happy with my response, but he just nods his head. "Okay. Well, heads up, now that practice is starting up soon, a lot of guys might be coming over afterwards. If you ever feel overwhelmed, all you have to do is let me know and I'll take care of it."

I shrug my shoulders at him. "I mean it beautiful, if you ever feel unsafe or uncomfortable just let me know." As I'm looking into his face, my hands are twitching from wanting to touch him. I don't know what is going on with me, but I have to try to get myself under control.

I simply nod my head again and thank him before I walk back in the direction of my room. At least there I won't be torturing myself looking at Matt.

## Chapter 16

KNOWING THAT I needed to get out of the house more often, I set up a shopping date with Kelly for the next day. My hope is that keeping a distance between Matt and me will help get these crazy feelings under control.

When she arrives the next morning, to say that I'm excited is an understatement. I finally get to get out of the house without Matt and with a girl, someone I can relate to. As we're in one of the stores, preparing to pay for our items, I begin to hear singing coming from somewhere around me. It's Big Poppa blaring near me, the ringtone is softened, but relatively close.

"Who would have that annoying ring tone?" I say, scrunching my nose to Kelly. I start looking around the store trying to find where it's coming from.

Kelly's face makes a frown at me as I look back at her. "Umm, Abi. I think it's your phone," she says, pointing at my purse.

Oh crap, it is my phone.

The ringtone stops, and then within a few seconds starts up again. I frantically start digging in my purse looking for my phone, wanting to shut it up. Once I've found it I look at the screen and see Matt's smiling face staring back at me.

That fucker.

I'm going to kick his ass when I get home.

I quickly answer the phone in an effort to shut the ringtone up. "Matthew Garcia, you are in big trouble," I say quietly, scowling into the receiver.

He's laughing on the other end of the line, knowing exactly how pissed I would be when I heard it. "Love my new ringtone, beautiful?" he mocks me.

Oh hell no, this shit is getting changed as soon as I can find a song to describe him, maybe something about being a heartbreaker or a tease. "What do you want Matt?" I snap at him in irritation.

I know I shouldn't be snapping at him, but I can't help it. He always manages to do these things and get away with them when it comes to me. Wait 'til I get my hands on his phone, he's going to regret it.

"I'm out running errands, I just wanted to make sure everything was okay. Do you have enough cash or do you need me to bring you my card?" he asks me.

I'm done shopping. I'm pretty much wiped out. "No, I'm fine, I think we're done for the day," I say, looking over at Kelly and she nods her head in agreement as she's paying the cashier.

"Alright, sounds good. If you need anything just give me a call. I should be out and about for the next couple of hours."

"Thanks, I'll let you know," I tell him.

He whispers into the phone right before he hangs up,

"Bye beautiful," which makes my irritation fly completely out of the window like it usually does.

He always knows how to do that. One minute I'm pissed at him, the next I'm melting at his feet, even if it's over the phone. Today's shopping trip was so I could avoid turning to mush with him around, and he's managed to do it over the phone. I need to grow a backbone and fast. Wanting to distract my lovesick mind, Kelly and I keep shopping.

We hit another store with no incident. It's when we decide to take a casual stroll of window-shopping that the chaos begins. People begin to recognize me and begin to approach. I try to be nice, wave, and smile while I continue going about my day. But as more and more people keep approaching me, Kelly and I agree that our shopping expedition is over and decide to leave. Then the crowd starts to grow, and they even begin to follow me, not leaving me alone. I panic, not knowing what to do, as they start trying to pull me in different directions demanding autographs, or pictures. When I to cover my face from the flashes they get angry. Kelly sees the panic in my eyes, but as she tries to ward people off me they start to get aggressive with her.

"Back off bitch!" one girl yells at Kelly while trying to shove a pen and paper in my hands. "It's just a signature!" the girl says.

Another person moves up next to me asking, "Can I take a picture with you?" and then proceeds to take the self-pic of us without me giving her an answer. I move away, feeling like I need my space. "What, too good for a picture?" she says when she sees me scowling at her.

I can't believe how rude some of these people can be. I hear everyone shouting at this point as I'm pushed in different directions and surrounded by flashes. A couple of security guards show up and usher me into one of the stores, where they shut the doors, and try to calm people down as they yell through the windows.

A lady inside ushers me towards the back of the store out of view of the crowds. She ends up being the owner of the boutique and asks, "Are you ok?"

I see the concern in her eyes as she's wringing her hands and looks back and forth between the front doors and me.

I can hear Kelly talking into her phone, "Yes, they just started attacking us. It really scared the crap out of me, David. Yes, she's okay. What do I do?" she asks into the phone, nodding her head at the same time. After telling him which store we're taking refuge in she hangs up and walks over to me.

Looking really agitated and worried at the same time she throws her arms around me to calm me down and asks, "Are you okay?"

The only thing I can do is nod my head and keep the tears at bay. The last thing I want is to give these rabid fans the satisfaction of knowing that I cried.

Rubbing my arm with her hand to comfort me, she says, "Had I known this was going to happen Abigail, I wouldn't have suggested we come."

Now I feel guilty because she looks like she's blaming herself for this whole ordeal.

"No, it's not your fault. I never thought this would happen either," I say. "This never happened when I was at a race or the Market with Matt."

We sit there hoping that the crowd will eventually grow bored and leave. Less than ten minutes later, I hear banging on the door and a guy shouting, demanding to be let in. I automatically tense up and Kelly and I both look over to the doors. We see Matt trying to resist being pulled away from the doors by the mall cops, so Kelly and I both walk over to the doors asking the owner to let him in.

She rushes to unlock the door. I notice that there are still a few people standing outside, as if they are waiting for me to come out. The security guards finally let go of Matt when Kelly lies to them, stating that he is my brother here to pick me up.

As soon as Matt clears the door, he rushes to me and immediately takes me in his arms and I start crying. The tears I have been holding begin to come out like a dam that has been broken.

"Shh, shh. It okay, I'm here now," he says, rubbing my back to calm me down.

Matt looks back at the crowd still waiting outside and then at the storeowner. "Don't you guys usually have a back exit or something?"

She nods her head, then leads us to the back of the store, into what looks to be an office. Once we're all inside she points to a door that is against the back wall and has an exit sign above it. Matt nods his head at her then faces me.

"Stay here, I'll be right back," he says right before he turns to leave. As I'm about to follow him, I notice that he is jogging to the front of the store, exiting it.

I'm left confused why he would leave me here. I'm still scared and I want to go home.

After what feels like forever, but in reality must have only been maybe five minutes, I hear pounding on the door that is against the wall under the exit sign. I jump in fear, thinking that the crazy people have found me again and are now trying to get in through the back door.

"Kelly, it's me, Matt. Open the door," we hear Matt shouting as he's banging once again on the door.

I calm down, relieved that it's only him. Kelly and I both head to the door and when she opens it I couldn't be happier to see Matt. Even though he said he'd be back, I still felt hurt that he left. I get even happier when I see his car behind him in what looks to be an alleyway. Matt looks slightly out of breath, like he usually does when he's done running, and he has a couple of drops of sweat on his fore-head. He must have run all the way to the car since he was only gone a couple of minutes.

He comes into the office, grabbing me by the waist with his arm, leading me back outside into the car. Kelly is slowly following behind us and climbs into the car, leaving me to sit in the middle of the front seat, between her and Matt.

As soon as Matt is in the driver's seat, he puts the car into drive, and we take Kelly to her parked car. As Kelly exits Matt's car, I'm about to scoot over into the passenger seat, but Matt grabs onto my thigh, shaking his head. I don't need any words to know that he wants me to stay sitting next to him, and I really don't want to move either. After we make sure Kelly is safely in her car, we drive off, and finally head home.

The whole time I am sitting next to Matt I have my head on his shoulder, staring out of the windshield, happy that I am finally out of the nightmare that just happened.

Matt's hand is still on my left thigh. He didn't move it after Kelly got out, but had started rubbing his thumb back and forth on it, sending a calming sensation.

When we finally arrive home Matt reaches to grab my hand. He exits the car, pulling me out of the driver's side with him, heading straight into the house, and leads us to the

GABBIE S. DURAN

couch. The minute we both sit down, the events of the day finally catch up to me, and I start crying all over again. I drop my head into my hands, but Matt grabs me by the waist, and pulls into his lap. He's embracing me tightly, letting me cry into his shoulder. The entire time his hand is rubbing my back as he's shushing me, trying to get me to calm down.

I can't believe that Bill was right when he said this would happen. I had always thought that he wanted me to take a security guard so he could keep tabs on me. I was just the ignorant one who refused to believe that this could happen. It's easy to do, since I didn't know anything about my old life. I had no clue what to expect, and I still don't sometimes. I finally run out of tears and I begin to calm down. I lift my head and notice that Matt's shirt is soaked with tears.

"I'm so sorry. I've cried all over your shirt," I tell him.

"It's okay, I'll just have you do my laundry this week," he says with a light chuckle. I really doubt he would make me do his laundry, but I'm relieved that he's trying to make a joke out of it.

"When David called me and told me what was happening, I was scared out of my mind. I felt like I couldn't get there fast enough. I think I must have broken at least ten different laws just to get there."

I feel him sigh and he keeps my head tucked against his shoulder, running his hand down my head and into the strands of my hair. "Please promise me you won't leave this house without me or Trey to protect you. I don't know how I would handle something happening to you."

I can't believe how I am feeling at this moment. My emotions are all over the place, but the only thing I can say is, "I promise."

I know I am taking the biggest risk ever by asking the next question, but I do. "Matt, why are you being so nice and protective of me? I'm nothing to you." I brace myself for his response.

As he pulls us apart, he stares at me with eyes hurt by my question. He sighs and runs his hands through his hair. He has a frown on his lips as he starts to talk.

"The reason why I feel like I have to be so protective over you is because I'm scared of losing you." He looks out to the backyard, taking another deep breath, he continues. "When I lost my sister, I felt like I lost a reason to live, I had no one to protect anymore. She was everything to me, but when you came to me that day claiming to have her memories, for a moment I thought I was getting her back. As crazy as that sounds."

I place my hand on his shoulder, saying. "It doesn't sound crazy, it sounds kind of sweet," I tell him smiling.

Right then, I hear Trey, David, and Kelly walk in the door, making me jump off Matt's lap to stand. As they walk into the living room they go straight to reflecting on how out of control my life was, leaving me reassured that they didn't see anything.

I once again had to promise, this time to Kelly, that I wouldn't go anywhere without someone to champion and protect me. David had offered to put the football team on rotation duty, two at a time, against their will if needed. Which makes Kelly and me laugh when she mentions that they wouldn't see it as a burden to protect me. This earned him a muttered curse from Trey, stating that he wasn't going to let half of them near me since they were a pack of horny college guys anyways.

When Trey suggested that we have a couple of drinks,

saying we all deserved them after the day I had, I knew it wouldn't be a good idea. I finally ended up passing out from the four beers and God only knows how shots of Patrón. The last thing I remember is putting my head on Matt's shoulder saying I was only going to rest my eyes for a moment.

The next morning I wake up with a pounding in my head and the worst feeling of retching coming from my stomach. I barely manage to stand up and make it to the bathroom before I'm dry heaving in the toilet. Once that is done, I somehow, manage to shower and get dressed. Even that feels like an obstacle.

From the way I'm feeling this morning, I know to never allow myself to get that drunk ever again. Unless it was for a good reason.

# Chapter 17

THE NEXT EVENING I'm sitting outside, taking in the view of the clear bright sky full of stars, watching the full moon as it illuminates the sky. It's so relaxing just sitting here, but before I let my mind wander off into a world of endless daydreams, I see Matt come out of the house.

He takes a seat in the lounge chair next to me. Instead of lying down like I'm doing he sits there, placing his elbows on his knees, just staring at me, making me feel a bit uneasy.

"I've been thinking a lot lately since the 10k." Yeah, the one where I clearly lost to you, I think to myself. "Since you were able to keep up with me I think you should run the half with me next weekend."

I turn my head to stare at him, like he's said the craziest thing in the world.

"What?" He's still looking at me. "I'm just saying. You can already run ten miles with me, what are three more? And I planned on running fifteen this weekend, if you can do that, which I'm pretty sure you can, then you can easily run thirteen," he casually says, like no big deal, as he always does.

What is up with him throwing these races at me?

I think about what he's said. "Can I even still run it? Isn't it full or something by now?" I ask, hoping he'll say it is.

"Actually I checked. It wasn't, so I signed you up," he responds, shrugging one of his shoulders.

"What!" I exclaim at him, while sitting straight up in my chair.

He gets a worried look and pleads. "Look, I have to run fifteen anyways this weekend. At least run them with me so I don't have to do it by myself. If you can't handle it, then I won't force you to run the half with me."

As much as I would love to refuse, with the pleading look that he is giving me, I can't. I take a moment to ponder it and think to myself, why not? "Okay, but if I can't hang I'm stopping to walk the rest while you keep running."

Matt nods his head. "Deal."

I'm hoping that I don't end up regretting this. The things I do for you Matthew Garcia.

I SURVIVED MATT'S preparation run of fifteen miles, proving that I *can* easily handle thirteen miles. I was now preparing myself to run the actual half-marathon that Matt had involuntarily signed me up for.

Therefore, Matt had cooked us a delicious pasta dinner the night before. There were definitely no complaints on my part. Anything he cooked was always welcome in my stomach. Trey was the surprised one when we had informed him that we were now eating dinner at the table like *normal* families.

According to him he didn't come from a normal family so he had no clue what that meant. He had even gone into detail regaling us with wacky stories from his family dinners, some which even had me practically rolling with laughter. They really helped distract me of my nerves for the race.

When I had explained how nervous I was to Matt, he said it was normal for me to feel this way. Especially since this was my first big race. I don't care how normal it was supposed to feel, it didn't help at all.

After dinner though, the nerves started to get to me again. Matt had forced me to go to bed early, claiming we had to be up *really* early the next morning, so he wanted me to be well rested to run. My nervousness kept me from falling asleep right away. I kept tossing and turning. After half an hour of fighting with the covers, I finally decided to get up.

I knew Trey had decided to go out earlier, so I thought that maybe if I paced the living room, it would help calm me down a little. A theory that was obviously proven incorrect; it only made it worse.

Matt must have heard me walking back and forth, even though I was barefoot, because after ten minutes I saw him standing against the wall leading to the hallway. He had his arms crossed over his shirtless chest, with his legs crossed at the ankles, looking sleepy eyed.

"Why you up?" he asked, squinting and blinking his eyes trying to get them to adjust to the kitchen light that I had turned on to keep me company.

"I'm sorry if I woke you up. I couldn't sleep," I say starting to bite my thumbnail as I stop and stand there in the middle of the room.

Matt's shoulders drop and he heads over to me. When he reaches me he grabs my hand, and pulls me to the direction of my room. He walks us both in, shutting the door behind us. I'm confused why he's still in my room, but he answers the question when he pulls us both to the bed.

My heart starts to speed up with excitement, even though I have no clue what he has planned. I'm hoping it's something good. I start to bite my lip to keep my smile from showing, even if the room is pitch black, and he can't see it. I'm giddy and the nerves I have now are for a whole other reason than the ones from moments ago.

I feel him climb into the bed pulling me down with him. He's wearing his usual black boxer briefs, and nothing else. So naturally I can feel his body since I only have on boy shorts with a tank top. His body is bare compared to mine and I'm tempted to make it equal. I'm quickly disappointed when he says, "Let's go to bed, beautiful. You have a big day tomorrow," with his sleepy voice.

Crap, all he wants to do it sleep. I roll my eyes in the silent dark, mentally kicking my perverted mind and myself.

I start to adjust my body against his, craving his warmth. He entwines our legs together, pulling my body tight against his, almost as if he's ensuring that I don't get up again. I bury my face into the crook of his neck, memorizing the smell of his body wash from his earlier shower, loving the way it combines with the natural smell of his skin. I wrap my arm under his, securing it up around his shoulder, wanting to hold him just as tight. I could feel the muscles in his back and shoulders. My mind goes crazy with the images that are swirling in my head.

Just holding him starts to make my hormones go into

overdrive. My body starts prickling, coursing through my blood, down to my toes. I want to run my fingers all over his body right now, touching every single inch of it. It's driving me insane with all the mixed signals that he's sending me. He can easily make me feel secure and safe, then just as fast push me away to prove that there is absolutely nothing between us.

His embrace calms my nerves and my body starts to relax. Within minutes I feel Matt's breathing begin to slow down, and by the stillness in his body, I know he's already asleep. Although I'm still frustrated, my body is getting so lax in his arms that I grow sleepy, and I finally allow my body to join him into the world of dreamland.

I wake up the next morning to my alarm blaring from my phone announcing it's time to get up. My body is yelling it's too damn early! I automatically reach for it, already knowing how to shut it up with my eyes closed. Remembering how I finally wound up falling asleep last night, I open my eyes to see if Matt is still in bed.

I'm disappointed when I'm once again alone in an empty bed, free of Matt. I want to scream from the dejected feeling that I'm getting right now, but instead I take a deep breath. I let it out, trying to push out the frustration that is building up in my entire body.

I eventually get up, heading straight for the shower hoping that the cool morning water will wake me up, or at least cool down my burning body.

We make it to the race with the usual time to spare, and I'm once again standing at the start line of yet another race.

We're surrounded by a crowd of people and I'm scared witless with nerves. I've had them for the last couple of days, and I'm about to go mad. This morning my nerves are a hundred times worse than the last couple of days. The first race I ran with Matt I had no idea what to expect, but this one is different. I knew *exactly* how many miles I was going to have to run, and I knew to expect a huge crowd compared to the last one. There were easily at least 20,000 runners today.

I try to distract myself by adjusting the armband that holds my phone, making sure it's not too tight, or too loose. I bought it before our "fifteen" miler, since I discovered at the 10k that it was driving me nuts having to hold my phone in my hand while trying to outsprint Matt.

As the announcers start to rev up the crowd, I actually begin to get excited. I look over to Matt feeling good about this race. Or maybe I am feeling cocky from everyone cheering. "Okay, what're the stakes this time?"

He looks over at me with a raised eyebrow, and then considers the question.

"You have to cook for two nights this time, one of them being for a group of friends that I'll invite over," he says with a cocky grin.

Uhh, what is up with him making me learn to cook? I'm not the one trying to get some guy's attention. Okay maybe just his, but we both know it's not going to be with my cooking.

"Why do you always throw the cooking thing at me? Isn't there anything else you'd rather get out of me?" I say without thinking.

His eyes turn sexy and hooded. His lips go into a half smile, as if he's getting the same picture I'm imagining if he were to take me up on my offer. I begin to feel an ache in between my legs with that look. His eyes are my weakness, but those lips are closely behind them in the ranks. I want to run my tongue along those lips.

"I know you hate it, so it's worth wagering," he says in a husky tone. "Anything else I wouldn't want to risk wagering for."

"What the hell are you putting on the table?" I quickly put my finger up to stop him from speaking, and continue on. "It can't involve cooking or anything domestic. We already know you can play the housewife in this friendship of ours."

He turns his head, staring ahead into the crowd. At first, I think he's ignoring me then he says, "I'll let you drive my car home," without glancing in my direction. I'm pretty sure it killed him inside to even suggest it.

I mouth falls open in a huge O, and my eyes go wide. I want to jump up and down, whooping at the same time, but I can't get to ahead of myself. I did that last time, and he ended up smoking my ass.

"Deal," I say with enthusiasm, lightly jumping up in down, unable to control myself. My nerves have now turned to total excitement and I'm ready to run this thing. I put my earphones in my ear and start my playlist as the crowd moves forward pushing us through the start line.

Matt and I keep up with each other, moving through the crowd, keeping a steady pace. He told me during our last run that you always want to pace yourself for the first eight to nine miles, increasing slowly from beginning to end. According to him, one problem runners always have is that they start off fast from the excitement of the race, then die down when they reach halfway which causes them to want to slow down or give up.

He was really good about touching my arm to slow me down when I would want to speed up. At first I had thought it was because he wanted to pull the same stunt as the last race, but he was right.

Once we hit the mile marker for the sixth mile, I began to notice what he meant by people dying down. The crowd slowly started to thin out from them starting to walk, but it allowed us to slowly increase our speed.

By the time we hit the ninth mile, I felt him start to run faster, so I followed his lead. Next thing I know I lose myself in the music blasting in my ears, and start to take off leaving Matt behind. I don't do it on purpose, but the song that happens to come on at the moment on my playlist gives me a jolt of adrenaline. I wanted to finish this race already.

We finally hit the tenth mile marker, which records our time, and I just keep running faster. Still lost in my world of music, I notice the crowd of people cheering us on, and it helps push me forward. All of a sudden I see the sign that marks "Mile 12" and grow ecstatic. I'm almost done and even if I feel a little fatigued; I know deep down inside it's almost over. My brain tells my legs to pick it up and they start wanting to move faster.

I begin to see the crowds increasing on the side, with people cheering, and I see the finish line in the far distance up ahead. I grow excited, and suck in a big breath, telling myself, let's do this. I dig deep down inside, trying to pull energy from my body, and pick up my pace. I can see the finish banner slowly start to come visibly close, so I start sprinting for it, finally crossing it a couple of seconds later.

I stop running, bringing my body to a walk, as they place a medal over my neck. The feeling of knowing that I've finally finished, mixed with the pride of receiving my first medal, makes it worth running this race.

That's when I realize that I had totally forgotten about

Matt a while back and I feel horrible about it. I turn around looking for him and see him running towards the finish line. Once he's crossed over he brings his body to a walk as well, with his hands on the side of his hips, and shakes his head as he drops it in defeat.

After they place his medal around his neck, he comes straight to me and hugs me, making the guilt disappear. After a couple of seconds he lets me go, but keeps his arm around my waist, and he walks me through the crowd of spectators.

My body feels spent, but there is nothing like the feeling of knowing that you just finished running thirteen miles and you also beat someone else in the process.

After gathering our stuff from the check-in where we left our bags, we begin to silently walk over to the lot where we left his car. The whole time we don't speak, and I'm already beginning to think that Matt is going to back out on his end of the deal.

I had totally forgotten about it until we started walking back. You would have thought this was the reason why I kept running faster, but in reality it wasn't. I was lost in my own little world of wanting to finish.

Once we get to the entrance of the lot with the car, I see him grimly start to dig through his bag. Looking worried he takes out his keys, tightly squeezing them in his fist, as if he's about to change his mind. He closes his eyes, tilting his head up to the sky before taking a deep breath. You can see his throat tightening up as he swallows and the strain in his jaw indicates that he's keeping himself from grinding his teeth. I see his head come back down as he solemnly opens his eyes, looks directly at me, and then throws the keys to me.

I catch them with a grin from ear to ear, jump up excited, pumping the fist holding the keys and start to jog to the driver's side of the car.

I get in, stick the key in the ignition, and turn it. The car turns on with a loud purr that I love hearing. I sit there, closing my eyes, gripping the steering wheel as I rest my forehead against it.

I can hear Matt groaning from the other side of the car, but I only ignore him wanting to take in my sweet victory.

Yup, this feeling right now *might* just be better than eating Matt's pancakes after a long run.

# Chapter 18

A WEEK LATER I'm lying outside in the backyard sun-bathing in a bikini, taking advantage of the sun that has decided to show itself in Portland. These days are rare, but when they do happen, I take full advantage. I feel a silhouette taking over the sun shining down on me, and I open my eyes to see a sexy looking guy looking down at me while he's licking his lips. Thank God for the sunglasses I'm wearing at this moment, because I'm staring intensely right back at him, imaging what I could easily do with those lips.

I shake my head, forcing myself to return to reality. "Is there a reason why you're out here, Matt? Besides blocking the only sun that decided to grace us with its presence on this day."

He stares at me, and I begin to feel my body heat up from his sexy eyes bearing down on me. Even the sun that is shining down on me doesn't heat my body as well as those eyes. My heart starts to race like it always does when he's near me, and I might have to take a *really* cold shower to bring my body temperature back down.

"I wanted to tell you that I went into the Portland Marathon's website to confirm my entry, and I discovered that there were still open entries. So I signed you up to run it with me," he casually says.

My body shoots up and I immediately stand up to stare at him in astonishment. "Why the heck did you do that Matt, and without asking me first? What makes you think I would even want to run it?" I practically shout at him. "My legs hurt for days after the last race. I was sore in places that I didn't like, and it's unfair because I didn't get any enjoyment out of it."

Matt looks at me dropping his eyelids with his signature beam on his face and I'm instantly regretting was I've said. "If you wanted some enjoyment out of it beautiful, all you had to do was ask."

I want to smack that smile off his face right now. "Don't you start with me Matthew, I'm not in the mood," I snap at him.

"Let me know when you are and I'll make it up to you."

"Look, I didn't want to run it alone," he says, trying to change the subject. "Since you already have the stolen memory, I figured I would make it a reality for you," he says as he walks away from me and into the house. The sadness when he said it makes me feel guilty, then I quickly remember what he said.

Stolen memory, my ass. It's not like I wanted these damn memories to happen. I don't even understand why they're happening. Especially when they're all about him.

I follow him into the house, still pissed. If I thought I was overheated earlier from his sexy stare, he is going to feel the wrath from the heat of my glare in a minute. *He's* going to be the one that needs the cold shower when I'm done with him.

"Matthew Garcia, you had no right to register me for another race without my permission. You have to stop doing that," I shout at him, because he's still walking away from me. "I haven't been training as hard as you. So there's no way I could even hang for, for… how many miles is a marathon anyways?" I ask, totally lost, not knowing the answer.

He stops in the hallway before his doorway and faces me with a serious look on his face. "It's 26.2 miles and I'm pretty sure if you can handle fifteen miles you can handle a couple of more."

My jaw drops open. "Did you flunk math? Because I'm pretty sure twenty-six minus fifteen is not a couple of measly miles," I say, dropping my hand on my hip, glaring him straight in the eyes.

"We'll run twenty miles this weekend at an easy pace for your body to adjust and then the week after that you'll take it easy during the race. You have seven hours to finish it anyways. I'm pretty sure you can finish it before that," he says, smiling down at me.

"Give me one good reason why I should run this race?" I throw at him.

"It's the last race that I can run before the season starts and being that it's the last race that I ran with my sister, I have a feeling it's going to be hard on me to run it alone. It would really mean a lot to me beautiful, if you'd run it with me." His eyes are pleading with me.

He's managed to make me push the anger completely away with his plea and the only thing I can say is, "Alright, but it's the last one," Pointing my finger at him in irritation, I declare, "So quit signing me up for the damn things, or the next time you'll be running alone, whether you like it or not."

I turn around, heading to the kitchen, not giving him a chance to give me an answer.

As I stand against the counter drinking some water I think about everything that just happened. What is up with this man? He knows how to push my buttons in all the wrong ways.

Since I'm still fuming a little, I decide to head to my room to take a shower. I'm hoping the cool water will temper down my mood.

Once I'm finally done and dressed in normal clothing, I head back into the living room and notice Matt sitting on the couch. He's leaning forward over a thick folder, concentrating intensely on it. I go over and sit next to him and see that he's staring at a page with a bunch of Xs and Os all over it. He turns a page and does the same with the next one.

I'm staring at the markings on the page and I'm confused out of my mind what it means, so I look up at Matt. He finally notices that while he's deeply concentrating on the page, I'm deeply concentrating on him.

Matt tilts his head to me with a half-smile. "Hey beautiful, you done with your tantrum?"

I roll my eyes at him and take a deep breath. I really don't want to start fighting with him again.

"What are you looking at?"

He lifts up the folder he's holding with the pages and states, "It's this year's play moves. As the quarterback, it's my job to know all the offensive plays."

I look back down at the folder and notice that there must be at least fifty pages. "That's a lot of pages you have to memorize, how do you do it?"

He smiles at me, saying, "Practice. If you want to help

me practice the moves, I'm all up for it."

I roll my eyes again, grab the folder from his hands, and start flipping through the pages as well. We sit there with him trying to explain what the different plays are, but to me it's a whole bunch of mumbo-jumbo. Instead, I sit there listening to him, just so I can hear his voice.

I learn that when he's in deep concentration his voice becomes husky without him trying, and it has a way of taking me to another world. I love the way his eyebrows move up and down when he changes his facial expressions with the different explanations. I wonder what his voice would sound like against my skin as he's kissing me.

As soon as the thought comes to my head I easily shake it off. I have to stop doing this to myself. I don't know why I'm even doing it. I know he's totally off limits, but then that's when I realize the old saying. You want what you can't have.

Willpower Abigail Adams, willpower.

"Matt, do you still talk to your ex-girlfriend, the one from Berkley?" I suddenly want to know.

He looks puzzled why I would ask. "I talk to her every now and then. Mostly when I'm drunk, and same with her. You know, the whole drunk dial call," he says.

I shake my head because I don't know what he's talking about. I can't imagine myself trying to call someone when I'm drunk. If I have in the past, it makes me feel better that I don't know.

Matt quickly chuckles and says, "Well, one of these days I'll show you how to do it."

"I really doubt I'll want to call your ex-girlfriend when I'm drunk," I tell him. This makes him throw his head back while he laughs. He laughs so hard he has to wipe his eyes.

His laugh is contagious and I'm soon doing the same.

When he laughs like this, it makes me feel so good. It brings back the small memory of his sister, when she told me that he needed me in his life to make him laugh again. At this moment I understand exactly what she meant, I haven't seen him laugh much since I've met him.

He's finally able to calm himself. "I really doubt she would want you calling her on my behalf anyways. That would be a very awkward call."

Yes, it would, I think to myself.

Matt reaches over and grabs my hand, then brings it to his lips, giving me a kiss on the back of my hand. Then he stands up and heads to the kitchen. I close the playbook, place it on the coffee table in front of me and follow him.

As I reach him, he's taking things out of the cabinets and fridge, while placing them on the island in front of me. "I'm planning on making lasagna for dinner. Want to help me?"

I shrug my shoulder. "Why not, I have to learn to start cooking anyways. There is no way I'm going to be able to beat you in the marathon."

He looks up from the counter and gives me a wide smile. "I hope not, because I don't know if I could trust you driving my car again."

"Hey, we made it home in one piece. As for your car, it's not my fault that it has so much horsepower that I'm not used to," I retort.

The problem I had with his car was that the gas pedal was very sensitive, and every time I would press on it, I ended up almost peeling out. I thought Matt was going to have a heart attack on the twenty-five minute drive home. I had him gripping the seat and dashboard more times than he wanted to, but he was a good sport about it. He never once yelled at me. He did give me some ugly looks, but never raised his voice. If looks could kill, I would have been dead upon arrival.

He had the biggest scowl on his face when he got home and all I wanted to do was kiss him to make him smile. Ever since that day I was obsessed with thoughts of kissing him. There wasn't a day that went by I didn't think about it. I just wanted to take those plump, juicy pink lips in between my teeth.

My lusty thoughts are instantly broken when I hear Matt say, "That's not the only thing that has a lot of power in it," waggling his eyebrows.

I'm already used to his perverted comebacks, so I merely throw my head back and laugh at his response. "Does everything always have to come back to sex with you? Don't you get enough from all the girls swimming around you all the time?" I ask.

He stops, stares at me, and then says, "Since you've moved in, I've calmed down quite a bit."

If you call often, leaving for a couple of hours during the day calming down a bit. I don't want to know how crazy his sex life was before.

"I haven't seen a girl come over since Lizzy, not that I could keep you from bringing girls to your house," I say, raising my hands in surrender. "But you must make it really quick since you only leave for a couple of hours. So you must be going to them?"

Matt shakes his head as he puts ground beef into the pan in front of him to cook. Keeping his eyes on the pan he responds, "I haven't been going to any girls, Abigail. I go to the gym at school. I have to keep in shape, especially with the season about to start soon."

His statement surprises me. Knowing that he isn't out screwing any girls makes me feel so much better. I know it shouldn't, but it does.

The rest of the night goes pretty smoothly, with me doing the easy parts of the lasagna. I learn that this is another dish that requires layering, but with Matt's help it gets done quickly. I help make the salad, and, as if on cue, once it's done Trey walks into the door.

Matt starts placing all the food on the dining table and Trey stares at him. "So we're serious about this eating at the table shit?"

"Yeah, so get over it," he says without even looking back at him.

I head over to the table to place the salad on it. "Families eat dinner at the table. Since we are now a happy family, according to you two, we eat our meals at the table."

Trey shrugs his shoulders and says, "Whatever makes you happy, supermodel.

We're almost done with dinner when we start discussing the recent nightmare that Matt has signed me up for, making Trey laugh from imagining how pissed I must have been when he told me.

I state that I was beyond pissed, but finish with, "If I need to, I'll walk most of it. According to Matt I have seven hours to finish. I'm pretty sure I have this one in the bag."

Matt quickly looks at me shocked, and then turns to Trey. "She's running most of it, even if I have to slap her ass most of the way to keep her going." Then he looks back at me, smiling. "Trust me, I would do it too."

I gawk at him. "You wouldn't dare."

Matt lowers his lips to my ear to say, "Trust me, beautiful. I *promise* I will." My eyes draw wide open at him as he stands, and begins to clean up the table.

Trey might not have heard what Matt said, but by the shock on my face I think he gets an idea. He's sitting there laughing at me, while shaking his head before he also stands up, leaving me alone at the table. I better make sure to pace myself, because as much as it turns me on when he slaps my ass, I don't want the whole public seeing him doing it.

I can already see the paparazzi catching the shot, head-lining it, "Supermodel gets slapped on the ass." Yeah, definitely not going to happen if I can help it.

# Chapter 19

SAYING THAT CRASH training for a marathon in less than two months is harder than it sounds, would have to be the understatement of the century.

It was torture.

My body would ache in places I didn't know existed. One of the benefits from all this was that my legs were starting to tone out very well. Even I couldn't help admiring them in the mirror sometimes.

Another plus was that I didn't really have to watch what I ate. I didn't eat junk food, Matt made sure of that, but I wasn't living the life that most people assume for a super-model. I was able to eat pieces of what I wanted, when I wanted it, and not have to stress about it.

Matt finally took me on his last long run before the marathon, and although twenty miles sounds long, it's even longer when you're running it. Matt never let me stop, and kept tugging me along. At around mile 16 I tried walking, this is where he kept his promise by turning around, coming up behind me, and slapping me on the ass.

Surprisingly, it didn't hurt though. Maybe it didn't hurt as much because I was awake. After that I would slow down, but keep moving, knowing that he'd keep his word. I don't know how in the world I was going to be able to keep up with Matt. He wasn't Speed Racer, but I wasn't as into it as he was, which caused me to slow my pace.

We finally finish the run and my body is already aching a bit on the walk back to the car. We climb in and I'm relieved that we are finally heading home. I just want to go home and fall asleep. My body feels exhausted, and a shower sounds so good right now.

I'm soon disappointed on the way home when instead of heading to the house he's headed in a direction that is unknown to me. We pull into a street that begins to wind and curve to some buildings that look like they are part of the college. He finally pulls the car to a stop in front of the building that says, "Athletic Department."

"Where are we?" I'm curious why he'd even bring me here.

He doesn't say anything, but reaches for a duffel bag that he had brought with him this morning and placed in the backseat.

"Come on," he says, opening his door and climbing out of the car. I have no choice but to follow him since he's already walking towards the building.

At this point my legs are killing me, and I don't want to walk anymore.

"Aren't we going to get in trouble for being here?"

He takes my hand and says, "Nobody's here right now, and I have a key. This is where I come to work out and recover after my really long runs."

I really don't feel like working out any more than I've already done this morning, and I'm pretty sure I can recover at home in the comfort of my own bed. Apparently, Matt has a different idea though. He uses a key attached to his car keys to open the door to the building, and then holds the door for me, and I walk in.

I notice right away it's a locker room, as he walks ahead of me. I follow him, and we end up in front of what looks like giant bathtubs that have plastic covers on them. He takes the cover off the one we are standing in front of, and pushes a button a couple of times. I see the numbers on the dial begin to drop, lowering the temperature.

"Take off your jacket, shoes, and socks," he tells me, while he starts to do it himself.

"Why?"

"We're getting in."

Does he mean in the tub? Is he crazy? I saw the low number on that dial. I'm not getting in there, so I stand there, refusing to do anything. Noticing that I haven't done my part, he bends down instead, and starts to untie my shoes removing them along with my socks. He stands up when he's done and removes the jacket I'm wearing. Which leaves me in only the sports bra I had underneath the jacket and my tight running shorts.

He places his hand in the tub, checking for the temperature. Satisfied, he grabs my hand as he walks over to the steps, and begins to climb them. With his hand stretched out, still holding mine he swings his legs over into the tub, and I notice he immediately sucks in his breath as he sinks in. His reaction scares the shit out of me and I stick the hand that he isn't holding into the water, yanking it back just as fast.

"Are you crazy? That water is freezing cold," I squeal

at him.

Matt stays sitting in it, ignoring my complaint. "It's good for your body to take an ice bath after a long run. It helps your body recover faster, and prevents injuries."

I shake my head and try to pull my hand from his, but he has a firm grip on it and holds on. "Come on beautiful, I'll keep you warm," he says with a sexy smile.

He doesn't give me a chance to protest as he stands up, grabbing me by the waist. Lifting me up off the ground, over the tub, dunking me completely, including my head into the water.

The shock of the freezing cold water hits me, and I stand up, gasping for air. My entire body feels like it's being pierced all over with needles, and I immediately start shivering from the cold.

I'm standing there, trying to focus on my breathing, wanting the coldness to go away. Matt pulls me closer to him, pushing his knees in between mine, forcing me to straddle him.

As I sit there, straddling his hips, he wraps his arms around my waist, placing his face into my neck to breathe his warm breath next to my skin. I wrap my arms around his neck in reaction, trying to pull him closer to me, and sit there against him. I lay my head against his neck as well, as my teeth and lips are rattling from the cold.

Since I can feel the warmth of his face against my neck, I start to relax a little, trying to ignore that we are in freezing water. After a minute, my body starts to forcefully adjust to the temperature, and it actually does start to take away the ache that was coursing through my body earlier.

My body starts to warm up, obviously not from the water, but because I know that my body is pressed so closely against Matt's. He slowly starts moving his hands up and down my back, heating the blood in my body with his fingertips gently gliding as they touch my naked skin. I try pulling him closer, even if I know it's not physically possible, since we're already practically glued to each other, but I want him closer. I want his body linked with mine. I feel him gently bite my neck and my body reacts with an explosion of shivers that run up and down my body.

I feel him come alive between my thighs, and I get excited, grinding myself against his groin in reaction. I hear a small groan come from his neck. I pull my head back to look into his eyes, wanting to see what they look right now, but they are closed. His face is strained, slightly thrown back, with his jaw drawn tight. His breathing is heavy and almost restrained, as if he's using all his willpower to control himself. I love the way he looks right now, and it satisfies me knowing that I'm making him feel this way.

He slowly opens his eyes to a slit, looking directly into mine, and his lips go into a slow sexy smile as he sees me. I start to lower my head to kiss him, closing my eyes, and the minute our lips touch my body feels like it explodes.

He pushes his tongue into my mouth, forcing me to meet his with mine, tangling them together as they move back and forth against each other. Tilting my head so I can have better access to his mouth, I grab his hair with my hands, practically digging my nails into his scalp.

I grind my body against his, feeling his erection grow harder beneath my core and his hands tighten, digging into my hips. Right now I'm cursing the fact that we both have a barrier between us. Why didn't he make us remove all our clothes before we got into this tub?

I love feeling him hard against me, as our bodies rub

fiercely back and forth. Our mouths practically fusing together as our tongues duel with each other, I moan loudly, not caring what he thinks.

I feel his hands begin to creep up my body. His palms slowly tease their way up my back.

We hear the door of the locker room opening and the shock of knowing that we might be caught causes me to instantly jump off Matt. I push myself off him, pushing myself against the other side of the tub, putting distance between us. I hear footsteps behind us. I turn to look back at the person entering the locker room and see an older gentleman walk over towards us.

"Hey there Matt, I didn't know I would be seeing you with company today," he says, looking down at me in the tub.

I must be beet red from the embarrassment of being caught. I sure feel like I am. "Hey Coach, this is my roommate, Abigail. We're training for the marathon next week, and I brought her in for an ice bath," he says casually.

The older man laughs, saying, "You actually managed to recruit someone to run it with you after all."

"I didn't have much choice," I mumble while holding my arms around my waist to try to find some warmth, since Matt's heated body isn't underneath mine to warm it any longer. I can feel the piercing feeling coursing through my veins all over again, and I don't like it.

This makes them both laugh, as the coach shakes his head, and he walks away. He waves his hand in the air yelling, "Don't forget to cover it up and turn it off when you're done, boy."

I hear the shutting of another door and once I'm sure the older gentleman isn't in the same room, I stand up and climb out of the tub. I don't even bother with the stairs, I need out as soon as possible.

Matt takes the hint and climbs out using the steps. I'm standing there wrapping my arms around my freezing cold body. Matt walks over to a stand with towels on it and brings several over, handing one to me. I automatically wrap one around my shoulders, wishing it would take the cold away. Matt takes one in his hand, and starts rubbing down my legs.

Once he's done with them, he takes the towel, and starts drying himself. After a few minutes of making sure we are both completely dry, he reaches for my jacket, helping me put it back on. He takes the wet towel I have and throws it with the others into a bin. He grabs another dry towel and wraps it around my waist.

He reaches down and unzips his duffel bag, taking out our sandals, placing them at my feet for me to put them on. Then he picks up our shoes and socks, placing them in the bag. He goes over to the tub, turns it off, and places the plastic cover back on it.

As I'm about to take off the towel he shakes his head. "Don't worry about the towel, I'll bring it back during my next workout. Let's get you home and fed. I know you must be tired too and wanting your nap," he says as he grabs for my hand, pulling me to the exit.

I take one last glance at the cold tub, wondering how far it would have gone. Even if I was freezing my ass off, I'm pretty sure it would have gone far enough if we hadn't been interrupted.

# Chapter

## 20

ONE WEEK LATER, I am once again standing at the start line of a race with Matt. As we are adjusting our phones into their armbands, he says. "Okay, fastest person has to do the other person's chores along with their own for a week."

I knew exactly what he meant. We had come up with a little system in the house between the three of us. Trey was in charge of cleaning and maintaining the outside of the house, including the garage. Matt was in charge of grocery shopping and cooking. Since I couldn't handle clutter, I was now in charge of the cleaning, something that the guys hated doing. I'm not going to lie and say I deep cleaned the house the first time I cleaned it.

Oh hell no.

That house was screaming bachelor pad from head to toe. I'm surprised I even went near the toilets to pee the first day I moved in. I ended up calling a maid service; I even paid extra for them to come over that same day and take the first round. After that I took over. Maintenance was a lot easier once you've set some ground rules.

"What, I don't get to drive your car again?" I say, pouting my lips.

He grunts before saying, "Beautiful, even if I was dying, I would still make you call an ambulance before I let you drive Eleanor again."

I laugh at his response. He's never going to get over that.

"Deal," I say, knowing that I'm going to end up losing anyways. The guys are going to have to eat a lot of canned soup for the next week, or else starve. It gives me a little confidence knowing that he doesn't want to do the cleaning just as bad as I don't want to cook.

It's still dark outside as we stand around waiting for them to start ushering us ahead. Since every corral was gathering in a different section of the city, you really didn't know when exactly you were going to start. Just standing around was making me nervous. The nerves were there all week, but I was too tired to let them take over. I've been so worn out from the running that we did during the week, I practically passed out last night. So I didn't need a repeat of Matt keeping me company, which I was grateful about. After the tub incident, I was scared of getting too close to Matt's body in fear of raping him.

I feel the crowd around me start to jog forward. I'm wondering where the hell the start line is, but as I'm jogging along I finally see it up ahead, and I start getting excited.

The beginning of the race goes very smoothly, with Matt and me weaving and bobbing our way through the crowds of people. With every mile that goes by we start to get a silent routine between the two of us, occasionally separating to get around people, but coming back together.

This race is a lot different from the half that we ran because it has long stretches of land before you have to loop back around and run the same stretch all over again. Since Matt had me study the course online, it was killing me knowing how much we had ahead of us.

The clocks alongside the course are what really keep me distracted. According to them we are keeping a faster pace that we normally did during our runs. I was starting to get a little worried since my body didn't feel fatigued yet. I couldn't help but wonder if we were going to crash and burn towards the end. We're definitely going faster than we did last week.

I keep the thought to myself, trusting that Matt knows what he's doing, and lose myself in the music blasting through my ears. As we cross over St. John's Bridge, knowing it's the first of two that we have to go over, I get excited noticing the crowd has really thinned out by this point. We are well over with the first half of the race.

I start to notice that my body wants to give up, but I see Matt speaking to me, and I pull out my ear bud to listen to him. "Your body is going to want to hit the wall soon, but try to ignore it, and push through it. It's all mental Abigail, your body can do it. Or you could start planning all the meals you're going to have to cook for the team as well, while you're running," he says before pulling ahead of me.

Oh hell no.

I think to myself that there is no fucking way I'm cooking for half of the team as well. I'll end up burning down the kitchen; no, the whole house!

So I pick up the pace and push forward. I have to win this thing. Or at least finish it. I'm not giving up, dammit. I see the sign that marks the 20-mile mark, knowing that I have never run more than this distance. I have to listen to Matt and tell myself I can do this.

When *"Firework"* starts to sing about feeling like a plastic bag drifting through the wind, I make my legs go faster as I see the Broadway Bridge. I know that the race is almost done past that bridge.

My body feels like it has found a second wind with excitement. Next thing I know, I'm passing Matt with speed as I'm going over the bridge. Forgetting about him, I promise myself that I'm going to beat his ass again, even if it kills me. Every time a new song comes on I use the tempo of the bass to keep me going. I had timed my songs, leaving my most motivating and fastest ones until the end, knowing that I was going to need the beat to push me harder.

I finally see the buildings of downtown up ahead, and know it's practically over. I dig deeper, moving faster than my protesting legs want to go, but I ignore them. I start using the visual of the screaming crowd on the sides of the streets to encourage me. I finally turn a left at a corner. Only a few feet ahead of me I see the banner, and I'm crossing the finish line while the announcer says my name.

As I slow to a walk they put a medal around my neck. I turn around to look behind me, and see Matt starting to run up to the finish line with a smile on his face. Almost as if he's laughing while the announcer says his name as well.

Matt comes straight to me once they are done placing the medal around his neck and says, "Just couldn't resist leaving me in the dust, now could you?" He throws his arms around me bringing his sweaty body against mine, and kisses me on top of my head.

I embrace him back, holding him around the waist with both my arms, smiling from ear to ear. I notice that there are at least three camera people surrounding us, taking pictures as they circle us.

I ignore them, wanting to take in the moment.

We collect our rose for finishing, memorabilia, and a souvenir shirt that we immediately put on. We leave the race, heading straight to my new favorite hangout. I'm starving right now and I want a big juicy burger to satisfy my hunger.

On the way I call all our friends. Once we've arrived at the Brewhouse, they're waiting for us, ready to celebrate. We walk through the door and they start cheering for us as we walk into the restaurant. I can't help but throw my hands up and down in the air taking the praise they were giving.

"So who won?" Trey immediately asks as we take a seat in the bench.

I start to smile, while biting my lip as Matt answers. "She did," he says, hooking his thumb in my direction, not sounding too happy about it.

The manager of the day comes over to our table and asks, "What can I get our runners to drink?"

I look up at him, beaming. "I want Matt's usual. A really big one, I think I've earned it today," I say to him, as he nods his head at me.

"Damn right you earned it," Trey says to me.

This makes everyone laugh, and we start to order our food while we sit there sipping our beer, and I savor the moment.

After looking back at it, I realize that no matter how much Matt has to push me, in the long run I've ended up finding something I like doing. I would have never thought that I would love running, but since the first day I started, I fell in love, and wouldn't change it for the world.

I'm grateful that Matt is finally going to start the season. He doesn't do races during the season, so I was in the clear of him trying to sign me up for any. I can finally give my body a break from *long* distances and just do it for fun. Which is exactly what I plan on doing.

THE NEXT DAY I wake up to Kelly's ring tone blaring through my peaceful sleep. Even though I want to ignore it, I know I can't, or else I won't hear the end of it from her about ignoring her phone calls. I reach over, and answer the phone, half-asleep.

"This better be an emergency Kelly, or else I'm not speaking to you for a week," I grumble into the phone.

"Have you seen the sports section of today's newspaper?" she says to me.

Knowing that we don't get the newspaper, I say to her, "No."

I hear the sounds of beeping, as if she's exiting the car, then a car door shutting. "Well, I'm at your front door, so get your butt up so you can see for yourself," she says before ending the call.

Knowing she has a key to the house now, I stay in bed, counting the moments until she walks into my room. I hear talking coming from the hallway and wait for Kelly to come to my room, which is 30 seconds later. What I didn't expect is for her to be dragging Matt along with her.

He comes over to the empty side of the bed, and climbs beneath the covers, trying to go back to sleep. If it weren't for Kelly in the room, I would have snuggled up against his body, and fallen back to sleep with him.

For that split second of a thought I did forget she was in the room, before she walks over to my side of the bed swatting both of us on the shoulder with what feels like a newspaper, shouting, "Get your asses up, you made the front page."

This wakes both of us up in a heartbeat. I sit up, grabbing for the newspaper in her hand. I see Matt and me on the front page. The headline reads, "Local celebrity runs marathon!" It's a picture of Matt embracing me, and I have a huge smile on my face as I'm leaning into his shoulder at the finish line. This must have been the photo all the photographers surrounding us were trying to get.

Crap. Right when I'd finally got Bill out of my hair, I'm out in the public all over again. I only had three more weeks to go to ride out the contract, and here I am on the front page of the newspaper.

Matt is looking at the newspaper with his chin on my shoulder, still half-asleep. I shrug it to wake him up. "Well, it only proves one thing. You missed Boston by 18 minutes, what a bummer," he says before he gets up and walks out of my room.

What is he talking about? What the hell is Boston, and why is it a bummer to miss it, if I've never even been there? At least I don't think I have. Wanting to know what he's talking about, I get up and follow him into the living room. He's sitting on the couch now with the remote in his hand, turning the TV on.

"What were you talking about when you said Boston? Why would I miss it?" This earns me a laugh from Kelly as she sits on the other couch, leaving me standing in front of Matt with my arms crossed over my chest, still waiting for an answer.

Obviously Matt is ignoring me, causing Kelly to answer my question. "Boston is the Super Bowl of running races. You have to run a marathon under a certain time in order to qualify for it," she informs me. "Even if you do make the qualifying time, you have to sign up in a certain time frame, which is super hard to get into."

I look over at her confused, wondering how the hell she knows all this info. As far as I knew, she wasn't a runner. She shrugs her shoulder, seeing my confusion. "My dad ran it one year when he was young. That's the only reason I know about it. It's his proudest race to date."

Still confused, I look back at Matt. "So how fast are you supposed to run a race in order to qualify?" I ask, throwing my fingers up in air quotes as I ask him.

He takes a deep breath like he's frustrated, as if he's finally decided to answer me. "Women your age have to run it in under three and a half hours. For me it's under three." His lips go into a grimace. "So you missed it by 18 minutes, being that your time was three hours and fifty-three minutes. Which is pretty good for your first marathon, and you had a lot of people to push out of the way."

Kelly pipes up and says, "Are you kidding me? You're just pissed 'cause she wiped your butt all over that asphalt again."

This makes me laugh, because that's exactly why he's in this sour mood right now. They had placed both of our times in the newspaper, making it seem like I did wipe the asphalt with his butt, for it being my first marathon.

I don't care that I didn't make this Boston thing anyways. I was proud of myself for even finishing, that's all that mattered in my mind. The only thing I was worried about at this moment was the fact that my face was plastered on the front page of the Portland newspaper, claiming I was a local celebrity. I was far from being a celebrity anymore, and I wasn't looking to be one.

# Chapter 21

"ARE YOU SURE you don't need any help?" Kelly asks, leaning against the island counter in the kitchen, as I'm placing the frozen lasagna dish into the pre-heated oven. I close the door as I look up at her, and say, "No, it has to cook for about two hours, and then we take it out. Put in the garlic bread while we are putting the salad together, and everything should be good."

I start the timer on the oven the way Matt had taught me the last time I cooked with him, and walk into the living room with Kelly following me.

As we sit on the couch she says, "I don't know why you're making dinner tonight. You did win the race after all." Then she lifts her eyebrows with curiosity. "Unless you're trying to score brownie points with Matt. You know, my momma always says, the way to a man's heart is through his stomach," she says with a mischievous smile, while wiggling her eyebrows.

I roll my eyes knowing exactly where Matt's heart is. "I

thought I would actually try to voluntarily make dinner for once. It's their first practice back, and I didn't want Matt to have to cook dinner. It has nothing to do with winning Matt's heart," I clarify to her.

Now she's the one to roll her eyes at me, and we both laugh. "What time are the guys done with practice today?" I ask.

She shrugs her shoulders, looking down at her phone in her hand. She's just as bad as I am with that thing. One time she left it here accidentally and drove back in the middle of the night to get it. She had woken us all up ringing the door-bell like crazy. That was the reason why she now had her own key. I had discovered I liked my sleep, so that night I was not happy she woke me up.

Since the team had started practice today, they had no clue when they would be done. David had mentioned when he dropped Kelly off to keep me company, that they were probably going to have a usual meeting for the new players and go over the rules with them. It shouldn't take too long. I was just hoping it was long enough for the lasagna to cook. I had forgotten that I wanted to cook dinner, so I was a little behind on time.

As I start to channel surf, the doorbell rings, surprising both of us.

Kelly looks over at me confused. "You expecting any-one?"

I shake my head, just as confused. Who would be at the door? My gut feeling says to ignore it, but then I hear a de-termined knock. Kelly gets up from the couch, and I stay there not wanting to attract any attention at the door in case it's someone I don't recognize. Everyone who would come over is at practice right now, besides Kelly, so this has me troubled.

From where I'm sitting I can see Kelly open the door a crack, and she begins to speak to someone, shaking her head. But as I see her try to use her body to force the door shut, she's instantly thrown back with it, and in walks Andre with Bill on his heels with a determined look on both their faces.

"Hey what the hell, you can't come in here!" Kelly shouts at them, while trying to grab onto Andre, but he shoves her aside causing her to fall to the floor.

I automatically panic, jumping off the couch. I try to run to the back door. But as I take my first step, I feel a pain in my scalp from my hair being pulled. I turn my body around trying to shove my attacker away, but I'm thrown to the floor, landing on my side.

I lift myself up with my arms, trying to stand. Just as fast, I feel something whack me on the side of my face. I'm thrown once again to the floor and I hit my head. My head is now throbbing, and my face is stinging.

My body doesn't have the strength to fight back, but I can hear Kelly screaming in the background for them to leave me alone, and she sounds very panicked. Since my hair has fallen forward, covering my face, I can't see anything. I try to crawl in the direction of her voice. After a couple of crawls, I feel my head being yanked up, and I'm looking directly into Bill's eyes. He looks ready to kill.

"You thought you could hide from me, bitch?" he says angrily. "You're lucky I need you, or else I would kill you right now," he growls into my face.

I try kicking at him with my feet, while trying to push at him, but he moves away from my legs. Then he throws my body again. As the side of my body hits the wall, my ears start ringing, leaving the room silent.

I'm expecting him to come at me again, so I brace myself in a fetal position praying to let me die right now. I can't take any more. I want it to end already. But after a couple of seconds I don't feel anything, and it scares me.

The ringing slowly starts to subside and I hear Kelly's shouting again, with grunts along with it. In the corner of my eye, through the cracks of my hair, I see two guys, David and another guy from the team, tackling Andre to the ground pounding into him.

I automatically start to look for Matt and when I finally find him, what I see is surprising. He's pounding into Bill as Trey is holding him back by the neck, keeping him from moving. Matt looks furious as he's repeatedly punching Bill in the stomach.

I start to hear shouting again, this time coming from the door as police officers start running in, guns pointing everywhere. Everyone stops, Trey dropping Bill to the ground as he lifts his hands up in the air, but Matt ignores them and runs over to my side.

"Abigail, are you alright?" he fearfully asks. "Don't move. Somebody call an ambulance!" he shouts behind his back.

There's instantly a police officer at my side asking where I'm hurt, but another is pointing a gun at Matt, while shouting at him to put his hands up in the air. I don't want them hurting Matt so I grab onto him as tightly as I can, "He's okay, he's my roommate," I tell the officer.

I see the policemen stare at each other hesitantly, but the one next to me nods his head, and gets up talking into his radio ordering an ambulance. I shake my head trying to get him to stop, but even that hurts too much.

Matt takes me into his arms as gently as he can. It still

makes me wince since I'm in so much pain, but I don't care. I just want him to hold me right now, even if it hurts. I bury my face into his chest while he uses his hand to push my hair up and out of my face. He keeps whispering into my hair that everything is going to be okay. I don't know what to believe right now, but his voice calms me, so I sit there and listen.

The ambulance arrives a couple of minutes later, and against my protests, everyone insists that I go to the hospital for X-rays. I don't have the strength to argue anymore, so I go. As I'm being wheeled on the gurney through the house, I see the cops arresting Bill and Andre, while David, Trey, and the fourth guy are being questioned by the policemen. Matt stays at my side, and climbs into the ambulance with me on our way to the hospital.

The whole ride to the hospital, I'm grateful that Matt and Trey showed up when they did. If they hadn't, I wouldn't be in the ambulance right now. I'm pretty sure I would be in a car on my way back to Seattle. There was no question in Bill's eyes that he wasn't going to take no for an answer. Especially since he claimed he needed me, and I'm pretty sure not in a nice way.

We finally arrive at the hospital and they take me to a private emergency room. A nurse starts taking pictures of my injuries for evidence and I'm soon questioned by a police officer for my version of the attack. As I'm sitting in the emergency room the familiarity of the IV machine and monitors are making me very uncomfortable. The surroundings remind me Bill and of the last time I was in the hospital. I really don't want to be here, but they insist that they need to do further testing.

I'm once again put through the cocoon of a machine, along with taking some x-rays where my body aches, just in case. The whole time Matt never leaves my side, except when needed. His presence is the only thing keeping me calm.

After a couple of hours, since nothing is broken, and my injuries are superficial, I'm given clearance to go home and take it easy for the next week. That's something I'm happy about, since I was not looking forward to spending another night in a hospital anytime soon.

As we're waiting for them to discharge me, Matt is sitting at my bedside, holding my hand. He's staring down at the bed, looking saddened.

"Matt, what's wrong?" I ask him.

He hears me and looks up. His somber eyes make my heart ache. "When I walked into the house, and saw what was happening, my heart stopped Abigail. It literally stopped. I didn't know who the fuck they were, what they were doing in the house, or why they were doing that to you. But the only thing I could think about was wanting to kill them for hurting you."

He takes a deep breath, and then continues. "I was hitting him so hard, if the cops hadn't showed up I probably would have tried killing him. I wasn't thinking right," he says before dropping his head against our entwined hands.

Guessing how guilty he must be feeling at this moment, I try to reassure him. "Matt, it doesn't matter what almost happened. All that matters is what didn't. I'm just thankful you showed up when you did. I had already given up Matt. I had no fight left in me, and I have a feeling he would have killed me. Even if he said he wasn't."

He stands up from where he's sitting, and hugs me. Tears fall silently from my eyes. "I don't know what I would have done if I lost you, beautiful," he quietly says into my

GABBIE S. DURAN

hair.

The nurse walks in the room with my paperwork to sign, and once I've signed them, we leave the emergency room. As I'm entering the waiting area with Matt I see Trey, and he looks worried as he walks over to me, and gives me a light hug.

"You okay, supermodel?" he hesitantly asks.

I simply nod my head, and keep walking towards the exit, wanting to finally go home. I'm starting to hate hospitals, since the only memories I have of them are not happy ones. I follow Trey over to where he's parked his Jeep, and I climb into the backseat. Matt follows, climbing in next to me, wrapping his arm around my shoulder, and envelops me against his chest.

Right now there's nothing in the world I want more than Matt's arms. Just being in them has a way of comforting me, instantly calming me, so I take advantage. The whole drive home we're all quiet. It's an eerie, but needed silence, since I really don't want to talk about the whole situation at all.

We arrive at the house, and I notice David's car is still in the driveway. "Why is David's car here?" I confusedly ask.

Trey responds. "They didn't want to leave until they knew you were okay.

When we told them you were getting discharged tonight, they insisted on waiting until you came home."

I smile, but then easily grow worried because with all the commotion around me, I totally forgot about Kelly. I start feeling like the worst friend in the world after everything that happened. We finally walk into the house, and Kelly immediately attacks me. She's hugging me, crying at the same time, and making me cry along with her.

She pulls herself away from me. "I was so scared," she says in between sobs. "After I was pushed by the big guy, I dialed 911. I left the phone on the floor as I tried to get to you." She sobs again. "But he kept holding me back, making me watch as that other guy beat the shit out of you. I'm so sorry Abi; I tried so hard to get to you," she says hysterically, crying.

David comes over to comfort her and I feel so bad for her right now. It must have killed her inside to have to watch. Knowing she had to watch the beating I was taking makes it so much worse.

"It's not your fault, Kelly. I'm just glad you didn't get hurt. That's all that really matters," I try to reassure her.

I quickly glance over my shoulder to Matt, and then back to Trey and David. "How did you guys know they were here?"

David shakes his head before answering. "We didn't, we actually got done with practice early, and headed here right away. Matt wanted us to go out to dinner, but now I'm glad we rushed back." As he mentions dinner, my face goes mournful, knowing that I had forgotten all about the dinner I was cooking.

Kelly sees my face and giggles. "Don't worry silly, your dinner didn't get ruined. We actually managed to take it out on time when we heard the timer go off. We were waiting for you to get home so we can all eat," she cheerfully says.

Matt turns my body a bit, with a really confused look. "You cooked dinner?"

"It wasn't from scratch, but it's lasagna," I muster.

"Shit, I don't care was it is, I'm freaking starving. Let's

eat," Trey says, walking into the kitchen looking for the food. I giggle at him, glad that he's able to lighten the mood.

Matt leads me to the dining room table, and orders me to sit. While everyone else brings the food with plates to the table, I notice that the salad is made, the lasagna is still warm, and Kelly is pulling the garlic bread from the oven. This makes me smile knowing that they actually saved dinner. When they had reminded me about dinner, I had thought it was going to be another failed attempt at cooking. It would have taken me a while to recover from it, if it was.

As I'm eating dinner, I think of the traumatic experience I just went through, and wonder what am I supposed to do now? I'm sure I'm not out of the woods yet, but I know I have to learn to live my life, one way or another not look back, but to keep stepping forward. At this moment, there is nowhere else I would rather be than here with my new family.

After dinner, we all ended up drowning our distress with alcohol. So Kelly and David stayed the night in Matt's room. Matt must have been feeling paranoid, because he insisted on sharing the bed with me, promising he wouldn't let anything happen to me.

As we lay there in the darkness, I can't sleep, even with the alcohol in my body. My body is facing in the direction of my bathroom, my back against Matt. By the sound of his breathing I know he isn't asleep either.

After the events of the day, I keep wondering how much longer I would have to hide from Bill, or if I am even safe still staying with Matt.

"Matt," I say, in his direction.

"Yeah, beautiful," he responds.

"Do you think Bill will come back?" I ask, almost not

wanting to know the answer.

"Even if he does, I won't let him anywhere near you," he growls, the anger radiating in his voice.

"Maybe I should move out, since he already knows that I'm here. I would hate for him to try coming back and you guys getting hurt or end up in jail because of me."

I feel the bed begin to move, then his arm wraps around my waist, pulling me closer to him. My back is now against his chest and he forces me to lift my head so he can place his forearm under my head. I feel his face find the crook of my neck, the warmth of his breath slowly striking my skin as he speaks, "You're not going anywhere. This is your home now as much as it's mine."

Silently sighing to myself, I knew it wasn't. But from the way he said it, I know he meant every word. I really didn't want to be anywhere else anyways. So as long as he wanted me here I wasn't going to argue.

With him next to me, comforting me, I finally fall asleep. I could have blamed the good night's rest on the alcohol, but I'd only be lying to myself. I knew it was really Matt's warm arms that kept me sleeping through the night, and I'd never felt safer.

## Chapter 22

WITH THE DRAMA behind me, I was finally able to slowly move forward. I stayed in the house for the next two weeks, which led to the weekend of the guys' first football game. It was an away game, taking place in Chicago, meaning they had to fly there. It also meant that I was going to have to be home alone. Matt and Trey were not happy about it, but they had no choice, since they *were* the captains of the team, and were obviously expected to be there.

Kelly had insisted that she was going to stay with me for the weekend, and it eased Matt a little. To say he was being protecttive was an understatement. The last two weeks sometimes felt like he was overbearing. I knew he was feeling really remorseful about what happened. I don't know why. I tried reassuring him that no matter how badly he wanted to, he couldn't be with me every second of the day. Although sometimes he tried, it didn't help alleviate my feelings for him, it only increased them, and I was now a willpower expert when it came to Matt.

It kind of sucked, knowing it was Matt's first game, and I couldn't be there. So making a rash decision, I told Matt I needed the credit card linked to my account to do some online shopping. I did most of my shopping online now, since the whole mall fiasco. He didn't think much about the request and just handed it over.

I ended up doing a lot of shopping the week before the game, but he never once questioned what it was. When I had told Kelly to pack a large bag for the weekend, she simply shrugged her shoulders, thinking that maybe I didn't want to leave the house at all. The day the guys had to fly out, I hugged them both wishing them luck, and waved them goodbye as they drove away in Matt's car.

When Kelly arrived at the house half an hour later, and saw that I also had a bag packed, she gave me a confused look. She screamed with excitement though, when I told her that I had booked us first class tickets to Chicago so we could fly to the guys' game. Five minutes later, we are piled into the car heading to the airport. We ended up flying out of a different terminal than the guys, so I don't feel worried at all about them catching us.

Two hours later we're on a plane, in the air, on our way to Chicago. With a bodyguard named Julio in tow, who I had hired for the weekend. After that last nightmare I wasn't taking any chances. He came highly recommended by a security agency, and the guy looked more like a linebacker who could be playing on Matt's team. He was currently on a trial basis only, but I had decided if he passed the Chicago test, I would keep him on the books.

As we are sitting in our seats drinking our champagne, Kelly looks over at me. "How in the hell did you plan all this without Matt blowing a gasket?"

I smile at her, knowing she's also not going to like my answer. "I didn't tell him. I wanted to surprise them."

Her eyes go wide. She already knows he's not going to be happy.

I lay out my defense before she can begin lecturing me. "Hey, I promised not to go anywhere without protection, hence my protection," I say, pointing my chin in Julio's direction, which is sitting on the other side of the aisle.

"Girl, you sure know how to get around those loopholes," she says, referring to how I was able to deprive Bill of my money.

I ended up telling her and David the whole ordeal the day we were drinking after the Bill incident. I don't know if it was that I trusted both of them because of what we'd just been through, or that the alcohol had given me liquid courage. Either way they both knew, and had sworn to the same secrecy as Matt and Trey.

Six hours later, with a slight buzz, we land in Chicago. I had arranged for a hired car to pick us up at the airport upon arrival, making the trip to the hotel easier. I had booked us the Presidential suite at the same hotel as the team, wanting to be as near to them as possible. This would also allow us to spend more time with them as well.

The hotel was in the heart of downtown, with Chicago's tall buildings all around us. The city was breathtaking, and I couldn't help notice how close we were to Lake Michigan. Upon seeing it, I was already itching to run next to it. The weather here was sunny and beautiful, making it harder to resist.

Upon checking into the hotel, we went straight to our room to settle in, and we decided to shoot the guys a text confirming that they had also arrived. Kelly ended up spoiling her end of the surprise for David. She kept asking for his room number, and he had gotten suspicious. She finally broke down and told him. I couldn't be too angry with her, since it also got me Matt and Trey's room number as well.

A couple of minutes after telling him, David was in our room attacking Kelly with kisses. Since all the team members had to share a room, I had a feeling that David would be spending a lot of time in Kelly's instead and I didn't blame him. Not wanting to put up with hearing sounds that make me jealous tonight, I left them alone in the room, and headed to Matt's.

Although I've stood at a door waiting for Matt before, I still get nervous when I'm waiting for him to answer. My stomach is turning and my palms are sweaty, but when I finally do see him as he answers the door, it all flies out of the window. The look on his face when he opens the door and sees me is worth all of it.

His mouth is gaping open and his eyes are wide open in surprise. "What are you doing here?" he says, before pursing his lips.

Trey comes up behind him, curious to see who is at the door. "Oh, shit supermodel. Whatcha doing here?" he says as his face lightens up.

"What you're not happy I'm here?" I tease them both.

Matt's eyes look past me, narrowing straight to Julio standing behind me, and his face grows in agitation. "Who is he?" he asks, not taking his eyes off him.

I look back at Julio, who raises his eyebrows, as if debating whether he should let Matt's remark slide or tackle him. He has his arms and hands crossed in front of his chest, just standing there, watching Matt like a hawk. So far he's doing well, I think to myself.

I turn back to Matt and laugh. I lightly swat him directly on the chest, to try to distract him. "Calm down, bad boy. This is Julio, I hired him for the weekend, *since* you made me promise not to go anywhere without you as protection."

Behind me, I hear a snort, then a quick throat clearing from Julio.

Trey comes to my defense, stating, "Dude, she's got you there," and laughing at Matt, while slapping him on the shoulder.

Matt shoots him a nasty glare, and Trey just walks back into the room. I follow him, pushing past Matt, causing Julio to follow.

The room now feels really small with all of us entering it, but I don't care. I didn't want to be standing out in the hallway any longer.

As Matt shuts the door, I walk over to what must be Matt's bed, since Trey is already sitting on the other one. I sit down at the head of the bed, leaning up against the headboard, and start to distract myself by picking at Matt's uniform. He has it tossed on the bed, with some of his other clothes. It looks like he's started to unpack.

From the corner of my eye I see him walk over and stop at the edge of the bed. Crossing his arms in front of him, eyes drawn to a slit, his lips are still pinched in a line. He still looks aggravated.

Trying to alleviate his tension, I figure I should tease him. "Didn't your sister ever tell you it's not good to look pissed all the time? You're going to get permanent frown lines," I say to him.

Matt's lips turn into a deeper frown and I instantly regret mentioning his sister. I know it's a sore spot with him, but I didn't think before I spoke.

"What are you doing here, and why didn't you tell me you were coming?" he growls at me. I don't know whether I liked the silent Matt or the snappy one.

This only makes me regret even coming, I thought he would be happy to see me, but I was wrong. Thinking about the other person who accompanied me, I hope Kelly is having better luck with David than I am at this moment. From the looks of them practically running to her room, I'm pretty sure she was.

I stand up, hurt in my eyes. "Obviously I wanted it to be a surprise, but by your reaction, it's the last thing you would want. So I'm sorry I even bothered you, Matt," I say, starting to walk to the door, with watery eyes.

Julio is standing in the tiny hallway entrance of the room, and looks uncomfortable as he sees me.

Matt yanks out his arm and blocks me from moving any further. He moves to stand in front of me, with regret in his eyes. "I'm sorry, beautiful," he says faintly, in a low voice. "I'm just shocked that you're here. I'm happy about it, really."

I don't know what to say, so I stand there, with my head hung low.

I feel his finger pull up my chin up so I could better see him when he asks, "Where are you staying?"

"Here, in the Presidential Suite," I say, pointing my finger at the ceiling.

I see Trey jump up, and off his bed from the corner of my eye. "You're shacking up in the best room in the house, and we're stuck in this piece of shit room? Oh fuck no. Party in supermodel's room," he shouts with a fist pump in the air.

I turn my head to him. "Oh, hell no, Trey. You are not trashing my room. If you want to party, you do it somewhere else," I say, pointing my finger at him.

Trey's face goes into a frown, but I don't care, I am not having my room trashed by a bunch of rowdy boys.

Since the guy's game isn't until the next day, we decide to go out to dinner, and grab some famous deep-dish pizza. After dinner, we head back to my room and sit around talking. The night starts to grow late and everyone decides it's time to head to bed.

I was saddened when Matt was about to leave, and I think he noticed. So he offered to stay with me for a little while, only until I fell asleep. We ended up lying in bed, facing each other, talking about his sister. I could tell how close of a bond they had, just by the way he spoke of her, and I loved listening to him. His voice did its magic trick as always, and eventually sent me into a deep sleep. As I started to drift away, I hoped Matt would forget about getting up and stay the night with me instead. I was sadly disappointed when I woke up the next morning, with the other side of the bed empty.

He always had a habit of leaving before I awoke. It's as if he had sneaking away down to perfection at this point. I wondered if he had perfected it due to his friends with benefits rule. Even though I didn't want to know the truth of that answer, I had to look at the bright side of the situation; he at least falls asleep with me.

Refusing to let it dampen my mood, I get up, and out of bed. I'm hoping that maybe if I take a run this morning, it will help cheer me up.

As I'm getting ready to go for my long awaited run, I hear a knock at the door. I'm hesitant to answer at first, since I'm not expecting any visitors. I'm sure we haven't ordered room service yet, but then I hear the ping of my phone, and look down at the screen.

*Answer the door-M*

After seeing the message I rush to door and see that Julio is already looking through the peephole. He opens the door, probably since he saw Matt at the other end.

"Hey beautiful," he says with a smile as he walks in the room and sees me. "Ready for a run?"

"I am now," I answer enthusiastically. "How did you know I would go for a run today?"

"I know you; you're probably looking forward to running near the water."

I chuckle, and go back into my room, leaving Matt to trail behind me. I finish lacing up my shoes, and grab a light jacket. Dressed and ready to go, we head out of the room and straight to the nirvana that awaits me.

An hour later, I'm back in my room, and feeling content. After showering and dressing, Kelly and I decide on a quick brunch to help kill the time. Since Matt had to go straight to practice after our run, I won't be seeing him until after the game, and I couldn't wait.

# Chapter 23

MATT WAS OUTSTANDING while he played. I had heard from his fellow teammates that he was good, but from what I saw, he was amazing. He always stayed focused, made almost every pass he threw, gaining his team a very considerable lead, and with Trey blocking for him, he was rarely touched.

Kelly and I had decided to wear the guy's home jerseys with their number on it. By the looks on their faces when they looked up at us, they were very pleased. Kelly had claimed that I was the reason why Matt was playing so well, but I merely rolled my eyes at her, refusing to believe that he wasn't always this good. How else would he be going to college on a football scholarship?

Another factor I pointed out to her was how much Matt and Trey studied that playbook any chance they got during the day. I had seen that thing pulled out so much, that I could have starting reciting the plays at one point. It didn't help with understanding how the game was played though.

Once I mentioned it to her, Kelly started educating me on the tactics of the game, and finally understanding the concept of what was going on, I was able to watch without wanting my eyes to glaze over. They ended up winning by 14 points. Although the home team was clearly disappointed in the loss, our crowds of following fans were very excited about the win, predicting a really good season.

When the game was over, Kelly and I ran down to the field to congratulate the team on their win and agreed to meet them back at the hotel. A couple of hours later, we were in the room, drinking away.

Trey ends up getting his party, although, we managed to keep it to only the closest of their friends to avoid having hotel security on our ass. However, with the alcohol flowing and Kelly pushing drinks down my throat, I manage to get a decent buzz, quick. Matt, who obviously celebrated his victory, was just as buzzed the last time I saw him.

I had needed to go to the bathroom, so I excused myself and headed to my room. After going to the bathroom, I eyed the bed on my way back to the party and it looked so inviting.

I was so tired I didn't want to head back out there. So instead I decided to go to bed. I stripped my clothes off and climbed into bed, not even bothering to look for my pajamas. Pulling the covers over my body and closing my eyes, I let the darkness drag me to sleep.

I START TO awaken from my deep sleep, but I don't want to, because I feel cocooned in warmth and I'm very comfortable. I could stay like this all day. I keep my eyes closed and

GABBIE S. DURAN

take a deep breath, savoring the feeling. I think I must be dreaming because my cocoon smells so delicious, like Matt. I definitely don't want to wake up now.

Mmm, it feels so good, so I simply cuddle closer into it. That's when I feel an arm squeeze me tighter against a rock hard wall, and then another starts to rub against my back. My eyes snap open, the room is dark, and it takes a moment for my mind to come out of its cloudy feeling. As I take in my surroundings, I remember that I'm in the hotel room and realize the cocooned warmth is a chest. When did it get here?

"Morning, beautiful," I hear Matt whisper into my hair.

I panic and sit up with a jolt. I look back at him, staring at him in shock. Even though the room is dark, my eyes have adjusted enough to see his features and he has a hooded, sexy look in his eyes, and damn, if I don't want more of that. But, first of all, how much of it did I get in the first place?

I realize that he's naked, except for the usual black boxer briefs that he wears, but my body is completely naked. Then I remember stripping my clothes off to get into bed. The cover had fallen as I sat up, so I grab it, pulling it up to cover my breasts.

"What happened last night?" I whisper in confusion, searching for answers in my head.

I know when I came to bed I was still buzzed, but I'm pretty sure if we'd had sex I would have remembered. At least I hope I would have remembered, because it would really suck not to. I start to run my fingers in my hair, not to tame it, but in frustration.

Matt sits up and grabs me at the waist laying me back down with half my body draped across his chest, tucking my head into his neck. He feels and smells so good. It should be damn sinful.

He chuckles lightly and I feel it all over my body.

"I decided to come in here and check on you. I was worried when you didn't come back out, but when I saw you passed out, I decided it was time to call it a night. I didn't feel like having to go back to my room, so I figured we could share the bed. It was big enough for the both of us. Although, as usual, you do like to hog the covers, so that sucked," he says laughing.

"We didn't do anything, did we?" I apprehensively ask.

He starts lightly rubbing my ribs with his left arm, sending tingling jolts through my body, while his other hand is pulling my leg to drape over his waist. He starts to rub my thigh with his thumb in tiny circles, and it sends a shiver that starts to creep deep down in my core. God help me, I'm going to lose control any moment.

"As much as I would have loved to do something with you last night, I want to make sure we both remember if it ever happens," he says in a haughty voice.

His voice is hypnotizing me and I'm falling deeply into his spell. I hug tighter against him, rubbing myself against his leg, and I instantly feel his cock jolt to life under my other leg.

"Abigail, you don't know what you're asking for right now," he warns.

I ignore him and start to kiss his neck, wanting to taste him. He moans and it turns me on, so I keep kissing. He squeezes my thigh, turning to rub his now awakened cock against my body. Damn Matt for always sleeping in his briefs, they're currently preventing us from getting what we both want.

I start to kiss my way down his neck and begin sucking his shoulder, loving the way he tastes. I feel his hand start to

GABBIE S. DURAN

move up my thigh and rub lightly on my core, teasing me. I moan into his shoulder and suck harder, causing him to tense a little. That's when he gently sticks his finger in me, without warning, making me let out an appreciative moan. He starts moving his finger around inside of me, adding another finger.

He seductively whispers in my ear, "Damn, beautiful, you're so wet and warm."

I start to move my hips along to the movement of his fingers rubbing in and out of me, wanting more. He takes his hand from in between my legs, leaving me confused. All of a sudden, he rolls me onto my back, with him straddling my legs, lifting my arms above my head with his hands. He's staring down into my face and he looks so sexy above me. He keeps my wrists locked above my head with one of his hands, while his other starts to rub down my neck, moving slowly down my chest to tease my breasts. He lowers his mouth down to my ear and I can hear his heavy breathing. His tongue starts to tease my ear, and then he starts sucking on my earlobe, driving me wild. My legs are locked together under him with his body, otherwise I would already have them spread wide open, grinding up against his cock.

"Matt, please, I can't take it anymore," I beg him.

He ignores my plea and gently starts to bite my neck, moving down to my breast. I lift my chest up in an open invitation, but he keeps kissing down the valley in between both breasts, killing me with the tension. He finally moves his mouth to one of my nipples, which at this point are both fully erect, and ready to be sucked. After teasing me by rubbing his closed lips over one nipple, he takes it into his mouth and sucks it deep and hard, making me thrust my chest further up towards him, as I moan loudly with pleasure. He moves over to the other nipple and sucks it even harder. If I wasn't so fucking horny, I swear it would be painful.

I try wiggling my legs open, but he keeps his legs tightly locked over mine, torturing me. He lets go of my arms and my hands automatically go to his shoulders, holding him tightly for fear that he'll stop, but he doesn't, and continues to kiss his way down my stomach, tickling me. I lightly squeal and I wiggle under him, trying to throw him off in reaction.

Matt lifts his head and looks directly into my eyes with a wicked smile. "I forgot that you're ticklish."

He grabs both my hands with his and locks them at my sides as he lowers his head again. Thinking that he's going to try to tickle me, I jerk my body up, but instead he licks my stomach with his tongue, dragging it from right above my belly button. I close my eyes and throw my head back in ecstasy. Fuck, if his tongue feels this good on my stomach, I can't wait to know what he can do with it when he goes down on me.

"Matt, you in there, fucker?" Trey yells, banging on the door. "Get the fuck up, we gotta go!"

"Fuck!" I groan in irritation.

I hear Matt lightly laugh. "Sorry beautiful, I have to go," he says, kissing my stomach one last time.

He quickly jumps off the bed, searching for his clothes, finding them, and begins to dress.

I lay there, dazed, trying to catch my breath, watching Matt get dressed. He dresses in lightning speed, probably from being used to jumping out of girls' beds and leaving in a heartbeat.

Once he's done he walks over to the door, grabbing the

door handle, he looks back at me one last time and says, "See you at home, beautiful." He winks right before walks out of my bedroom, shutting the door behind him.

I'm lying there still spread out naked, trying to figure out what the fuck happened. Then I realize, against all the advice I gave myself, I was just *added* to Matt's list of friends. I throw my arm over my eyes and think, fuck my life.

# Chapter 24

OUR FLIGHT WASN'T scheduled to leave until four hours after the team, so I took this extra time to let out the sexual frustration that I had pent up from that morning. I found out that Julio also liked to run to keep in shape; that was another plus on his behalf, so an hour after Matt had left my body high and dry of satisfaction, I was out running along the Michigan Lake.

After forty-five minutes, I discovered that I couldn't find the nirvana that I had always found while running and it only frustrated me more. I was thinking too much of Matt. I don't know why the hell I was letting the encounter get to me, but I knew I had to find some way to get over it. Apparently today's run was not it.

Even though I was up in arms about the earlier situation, I had an overwhelming smile on my face. Matt had a way of making my body feel animated with joy, and both Kelly and Julio were noticing. On the way to the airport I was very quiet, thinking about the morning the whole time.

Kelly had noticed, but she didn't say anything.

As on the way to Chicago, we are sitting next to each other in first class, with Julio in the seat across the aisle. I had made the decision to hire Julio full time. I liked how he was able to keep people at a distance and not make me feel suffocated by hovering over me. That alone was the deal breaker.

I had notified him that I was going to keep him on an on-call basis for now, but would pay him as if he was with me 24/7 so I would have access to him when needed. He was happy with the decision being that he was tired of working as a hired security guard for a lame company. That only made me laugh. I don't know if he knew how lame his job was going to be when he was sitting around waiting for me to call. But I was happy nevertheless.

When the plane was finally in the air, I noticed Kelly starting to grow impatient. By the way she kept looking at me, then back at the magazine, I knew she wanted to know details, so I was already bracing myself for the question to leave her lips.

"Did something happen between you and Matt last night?" she asks me in a whisper, looking up from the magazine she'd been pretending to read for the last ten minutes.

"No nothing happened last night," I say, which technically isn't a lie since it happened this morning. I was trying really hard to keep the smile on my face under control, but that proved difficult.

She has a puzzled look on her face, like she really wants to know the details. "But something might have happened this morning," I tell her.

She looks at me with eagerness to know and says, "Please tell me you want to talk about it."

I want to keep it to myself, but she *is* my closest friend at this point so I take a chance. "We might have fooled around a little. We didn't get to the actual deed because we were interrupted," I say quietly near her ear with disappointment.

She drops her jaw, and then recovers, with a frown. "Just be careful, Abi. I'd hate for you to get hurt expecting more when he doesn't give it to you," she cautions.

I sit there taking in her words. She's right. Matt has been playing the field with no obligations for the last couple of years. What would make me any different? He's probably only seeing me as a convenience since I already live with him.

Then I think to myself, maybe I *could* be different. He's actually been showing me how much he cares by being concerned and protective. Maybe I'm the one that could get him to change his mind. That's the thought that I keep thinking as we are in the air and as soon as I see Matt I plan on asking him.

We land in Portland and since we had taken Kelly's car to the airport we were once again piled in her car driving back to Matt's. On the way there Kelly was complaining that she had one to many Diet Cokes and now needs to pee, so of course when we arrive at the house she gets out with me. As we walk in the door, we hear loud moaning coming from inside, and I cringe remembering what happened the last time I heard these noises, and as the last time, I am once again shocked by what I see.

Matt has some naked girl spread out on the dining room table in the kitchen. He still has his shirt on, but his body is leaning over hers as he's pounding his hips back and forth in between her legs, with his hands holding her breasts, for support.

What is up with my body freezing when I walk in on people having sex? It's not like I want to stand there with my feet planted to the ground feeling like they've been cemented there, but that was exactly what was happening at the moment. I couldn't breathe, my head felt like it was spinning, and all I wanted was for the earth to open up and suck me into oblivion.

Kelly's voice snaps me back to reality. "What the fuck, Matt?" she shouts at him. "Obviously, you've proven my point to Abi."

He snaps his head in our direction and I'm staring at his deep brown eyes. They aren't the ones I like, because they are full of regret.

Kelly must have comprehended that I couldn't move, because she grabs my arm, pulling me back out of the house and straight to her car. I'm still in shock and my brain is still trying to unscramble what has happened. All I can do is allow Kelly to lead me like a rag doll. She opens the passenger door and guides me into the car, shutting the door once I'm in.

She runs over to the driver's side, gets in, starts the car, and we are driving away a minute later. The whole drive to her apartment I'm just sitting there staring out of the windshield in silence, not knowing what to do with myself.

I hear my phone start to ring with Matt's ringtone and I ignore it. He's the last person I want to hear from right now, he has no reason to have to explain anything. Shit, for all I know, I could be wrong and he's really calling to chew my ass out for interrupting his sex session.

It stops ringing, but starts up again, and the last thing I want to hear, is what Matt likes for me to call him. So I keep ignoring it. Kelly doesn't have the same patience. She grabs my purse from my hand and digs through it.

Taking my phone out, she answers it, snapping, "Leave her the fuck alone Matt!" before hanging it back up.

A minute later the phone starts to ring again and Kelly pushes the ignore button, then turns it off. I start quietly crying, I can't help it. Just knowing that I have the worst luck with guys, and it's finally caught up with me.

We finally make it to Kelly's and since she had called David on the way to give him the details, he was already waiting for us at her apartment. He took one look at me and instantly came over to give me a hug and lead us back into the apartment. Once inside, Kelly led me straight to her couch, leaving me there as she walks away.

She comes back with a bottle of tequila and hands it to me. She hands me the shot glass to go with it, but I ignore it, taking the bottle from her hands. I take a big giant swig, straight from the bottle. It burns going down, causing me to gag and cough. I take in a big breath and do it all over again. Kelly sits down next to me on the couch taking the bottle from me, then does the same. David decides to avoid partaking in our tequila misery-binge, but instead sits there shaking his head at us with a chuckle.

"That's how I found my fiancé," I say to them, finally breaking the silence.

Kelly sits there like she's debating whether to say something, but decides to just nod her head at me. David sits there, looking compassionately at me with his elbows on his knees.

Looking over at him, I sit there confirming to myself, this guy must really love Kelly to put up with me as well. Most guys would have run to the woods to avoid a woman in misery. Then I think to myself, I wanted that so badly. Right when I thought I had found someone like David, I find him fucking some girl's brains out on the dining room table.

I sniff my nose, wiping it with my sleeve. "I shouldn't have let anything happen this morning because of his whole friends with benefits shit, so in reality it's my fault. I let it get too far," I say out loud, the words coming out of my mouth uncontrollably.

That's when David's eyes go wide with the realization of why I was like this. Poor guy was stuck in the soap opera of my life. He considered Matt one of his closest friends, but since he loved Kelly and she was on my side, he's obviously torn. David gets a worried look on his face before asking, "Do you care about him? I mean like, have you fallen in love with him?"

I know I should not admit my answer but I simply nod my head, because that's all I can do at this time. Kelly hands me back the bottle and I take another drink, hoping the fuzziness from the tequila will replace the misery.

Another hour later, David is passed out on the couch. Kelly and I have made our way to her bedroom so our talking wouldn't wake him. We are sitting cross-legged on her bed, discussing what I should say to Matt the next time I seen him.

I am so wasted that I'm not thinking straight and I'm pretty sure Kelly isn't that far behind me. Wanting to give Matt a piece of my mind at this very moment, I dig through my purse looking for my phone. I turn it on and look for Matt's number. I look over at Kelly and put my finger to my lips signaling her to be quiet.

Matt answers almost immediately. "I'm so sorry, beautiful," he says to me.

It pisses me off that he's trying to be affectionate with me right now. "Don't fucking beautiful me, Matt. I bet you call all your fuck buddies that to get in between their legs, and to think, I almost let you put your dick between mine," I shout at him.

I look over at Kelly as she's trying to catch her herself from the swaying caused by nodding her head once, really hard at me. Knowing I have her encouragement makes me carry on.

"I bet the only reason you even let me live with you is so you can say you fucked Abigail Adams, right? Well, here's a wakeup call for you Matthew Garcia, it's going to take a lot more than you calling me beautiful to get in between my legs. Because I'm worth a lot more that a quick fuck!" I say, staring directly at the phone that I have taken away from my ear so I can look at his picture. For some reason I needed to see his face as I bitched him out and the screen with his picture on it was the closest thing to it.

Kelly grabs the phone from me and hangs it up. After fumbling with it, she finally manages to turn it off and we sit there laughing at each other. I already feel drowsy, so lean back to lie down and finally pass out.

I wake up the next day, with Kelly lying next to me in her bed and I start to chuckle to myself when I see her drooling all over herself. She looks like she isn't going to have a good morning, and I'm pretty sure the nauseated feeling coming from the pit of my stomach confirms the same for me.

Staring at her, I think, this girl has stuck with me through the worst of my crap. Without me even asking. She's a keeper.

We both eventually get up and eat breakfast a couple of

hours later. David sits there with a grin on his face, and I'm pretty sure that if Kelly didn't feel just as bad as I do, she'd be smacking it from his face. My head is still spinning a bit and my stomach is worse. My throat feels like it has a frog lodged in it wanting to come up.

As much as I don't want to go home and face Matt, I know that I have to do it sometime, so I finally turn on my phone thinking about last night. The crazy thing is I don't remember much after David falling asleep. Saying that the night was a total blur is an understatement. Once the phone is finally powered up, I notice a text message left by Matt a couple minutes after we left.

*Abigail I'm sorry about you walking in on me like that, it won't ever happen again. I'll use the bedroom from now on. M*

I don't care if he uses the bedroom. I don't want to know when he's fucking someone else, period. After checking my voicemail, it only confirms that he left a message pretty much saying the same thing and stating the house was safe to come home to now. Being that Kelly knows why I was really upset, this makes her even angrier with him when I give her the details.

I reach over the table to give her hand a squeeze and tell her, "It's not his fault, and he has no idea how I feel about him. Especially because we made a deal not get involved with each other."

Her face goes pissed. "You must really care about him, since you're defending him for fucking someone else the same day he almost had sex with you."

I wince, taking in the reality of the situation. "It's not about caring about him; it's about knowing that I could never have a real relationship with him. After what happened with the last guy, I've now learned my lesson and the last thing I need to do is jump into a relationship with a guy who is used to passing his dick around."

This earns me a full laugh from Kelly, making her eyes water, while David sits there trying not to be judgmental.

"Okay, but if he breaks your heart, not even David will be able to stop me from kicking his ass," she says, pointing her finger at me.

Now I'm the one laughing along with David. "From what happened to the last guy I won't need your help. I'm pretty sure I could handle Matt myself. You're welcome to finish him off a second time though," I say smiling.

Kelly throws her hand up for a high five, which I give her. David just shakes his head at both of us saying, "Remind me to never do anything to Kelly that will have both of you coming after me."

I look over at him. "Damn straight," I deadpan, making us laugh again.

She eventually gives me a ride back to the house and I only see Trey's Jeep in the driveway, leaving me relieved as I walk into the house. When I walk in Trey is sitting on the couch eating a bowl of cereal, while watching TV, so I go over and sit on the other end of the couch. "The table isn't good enough for you to eat on?" I ask with a smirk.

He raises an eyebrow at me and says, "I figured since you weren't here to force me to eat at it, I choose not to." After eating another bite, he adds, "Anyways, who knows if he's cleaned the table?"

Even if he's trying to lighten the situation, it isn't helping. "So he told you?" I sadly ask.

Finishing his cereal, he places the bowl on the coffee table. "Yeah, I came home from having my own fun to find

Matt all fucked up with a weird look on his face. He eventually told me."

"Why would he be upset about me walking in on him?"

Trey shrugs his shoulders. "Fuck if I know what's going on between you two."

My body tenses up, wondering if he suspects anything. I mean, it's not like Matt and I advertise our little escapades. As far as I know, Kelly and David are the only ones who know something even happened between us at all.

"Where is he by the way?"

"Where the hell would he be? Running off his steam. I don't know how he can do it with the hangover he had, but shit if I care," he says, looking back at the TV.

Wanting to be alone right now, I get up and head to my room. I decide to take a shower and try to wash away the awful feeling I have. When I'm getting out of the shower I hear voices coming from the living room and realize it's Trey talking to Matt.

My body immediately tenses up thinking he's going to come straight to my room, but I hear the hallway bathroom door shut, and the shower start up. Feeling relieved, I quickly get dressed. A couple of minutes later I'm lying on my bed changing the ringtones on my phone, and I hear the knock on the door that I've been dreading.

"Abigail, can I come in?" I hear Matt ask through the door.

"Sure," I answer automatically.

Matt walks in and he *does* look like shit. He comes into the room and shuts the door behind him, walks over to the edge of the bed, and sits down. I know he's trying to keep his distance from me, because usually he would have come and sat next to me on the bed. But this time he's purposely putting distance between us.

He must have come straight to my room after the shower, because he only has on a pair of running shorts, his chest is bare. Normally I would have already been fighting my body not to react at seeing him like this, but after yesterday, I think my body won't have that problem anymore. I'd only have to remind myself of the image of seeing him with another girl, one that will forever be engraved into my memory.

As he's sitting there, my eyes automatically start roaming up and down his body. I've made my way up to his upper body and that's when I notice he has what looks like a bruise on his left shoulder. I narrow my eyes to try to get a better look at it. "What the hell is that thing?" I demand, scrunching my nose. Then it dawns on me, that it's a huge hickey on his shoulder.

Astonished at it, I cross my arms on my chest. "What the fuck Matt, does she like to play rough while you're fucking her?" I say, pointing my chin at his chest.

Matt looks down at what I'm looking at, then he looks back at me with a smile, and his brown eyes are boring right back into mine.

"Actually Abigail, that was a lovely souvenir from you," he says, cocking his head to the side, looking at me through his half-closed lashes.

Growing confused by his answer, I quickly scan my memory of what happened yesterday. Then I remember that my lips were on his shoulder, but I didn't know I was so out of control as to the point of giving him a hickey.

"What is it you want?" I ask, practically scowling at him.

He morosely says, "I wanted to talk to you about last

night."

"Look Matt, there's nothing to talk about, it's your house, you have a right to fuck whoever you want, when you want," I say to him.

He just winces, as if he wasn't expecting me to say that.

"She came over looking for Trey and since he wasn't here she practically threw herself at me, and it just... happened," he says, his voice full of regret.

My eyes go wide because the last line I wanted to hear is that one. I would have preferred any other excuse but that one, and it angers me.

Sitting straight up on the bed, my eyes going wide before I attack him with, "Don't you fucking say that it just happened. Nothing just fucking happens. So don't give me that fucking line. It's the same line he gave me and it's the same shit I walked into. So unless you want to start comparing notes with him... Don't! Fucking! Apologize!" I yell at him.

This time it's his turn to throw his eyes wide open and he's opening and closing his mouth in disbelief as if he wants to say something else. Instead, he gets up off the bed and walks out of the room leaving me staring at the door that he just slammed. I sit there, forcing myself not to cry. I don't want to let him win this time.

Knowing that I don't want to risk facing Matt today, I keep myself in my room for the rest of the day, sleeping my depression off. I only leave the room once to make myself a sandwich and take it back to my room to eat.

I purposely avoid looking at the table, because the last thing I need right now is a flashback of last night. Knowing how hard I fought for us to actually eat on that table and then for him to use it to fuck someone on it only hurt more. Like

Kelly pointed out, hours after he left me sexually frustrated. It makes me want to go in there and rip that damn table to pieces. I really need to get myself under control or I might just go crazy.

IT'S THE NEXT day and I'm lying down on the couch and turn on the TV. Of course it's on the damn sports channel as usual, I really doubt at this point that they watch anything else. The guys are at practice, leaving the house quiet and I hate it. It only makes me think of things. Things I don't want to think about.

I leave it on the channel since it reminds me of them and start watching a re-run basketball game that is playing. It must have started to bore me because I close my eyes and drift off into a dream.

*I'm at a basketball game. It's for a school, high school to be specific. Teenage boys are scrambling around on the court and I'm concentrating closely on number 11. He currently has the basketball and is dribbling it. He can't seem to find a player on his team to pass it to and it's frustrating him because he only has 12 seconds to do something.*

*As I look at the scoreboard, the home team, which is the team he plays on, is down by two points. The time is running out on the clock for the fourth quarter. The guy blocking him is shoving him, with his arms out to the sides, obviously keeping him from seeing where he wants to pass it.*

*The teenager takes this chance, faking that he's going to move to the left, then moves to the right as the player behind him goes to the left. Allowing him the opportunity to move forward. He dribbles the ball across the court just out-*

*side the three-point line and stops. As the clock dies down to two seconds left he shoots. I hold my breath, I'm so nervous. My heart feels like it has stopped, as I watch the ball fly through the air, praying that he makes the shot. The ball is in mid-air when the buzzer goes off, then I watch it sink right into the circled rim, through the net, making the winning basket.*

*The crowd goes crazy and his team all run to congratulate him. As I'm cheering with the crowd, he turns around to face me, he points to me, and I point right back at him with tears running down my eyes from the happiness. As he turns around to continue to celebrate the win with his teammates I see the back of his jersey that says, Garcia.*

I wake up, shocked as I'm gasping for air. I have tears running down my cheeks from what I've just seen. As much as I love seeing Matt's past, I'm really starting to hate these memories a little. They allow me to see a side of Matt that I want to ignore when I'm upset at him. It's as if they appear to help me understand him better, even though I want to be mad.

Remembering what I've promised Matt's sister, I realize that no matter what happens in my life I have to keep my promise to her. Even if it means never having a relationship with him because I could risk jeopardizing that promise, as much as it pains me, I know I can't break it. He means too much to me.

# Chapter 25

A COUPLE OF days go by with Matt and I dancing around each other, and it's killing me. Although we don't ignore each other completely, we only make enough small talk to not make it seem awkward around other people.

As I'm getting ready to go out shopping with Kelly this afternoon I need to call Julio to notify him of my plans. I can't find my phone, which is strange for me since I take that thing with me everywhere. The last time I had it I was in the living room. So I head in that direction on a mission to find it. As I walk into the living room I notice Matt and Trey are watching the sports channel as usual.

As I bend over and start digging my hands into the recliner, thinking it must have fallen into the cracks of the cushion, I ask, "Have you guys seen my phone? I can't find it."

They don't answer, so I turn my tilted head and see them both staring intensely at my ass. I feel something at the bottom of the cushion and get excited. Only to wrap my hand around the remote for the sound systems we've been searching for. So I dig it out, turn around, and chuck it at Matt with all my might since he's the one I'm angriest at right now. He instantly reacts by ducking his head, causing the remote to whiz by him knocking into Trey's head instead.

Matt throws his head back laughing while Trey rubs the spot on his head where the remote connected.

Pleased with myself that I was at least able to catch one of them, I say, "That will teach you to stare. Will one of you call my phone? I need to call Julio, or else I'm recruiting half the football team to take me shopping. As you guys requested."

Matt only groans. He digs out his phone from his pocket, and after tapping on the screen a couple of times, I begin to hear my phone start to sing. It's vibrating and *I knew You Were Trouble* is blasting for all of us to hear.

I hear the music come from close to Matt's feet and he looks down at the ground. My phone is on the floor under the couch at his feet. He picks it up and the words resister to him and his mouth goes into a deep frown.

"You changed my ringtone?" he says with his eyebrows drawn.

Trey says, chuckling, "That one is better, it suits you dude."

I grab the phone from his hand, practically yanking it from him, ignoring his scowl. I walk away shooting Julio a text with my plans, asking him to meet me at my house as soon as he can.

As I'm walking into my room, I'm about to shut the door, when I feel a hard body behind me pushing me further into the room. I turn around and see Matt shutting the door behind us.

"Look, I'm not going to apologize about what happened because you told me not to, but I can't keep living like this anymore," he says.

My breath catches, as my body freezes up, my body automatically growing panicked.

"Do you want me to move out?" I ask in a whisper.

His face turns to disgusted shock. "No. That's not what I meant. What I'm trying to say is that we need to talk about this, Abigail. Ignoring it is only making the situation worse.
"

I notice he's called me Abigail again. He's been calling me that since the night I walked in on him. He hasn't once tried calling me beautiful like he usually does.

Knowing this is going to go nowhere, I respond, "I already told you there's nothing to talk about. You'd already told me about your life, I should have expected to walk in on you having sex with someone eventually. I just didn't expect it to bring up things I didn't want to remember."

His shoulders drop, sagging even more than they were before and he has a disappointed look on his face.

"I know you don't want to hear it, but my only excuse for doing it was that I was frustrated from what didn't happen that morning. She threw herself at me and I took advantage. I wasn't thinking about the consequences, all I could think about was how pissed I was that I didn't get to finish what I had started that morning with you," he declares.

I stand there silently because I can't say anything. I don't want his excuses. He shouldn't have had a reason to be giving them to me. "Matt, you think you were the only one left frustrated? It's not like I asked for you to stop, you jumped off that bed as fast as you possibly could," I point out.

He sighs, walks over to me and takes me in his arms and I instantly wrap my arms around his waist, embracing him back. "I had to leave or the coach was going to chew my ass out. If not, I would have stayed in that room all day with you."

"I'm sorry Abigail. As much as I want something to happen between us, I'm scared I'm going to fuck things up. I like how things are going right now and I'm scared to even try to push it further."

His declaration only leaves me disappointed. It proves that he's never going to change. He will never want to try for anything more.

We hear a knock at my door, interrupting us. We both turn and see Trey walking in the door. We haven't even bothered to pull away from each other. When he sees us he raises his eyebrows curiously and has Matt's phone held against his chest.

"Dude, there's some guy on the phone asking for Abigail's assistant," he says in a questioning tone.

I'm confused why someone would be declaring Matt my assistant, but he pulls away from me, taking the phone from Trey. "This is Matt Garcia, Abigail Adams' assistant."

Trey and I stand there watching Matt bob his head up and down, with a couple of "Hmm, mmm" every now and then while he listens to the other person on the phone.

"How about in half an hour? Yeah, that's the address, okay see you then," he says into the phone and after nodding his head one more time he hangs up.

Trey and I are both looking at him waiting for him to say something, but instead he walks past Trey and into his room, leaving us to follow him. He's rummaging through his clothes and when he finally finds jeans and a shirt he likes he starts changing into them.

Still confused, Trey and I just stand there staring at him, and then I finally speak up.

"Matthew Garcia, if you don't tell me what that phone call was about, I'm going to come over there and drop kick you to the ground, and if I can't do it myself, I'll recruit Trey to help me," I say, tilting my head in Trey's direction.

As he's pulling his shirt over his head, he starts laughing. "That was a rep for the Marathon in San Francisco; they want to talk to you about running it."

"What do you mean they want to talk to me about running it? Why me?" I ask, just as confused.

As he's removing the track pants he's wearing he answers, "He only said he wanted talk to you about it. He didn't give me any other details. Only that we'd discuss it when he got here."

Why the hell would some guy want to talk to me about a race? Did I do something wrong?

Half an hour later, the doorbell is ringing. Matt goes to answer the door and when he returns he's being followed by an older gentleman in his forties, and Julio, closely behind. Crap, with the confusion of the situation I had forgotten to text Julio to cancel.

This reminds me to text Kelly about the change of plans promising a rain check. Julio, being in bodyguard mode, stays near the entrance of the house with his hands crossed at his stomach waiting, while he eyes the other guy.

Matt leads the older gentleman to the living room towards us. As he approaches Trey and I. Julio starts to move closer to us. He stops to stand near us by the fireplace as if he's ready to attack the guy in case he gets out of line, still looking firmly at him.

The other guy notices Julio's reaction and grows nervous. "I'm sorry, I forget you're someone famous," he says, chuckling in Julio's direction.

"I like him like that," I say, smiling at Julio, which earns me a smile back.

He holds out his hand for me to shake. "My name is Paul Henderson."

Once I'm done shaking his hand, I go to take a seat on the larger couch, inviting Paul to take a seat on the smaller couch. Matt comes over and sits next to me with Trey taking the recliner.

Paul starts up again, "I'm part of the promotional group for the annual Women's Marathon in San Francisco. It's a race that is held by invitation only, and we choose our participants by what we call a raffle drawing." He looks between Matt and I, then continues, "We first noticed you when you ran your first half-marathon back in July, then again when you ran the Portland Marathon recently. Your times were amazing."

I don't know about amazing. I practically dragged my ass to cross that finish line both times. The only reason I ran the darn things was sitting in the room. Another reason to remember why I should be pissed at him.

I shrug my shoulders saying, "I really didn't want to have to cook again; the first time was a disaster."

Being that he doesn't know about the bet, he simply looks at me confused. But this earns me a full laugh from both Matt and Trey, making me smile.

He looks back at me, his face turning serious again. "Anyway, we would like to invite you to run it this year."

Another darn race to run, but why? Knowing that everything in *my* life comes with a price, I give him a skeptical look. "What do you want from me in return?"

This throws him off guard and he states, "Actually nothing, we only want you to run it." But by the way he's beginning to fidget, I know he's not telling the whole truth.

"Are you sure?" I ask again.

"Of course. Like I said, it's by invitation only and we'd be honored if you'd run it this year." He gives me a forced smile.

I know he's keeping something from me, so I decide to test him. "In that case I appreciate the offer, but I'm going to have to pass. I told myself I wasn't running any more races and I don't plan on doing so. Thank you for coming out to-day Paul," I say, standing up.

"Wait," he says, standing up just as quickly.

"The word is out how fast you are running. You missed a Q time for Boston by only eighteen minutes in Portland. If you manage to qualify for Boston at our race it would be great publicity for us," he says, looking desperate.

Matt is just as curious. "Your race is one of the most popular ones in the country, why do you want Abigail? I really doubt you need her for publicity reasons," he states.

I sit back down on the couch, now interested in what he has to say.

Paul sits back down as well and answers Matt's question. "Think about it. She's only run two big races, and in both races she starts off slow because of the crowds. But as she clocks in at the second and third time marker before the finish line, she advances her speed by minutes. This only proves that if we can put her in a higher start corral, avoiding most of the crowd she'll definitely qualify. We'd be able to claim that she used our race to achieve her goal of Boston."

I don't like the sound of this and look at Matt with apprehension my face.

"That's it; you only want her to run the race, nothing more?" Trey speaks up and asks him.

Paul's lips go flat. "We'd also like her to do a little promotional appearance at the expo," he says.

"No," Both Matt and I say at the same time.

Paul frowns. "I'll do it only on the condition that everyone thinks I'm running it like a normal runner who has signed up to run. I have no intention of gaining publicity for myself," I sternly state.

He shakes his head. "That's impossible, the race is next month and like I said, the raffle spots have all been taken. The only entrants allowed now are for charity and there's not much of those left."

"Fine, I'll do it that way. I don't want anyone thinking I got a free ticket into this thing, and I definitely don't want any money in return."

"Are you sure you can't do the expo?" he says, hopeful that I'll change my mind.

I shake my head again. "I have my reasons for not doing any work right now. I just want to run; it's something I found that I really love doing and if I have a chance to qualify this time for Boston then I want in."

He instantly cheers up. "Okay, but let us at least put you up in one of the promotional rooms that will be reserved at the hotel holding the expo."

I look at Matt and he shrugs his shoulders. "Okay, but it has to be big enough to hold at least six people. I don't go anywhere without Matt or Julio, my bodyguard," I say, pointing my chin at Julio. "And they both need full access to me inside the race, anywhere I go, they go, if not the deal is off." I almost hope my demands will make him change his mind.

Matt takes this moment to put his request in as well. "We also need a private plane to get us there. She doesn't like having to travel commercial."

I turn to him with a questioning look. He's making me sound like some rigid stuck up model that doesn't like people. I thought we're supposed to be salvaging my reputation, not taking advantage of it.

Paul purses his lips again and considers my request. "Fine, we'll keep in touch with your PA here and look forward to seeing you next month," he says, standing up and holding out his hand for me to shake again.

Wondering if I'm doing the right thing, I shake his hand and leave the rest of the details to be arranged between Matt and himself. I walk over to Julio wondering what the hell I just got myself into.

"You up for the task?" I ask, tilting my head to the side, joking at him.

His only response is a chuckle, as he lets his body relax and says, "Piece of cake. I don't know how you did it without me at the first two."

I consider his meaning, as I look back at Paul and Matt. "People weren't expecting me to be at the other races. In a nervous crowd of runners, I knew I didn't have to worry about anything," I say to him. "This one, I have a bad feeling it's going to be known that I'm there. So I'm scared shitless about it and it has nothing to do with the race. If it's as popular as Matt says, then I'm really going to need you."

He nods his head in understanding and I stand there with him as I watch Paul walk out the front door.

# Chapter
## 26

AS THE DAYS that count down to San Francisco, Matt lays out a training schedule for me. When I look at it, I start to hyperventilate a little. All the other races I just showed up without any expectations, the only thing I had to do was make sure I finished. This time I had a different goal to accomplish. Qualify for Boston.

"Since I've started the season I can't really train with you as much as I would have before. I'm going to have too many practices and away games this month, so I've spoken to Julio and he's agreed to go with you on your long runs. I can still go with you on the shorter ones," he tells me as he's entering the schedule into the calendar of my phone.

This saddens me, although Julio is a great runner, I always looked forward to running with Matt. It was our special time alone. At least before the shit hit the fan.

As he's still opening and closing dates on my phone he says, "A running company contacted me yesterday and they want you to do a photo shoot for them." As I'm about to protest, he says, "They won't pay you for it, but they are willing to provide you with training gear to wear during the race. I only agreed because hopefully this will start opening doors for you again, Abigail. You're a model and since you're no longer under Bill's control you should start doing it again. Maybe you'll like doing fitness modeling instead."

I sit there in silence and think about what he's just said. He's right, I've been sitting on my ass for the last couple of months in fear of Bill finding me, and when he did, look what happened. I couldn't live my life hiding behind the walls of this house. I had to live my life again.

My contract with Bill was officially over, so I was technically what Matt had referred to a while ago as a free agent. I could go wherever or do whatever photo opportunities I wanted now. The only thing that scared me was, since I've woken up, I haven't done any photo shoots and didn't know whether I still knew how. What if I didn't remember how to do it? I guessed I would find out soon enough.

Once he's done fumbling with my phone he hands it back to me while saying, "I'll still look forward to waking you up for your runs." He wickedly grins.

"Of course you would," I grumble.

Just then the doorbell rings and my body goes tense. This always happens when I'm unaware of someone coming over. I hate it. I'm letting the whole Bill incident still get to me.

Matt notices my tension and squeezes my hand. "It's okay beautiful, it's only the delivery I'm waiting for," he says as he stands up from the couch.

I watch him go over to the door and when he opens it I'm looking at a couple of guys holding what looks like a table. I promptly stand up and head in the direction of the kitchen following the deliverymen who are bringing it in.

Very confused, I lean against the island, crossing my arms. I stare at Matt wondering what he's up to. "Why a new table?" I ask.

He walks over in my direction, stopping directly in front of me, placing both of his hands on my hips. "I noticed how you refuse to eat at it anymore, or even look in its direction. I know why and I don't blame you. I'm sorry. This is my way of trying to make things right again," he says apologetically.

Sighing to myself, I stand there and watch as they set up the table. I want to still be mad at him about what happened on the table, but him buying a new one is proving that he's trying.

"I did miss eating with you guys, but you're right. I refuse to eat at a table that you fucked some girl on," I say out loud. The delivery guys stop in their tracks, as if shocked, but after a second they resume setting up the new table.

Matt leans down and places a kiss on my temple before turning around to monitor the deliverymen.

"So what exactly are you going to do with the old one?"

I'm hoping he'll say we get to burn it, but I really doubt he'll let me. Actually, the way things are at this very moment, I'm pretty sure if I were to ask he'd let me. The thought makes me giggle.

He hears me and turns around. "I figured I'd have the delivery guys take it and let them dispose of it. I don't care what happens to it, as long as it's out of here, and you don't have to look at it anymore."

The deliverymen finish setting up the table and walk out with the old table, Matt following at their heels. I head over to the new one sitting in front of me. It's a cherry wood color and huge. It looks sturdy, well built, and seats six. I stand there and admire the beauty in it. Matt may not think so, but I really think some of his sister's eye for furniture has rubbed off on him.

I feel Matt come up and stand behind me placing his hands on my waist. "You like it?"

"Of course, it's beautiful," I exclaim to him.

I feel him place a kiss on the top of my head again. "Not as beautiful as you," he whispers.

Sighing, I lean my body back against his. Savoring the comfort it's giving me. Against my will, he was slowly breaking down the walls of protection that I had built around my heart. I already knew that it wouldn't take long until they were completely gone.

# Chapter
## 27

I SOON DISCOVERED that although Julio ran to keep in shape, he was not fast enough when my legs wanted to move. It made me laugh knowing that I was now the one having to slow down for someone else.

Distance running was not his thing either. The first time I took him on a run that required more than 10 miles he almost collapsed on me when we were done. Poor guy, I felt really bad, but I think Matt's pancakes made up for it. He made a new fan of Julio with those pancakes alone.

Matt sure knew how to make the fluffiest pancakes I'd ever tasted. Betty Crocker had nothing on that man. He always made them from scratch, flour, eggs, and all. What amazed me even more was that he never used measuring cups, he would only eye all the measurements. So I was screwed if I ever tried to make them myself.

After eating our pancakes Matt had come up with the brilliant idea that Julio start taking a bike on my longer runs. That way it would allow me to keep the pace I chose, yet make it easier for Julio to keep up with me. Especially since my next three runs leading up to the race were going to have to include hills.

Upon studying the elevation map for the race, I realized I was going to have to train my body to get used to the increase of inclines as well.

The following week, with a map in hand, Julio and I were driving out of town to a road that included some elevated inclines that I'd be able to safely run. I don't know how much the bike helped, but it did give Julio a workout for his legs. He *was* able keep up with me a little easier, being that I was a bit slower from the climbs, but according to Julio, it did burn his legs pedaling up them. I would joke with him to stop whining, and to look forward to the way back down.

Another dreadful thing I had to endure was the freaking ice baths. Matt had showed Julio how to fill the tub with bags of ice and cold water, so when I was done with the run I could soak my legs in it. Despite my protesting, Matt said it was a necessity for my legs to avoid injury. Trust me, I was thinking of Matt the first time I got into it. But it included a lot of cursing, which only made Julio laugh hysterically. Matt was a lucky man that his game was away that weekend, because if he was anywhere near me I probably would have made him get in with me. Why should I have to suffer alone?

During that week I had the photo shoot for the running company, which made me a bit nervous. I asked Kelly to accompany me, since it was during one of her days off, and Matt would be at school. She was ecstatic about the idea of the photo shoot. Good to know one of us was.

When we arrived I realized we were doing the shoot at one of Portland's famous trails, and my only job was to act like I was running as they shot photo after photo. When they told me this I wanted to laugh. I'd been so nervous that I wouldn't be able to perform as a model. I was almost at the point of hyperventilating. Had I known I was going to be doing something I loved doing I wouldn't have felt pressured.

Once I was dressed in an outfit from the selection they had provided, it was time to start. They had marked off a section of the trail for me to run on. My sole job was to start at the beginning of the mark, and run up the trail while the photographer took photos. When I reached the end, I would have to stop, then head back up to the start again and do it all over again.

I did this for half an hour, and then they had me stand around in different poses in the different outfits, looking vigorous from the run. I did this for the next hour and once the photographer was satisfied he had enough good shots I was done.

It was easier than I'd ever thought it would be and the company was satisfied with my work. They even let me keep everything they had brought to the shoot that day. I left a very happy girl.

With the help of the crew, I started collecting all my goodies from the day. All of a sudden I feel my phone begin to vibrate, singing at the same time to *Just the Way You Are*.

Confused, I look at the screen to see a picture of Matt smiling back at me. I instantly feel butterflies flutter throughout my stomach at the thought of Matt singing it to me.

"Hi Matt," I say into the phone. "You know you really need to stop changing the ringtones on my phone." Looking up, I notice some of the camera crew, Kelly, and Julio staring at me with a smile on their faces as well. The camera crew immediately goes back to packing up, but Kelly and Julio keep intensely staring at me, interested in my conversation.

I can almost feel his smile on the other end of the phone as he speaks. "Hey beautiful, you almost done?" he says back at me. "How's it going?"

I turn away from the curious eyes. "I'm actually done," I tell him.

"Already? That was quick. You're that good?" he says, chuckling into the phone, which makes me feel dizzy again.

I chuckle back at him. "No, actually. I would have done this all day if they let me, but they said they got all the shots they needed."

"That's good."

"What time are you done with classes?" I ask.

Matt has been so busy with practice and now classes that I rarely saw him anymore. I was starting to get a little sad about it. When he was home late at night, he was usually studying. The only time I did get to spend time with him now was when I'd help him study; it was his way of trying to spend time with me, while getting his school work done. I couldn't complain though, he was making an effort by including me.

"I'm done with classes, but I'm going to head over to the gym before practice. I was thinking that maybe we could all go out to the Brewhouse for dinner, the game's on tonight. What do you think, you up for it?" I could hear the hesitation in his voice as he asks, which makes me feel guilty. Why would he think he needs my approval?

"Matt, you don't need to ask for my approval, if that's what you think. I'm fine with whatever place we go to for dinner."

"It's not about me asking for permission, beautiful. It's because I know I haven't been spending much time with you lately and I feel really bad about it. Tonight's the first night I don't have the pressure of schoolwork or studying, so I thought we'd go out." His cheerless voice intensifies my guilt.

I feel like I need to reassure him. "Sure, sounds fun. Do I need to tell Julio to come with us?" I ask, looking back in Julio's direction, thinking he heard me, but he's already walking over to Kelly's car carrying the bags with my stuff.

"No, a bunch of guys from the team are going to be there too. They should be enough man power." His response makes me laugh.

"Okay. I'll see you after practice then," I say to him before hanging up.

I start thanking everyone in the camera crew, along with the running company, and begin walking back to the car.

As I get into the front seat of the car, Kelly starts it up. "So missy, what's really up with you and Matt? Have you guys kissed and made up?" she says, driving away from the trail.

"Matt has a way of getting me. I can't seem to stay mad at him," I grumble.

I hate saying it out loud. Even in my head it sounds lame. I'm pathetic when it comes to Matt.

"Mmmm, hmmm," she says, while keeping her eyes on the road.

"What is that supposed to mean?" I snap back at her.

Keeping her hands on the wheel she quickly looks at me. "I'm only saying, that there's something definitely going on between the two of you. Whether you see it or not, it's there," she says, refocusing on the road ahead of her. "And Julio could back me up on it," she says, her eyes darting to the rearview mirror.

I whip my head around to look at Julio, but he's acting like he's ignoring us by looking out of the side window.

Snapping my head back to the front to look back at Kelly, I argue, "I don't know what you're talking about. He obviously cares about me, but not in an *I want you as a girl-friend way*, and I'm not going down the road of adding myself to his special list of friends," I assure both of them. "He's really protective of me, that's all, and with all the shit going on in my life right now, I'll take it," I finish telling her.

She groans, pinching her lips together. My eyes avert to look in the rearview mirror to Julio in the backseat. He looks suddenly uncomfortable with the conversation, like we're discussing tampons and periods.

Deciding that a change of subject is needed, I inform Kelly of dinner plans, and let Julio know he's done for the day. He tries reassuring me that he doesn't mind tagging along, but I tell him exactly what Matt said about the team being there, and this makes both him and Kelly laugh. Matt might not be telling me how he really feels about me, but he sure is declaring how protective he is.

## Chapter 28

I'M SITTING AT our new table finishing a salad when Trey comes into the room. He keeps looking deviously in the direction of the hallway, where Matt's currently in the shower.

They had both came home really stinky after practice. After the usual game of rock, paper, scissors, Matt won the shower leaving me stuck with a stinky Trey. We couldn't use both showers at the same time, unless you wanted to take a really, really fast one. Having seen what guys do to each other, I was getting a bit worried about why Trey kept looking behind his back.

"Care to tell me what exactly you're trying to hide from Matt," I ask amusedly.

He checks behind him one more time. "I've arranged for us to go out for Matt's birthday and I want it to be a surprise," he says. "He insists on not wanting to celebrate this year, being that Emily is gone and everything, but I thought it might be better if we celebrate anyways. You know, maybe cheer him up."

It makes me sad to think that this would be the first year he'd have to celebrate without his sister. I don't know what's it's like to have siblings, but I've become really close to my new set of friends and I would be sad if I didn't have them around during my birthday.

Trey walks over and leans his hands on the chair across from me, the one facing the hallway, before continuing. "I booked us a VIP section at one of the new clubs that just opened. It's really hard to even get in so it should be awesome," he says, dragging out the last word.

Okay, now I know why he's being sneaky other than wanting it to be a surprise. "Trey Johnson, how is it exactly you got us into this club?" I narrow my eyes at him not wanting to hear the answer I already know he's going to tell me.

His face immediately becomes worried. "Come on super-model, it's for Matt." He pleads, "You know I had to drop your name in order to get us in. It's really no big deal, I told them you've really been wanting to go, but couldn't get in. The manager practically groveled at my feet with apologies, so I took advantage."

I angrily groan out loud. Being that it's Trey this doesn't surprise me. But he knows damn well that I wouldn't use my name to get us in anywhere. I'm pretty sure that if Matt got wind of it, he would be just as pissed. No wonder he's being so sneaky when he's telling me, it has nothing to do with it wanting to be a surprise for Matt.

Rolling my eyes, I brace myself and ask, "When is Matt's birthday anyway?" I wonder how much time we have to soften him up to the idea.

Trey drops the bomb on me by saying, "The end of this week."

If I was currently eating something I swear you'd need to do the Heimlich on me to prevent choking. "Trey Johnson, why are only telling me this now?" I practically shout at him, but keep my voice down since I heard the water turn off a minute ago.

"It took a couple of phone calls to get to the right person who would definitely get us into the club. I finally got through just a couple of minutes ago. Like I said, Matt doesn't want to celebrate his birthday, so that's where you come in," he placates me, smiling.

My temper is starting to flare and I'm about ready to walk around the table and smack that smile off his face. "Besides using my name against my will, what is it I'm going to have to do?" I seethe to him.

He desperately tries to plead his case. "I need you to somehow convince Matt that you really want to go to the club this weekend. We'll act like it has nothing to do with it being his birthday, even though he'll probably know it is."

I finally find an excuse to avoid the club, shaking my head at Trey in disagreement. "We can't go out this weekend, we leave for San Fran on Friday for my race," I say. "Or did you forget?"

"We can leave really early on Saturday. I checked your schedule and you were technically going to sightsee anyways." He's still supplicating. "Come on Abigail, don't be a meanie. That boy has done a lot for you lately, the least you can do is make him happy on his birthday." He throws that last piece in, while pointing in the direction of the bathroom.

Oh great, he's going to play that card on me. Does he really think I don't know how much Matt has done for me?

"That's low, Trey, even for you," I snarl at him. I hate the fact that I'm taking a chance at upsetting Matt. "Fine.

We'll leave on Saturday, but don't expect me to be happy about it."

"Be happy about what?" Matt says from the hallway, and I instantly go rigid. I look at Trey pleading for help, because God knows I can't lie to Matt. Well, maybe I would be able to, but I don't want to.

Trey looks up in Matt's direction with a smile. "Abigail got a phone call from that new club downtown, you know, Ardent, so she agreed for us to go this Friday. Isn't that cool?" he eagerly tells Matt. "She's not going to be happy about the lack of sleep, but oh well." He shrugs his shoulders.

My eyes are now shooting daggers at Trey for putting me into this situation.

Matt walks over to us dressed in his usual boxer briefs with a towel around his neck, holding an end in each one of his hands. I have to bite my lip to keep myself from drooling at him. When he's half-naked like this you can see every ripple of muscle lining his body and I just want to run my tongue over every... single... one.

Matt's stern voice snaps me out of my imaginary lick session. "No. This race is very important to you Abigail. The club thing can wait for another weekend."

Trey is looking at me with desperation in his eyes, ready to throw me under the bus. How in the hell did I get stuck with this task? I know the only way I am going to convince Matt is to use the female power I had over him. "Matt please, it sounds like it'd be really fun," I beg him.

Deep down inside I feel like the biggest traitor in the world right now as I stand up from the table. I walk over to Matt with my pouty lips and think to myself, I'm going straight to hell for what I'm about to do. "Please Matt, it would be really fun to be able to go out to a club. You haven't taken me to one, and I got really excited when they invited me. Come on Matt... for me?" I say to him as I'm standing directly in front of him, tugging on the towel ends he's holding to pull him to my body.

His eyes go dark as he's staring down into mine. I know exactly what I'm doing to him right now, and I'm pretty sure he knows it.

"Fine, but don't complain when you don't make the 3:30 mark," he says out loud so Trey can hear. Then he lowers his lips next to my ear to whisper, "Beautiful, I expect you to be the cake I'm eating that night."

I take in his husky voice whispering in my ear, imagining exactly what he means by that. He takes my hands, releasing them from the towel. He turns around, leaving me swaying to catch myself as I watch his hard ass walk away. Thinking about what he just said, combined with the sight of his sexy body in front of me, I swear I feel like I am about to come at this very moment.

I hear Trey's shout of triumph behind me and pull myself together. I feel like I'm going to have a heart attack from my rapid heart rate. I turn around and give Trey the evil eye before stomping off to my room to take the next shower.

There probably isn't any warm water yet, which is fine with me, 'cause right now I need something just as cold as one of those damn ice baths I dreadfully hate.

KELLY AND I decided to go shopping the next day for Friday night. We were both really excited, but I don't think Julio enjoyed it as much as we did. We must have gone to more than ten stores and I still hadn't chosen anything. Kelly had found her dress at the second store, but as she was claiming, I was being difficult.

The problem was that I wanted the dress to be perfect for Matt's birthday. Trust me, at that point I was frustrated too.

As we are in a small boutique, browsing around, frustrated again, I hear Kelly say, "I bet your old closet is filled with all the right dresses that you needed."

Thinking back to the enormous closet that held a massive amount of clothes, I nod my head before saying, "Yeah, it was huge, and it probably did have a dress I would have been satisfied with. But the size of that closet and the amount of clothing it had, it only proved one thing, how shallow and unhappy I was. I don't care what anybody says, money and clothes won't buy you happiness. Your friends and family give you that," I say, smiling over at her.

She smiles back, "Have you ever thought about going back for your stuff?"

I take in her question, then say, "No. Especially since I would risk coming across Bill again. I'd rather take the loss than run into him."

She nods, satisfied with my answer and we exit the boutique, moving on with our shopping. I'm about ready to make Julio drive us to Seattle if I don't find the dress soon. I'm so frustrated by that point that I'd even take the risk of being seen by Bill.

As I was about to give up we go into a shop claiming to hold high end couture dresses and the moment I walked in I saw it at the back of the store. It was on a mannequin, but I couldn't take my eyes off it. Needing to try it on, I quickly asked the store attendant to take it off the mannequin and I headed straight to the dressing rooms. Five minutes later I had the dress on and it fit perfectly. I was about ready to cry from happiness of finally finding the dress.

It was white, with a v-neck front and back that fitted tightly at my waist and flared out at the skirt. It had a bit of tulle under the skirt giving it a puffy look. I was in love with it and I knew Matt would love it as well.

"Damn girl, if that boy doesn't declare his love for you when he sees you in this dress, I'm going to have to hit him upside the head with that football he throws around," Kelly says behind me as she's looking at the mirror.

I turn around to look at her. "You think he'll like it?" I cautiously ask.

She snickers. "I should have known you were shopping for him. I wish you had told me that five stores ago, I could have helped a little. You sure this is the one?" she asks, tilting her head to really examine the dress. "Of course it is. You look smoking hot."

I nod my head in approval and begin taking the dress off so I can pay for it. Finally satisfied, I leave the store, with dress in hand, thinking that tomorrow night was going to be perfect. With Kelly's help, I quickly picked out some shoes to go with it and we were out the door.

# Chapter 29

THE DAY OF Matt's birthday comes sooner than I expected. After a quick lunch at the Brewhouse, we all head back to the house to get ready for our night out on the town.

Since we were leaving early in the morning we had agreed it would be a good idea for David and Kelly to stay over for the night. So they're here getting ready with us. Kelly helped me with my make-up, and also did my hair, throwing it into a stylish ponytail.

I finally got my dress on and was about to dig into my closet for my new heels when I hear a knock at my door. Since I'm on my hands and knees I just yell, "Come in," over my shoulder as I grab the box containing the heels. I'm already standing up when I feel a hand reach for my arm to help me up. I look up to see Matt smiling down at me with a thin jewelry box wrapped in black with a big red bow tied around it.

He hands me the box. "I saw this online and knew you had to have it."

"Matt, it's your birthday, I should be buying you something," I say to him, grabbing for the box. I hesitate about opening it, but Matt has a very anxious look on his face, so I start unwrapping the bow and paper.

What I see inside takes my breath away.

It's a charm bracelet, but it's breathtaking. Its links are made of beautiful sliver links, similar to a Tiffany's bracelet. Throughout the links are several tiny rounded charms, and when I lift the bracelet to take a closer look, I can see numbers engraved into them.

"It's the distances of the races we've run together. I wanted to get you something that would always remind you of those races. Of us," he says, as he looks down at the bracelet with me.

As I start to run my fingers over the charms, I noticed that he's also included the most recent race. It's of the Portland Marathon. They had included a small charm in their finishers' swag packet. At the time I had thought to myself, *what am I supposed to do with this?* Now that I was looking at it, I'm so glad that they had included it.

Matt also runs his thumb over the same charm as he says, "This one is the most important to me. Deep down inside, I believe it's the one that brought you to me."

My eyes start to tear up as I look up to Matt. "Thank you, I'll cherish it forever," I say, clutching the bracelet in my hand.

Matt reaches down and opens my hand. He takes the bracelet, opens the clasp and wraps it around my right hand.

I lift my head and look at Matt with tears in my eyes.

He takes my head, engulfing it with his hands, and tilts it up to meet his lips. I feel the electricity that courses in between our lips burning deep down to my toes. At first his kiss is soft and sweet, but I want more. I drop the box I was still holding and grab for his hips pulling him flush against my body, forcing my tongue into his mouth. Our tongues dance together, as our breathing becomes intense. I want him so badly right now. I can't control the need any longer.

Matt apparently has a different idea when he pulls us apart for air, pushing me away from his body. He reaches down and gives me another peck on the lips, clearly implying that we're not going to continue.

Why is he stopping? I let out a small whine and try to pull him back to me. "Not tonight beautiful, we have to go."

"Why not Matt?" My question makes me sound desperate, but I am.

"Abigail, it's not what you think. I want you, I do, but I'm not willing to risk messing up what we have. It's not worth it for a quick fuck."

A quick fuck? That's the way he sees it?

"That's all I am to you, aren't I Matt? Just another pawn in the game you're used to playing, one where you're used to making the rules? Nothing is ever going to happen between us because you'll always use that as an excuse. You've already made the decision for both or us."

He stays quiet, refusing to answer, but his eyes are conveying the message that I'm correct.

He probably sees me as one of the girls he's used to tossing aside since I'm always the one throwing myself at him. He's never tried to push for more when it came to me, which only proves that I'm right. If he had any intention of something happening he would have pushed for it a long time ago. He's always had the opportunity since we live together.

His continued silence hurts and I push him away, reaching down for the shoes. I walk barefoot out into the living room, not wanting to spend another minute alone with Matt. I want to cry so badly, but I bite the inside of my cheek and face the crowd, needing the distraction right now.

"Damn supermodel, Julio is going to be earning his paycheck tonight. You're going to have men all over you," Trey says as I walk over to him. When I reach him he grabs for my hand to twirl me around.

Matt's arms can always make me feel better, but Trey's words can always make me smile. I had to love him for that. Knowing that Matt is probably watching, I purposely avoid looking in his direction and start putting my shoes on, holding on to Trey's shoulder for support.

Kelly must have noticed my expression when I walked out because she gets up. "I think we all need a drink before we leave," she yells, walking over to the island containing all the alcohol.

I purposely go stand next to Kelly, dragging Trey up next to me, not allowing Matt a chance to come near me. He's studying me with piercing eyes from across the island, and it's driving me crazy. Those damn eyes have a way of reaching down into my soul, even when I'm mad at him. He knows I'm pissed right now and it's showing as he's glaring at me with his eyes at a slit.

I quickly tell Kelly that I'm refusing to drink tonight because I don't want to get dehydrated before my race and she just rolls her eyes at me and hands me a shot. I automatically shove it back at her and throw my hands up while I back away from the counter.

She looks irritated that I'm refusing to drink, but I inform her that I'm standing my ground. The reason I'm really refusing to drink is because I know the minute the alcohol hits my system, all bets are off, and I won't have any control over what happens with Matt.

Everyone takes his or her shot, then another for the road as Julio comes into the house stating that the party bus has arrived. I had instructed Trey to hire the vehicle because I was *refusing* to allow anyone to drive and I thought it would be easier than waiting around for a taxi as we left the club. It was paid for the whole night, so it would wait for us. But I think what sold everyone was that they could keep drinking on the way.

I already knew from the cheering on the way to the bus, that this was going to feel like a very long night.

# Chapter 30

AS WE WALK into the club, the music automatically begins to flow through my blood, taking over my body. I immediately pull Matt by the hand and straight to the dance floor, letting my body free. I need to let out a lot of sexual frustration and this is the only safe way I know without Matt pushing me away.

My hips move along to the beat pounding out of the speakers, the bass taking my mind away as my body grinds up against Matt's. With his hands roaming all over my body, making me feel sexy and alive, I keep rubbing against him. Although people surround us, it feels like it's only Matt and I on the dance floor, alone in our own world of ecstasy.

Moments like these are what I crave, yearn for, knowing that his hands will be touching me, and no one will judge me for it. I live for the feeling of his body next to mine, and the excitement that it sends to my blood. I close my mind and take it all in, dancing like this for at least half an hour, until Kelly taps me on the shoulder, bringing me back to reality.

"When are we going to start drinking, I'm thirsty," she shouts into my ear, pointing to the VIP section up above. I look back at Matt hoping that he's heard her as well, since I don't want to have to bust his eardrum like she did to mine. He nods and tilts his head in that direction confirming that he heard. He wraps his arm around my waist to lead me off the dance floor making me intoxicated from the contact that he constantly has to have with me.

We make our way over to the VIP area that has been designated for our little group and I immediately reach for the water, opening it, and downing it with one breath. I hadn't realized how thirsty I was until that first drop hit my tongue, or that I was still standing until I feel Matt's arm pull me down onto the seat cushion next to him.

He keeps his arm wrapped around me, pulling me tighter to his hip, clearly stating that he needs me next to him. I almost want to pull away, as if to prove that he has no claim on me tonight, but I would only be lying to myself if I did. Even my body knows who it belongs to, and he was sitting right next to me, branding me with his touch. He was driving me crazy and I was allowing it to take over me.

Thinking back to what happened earlier in my room was like a bucket of cold water being dumped on me, waking me up to reality again. I can't allow him to keep winning, so I stand up, using the excuse that I needed to speak to the waitress to order our drinks. I hope that the distraction will put some distance between us.

He tries holding me to stay next to him, but I ignore him and get up anyways. Even though Matt looks disappointed that I stood up, I couldn't let him make me weak.

Once I'm done ordering more alcohol than we really

needed, I look over to Matt, wondering what he's doing. He's having a conversation with Trey, and I stand there taking him in.

As if he sensed that I'm watching him, he looks up with his hooded eyes, and his long lashes that drive me insane. His lips go into their usual sexy grin as he looks at me, and it takes all my willpower not to go over to him. He knows exactly what he's doing to me exactly at this moment.

Biting my lip, I force myself to turn away, breaking from his spellbinding gaze. I walk over to a darkened corner where Julio is standing off to the side, observing our crowd. I grab on to the rail, facing forward, distracting myself by looking out onto the dance floor below us, watching as the crowd moves with the music.

I feel him come up behind me, my body already recognizing his touch, like it's always expecting it. He places both his arms along the sides of my body on the rail in front of me. It locks my body into place, giving me nowhere to go. I stand there and let his body press up against mine, savoring the feel of his chest against my back. I close my eyes and lean my head onto his shoulder, losing myself against his body. He slowly starts to rub his lips against my neck, behind the sensitive spot of my ear. The warmth of his breath sends shivers throughout my whole body, electrifying it.

"Hey beautiful. Why are you running away from me?" he whispers loudly into my ear before taking the lobe into his mouth and biting it gently.

The jolts of electricity are intensifying with every word he says. Coursing through my veins, making me weak, and wet with pleasure. I fucking hate how he does this to me. He knows why I'm keeping away from him, and yet he keeps coming to tease me. It makes me suffer and I want to run away some more.

He starts kissing my neck and I tilt my head to the side giving him better access. As he keeps kissing my neck I say loud enough for him to hear over the music, "Matt, we have to stop this."

"Stop what, beautiful?" He's acting like he has no clue what he's doing to my body.

I dig for the willpower to speak. "You know exactly what you're doing to me, you're teasing me, it's killing me, and it's torture," I tell him, gripping the handrail harder with a force that is hurting even my palms.

He simply laughs and grabs my hips pulling my ass up against his hardened erection. "Who says I want to keep teasing you?" he states with determination into my ear.

I force myself to turn around so I can look into his eyes and see for myself how serious he is. "If you wouldn't give me a reason to run, I wouldn't," I reply before kissing his neck, lightly sucking on it, giving him a taste of his own medicine.

I stop and pull back so we are looking directly into each other's eyes. I notice how close our lips are to each other right now. If I were to move forward just an inch, we would be kissing, and I know all hell would break loose then. I wouldn't be able to stop myself once I'd started. I can feel his breath on my lips and it feels so good. It makes me bite my lip to try to keep myself under control.

Trey's voice breaks our world of enchantment. "Hey birthday boy, alcohol is here. You can always get dessert later," he yells to us over the music and walks away, pulling Matt with him.

I take a moment to catch my breath, looking around to distract myself. I notice that Julio is standing there, staring in the direction of my friends. I take another deep breath before heading over to the table to join them. As I get there Kelly hands me a shot glass, refusing to let me slide this time.

"I told you, I'm not drinking tonight. I have to run this weekend," I plead, trying to force the glass back at her.

She scrunches her nose at me, before saying, "Quit being a sour puss, it's your man's birthday. Take the damn shot." She shoves my hand back at me.

I'm about to remind her that Matt is technically not mine to claim, but Trey and David begin the usual birthday toast, and I'm left standing there watching everyone throw their drinks back into their mouths. I place my full shot glass on the table with the rest of the empty ones and hope that no one notices it.

That plan is a complete bust. As Kelly starts refilling the glasses she notices that mine is still full. "Hey girl, you didn't drink yours," she says out loud, scolding me with her eyes. I laugh and tell her to drink it for me, which she does after shrugging her shoulders.

After another round we all head to the dance floor again. Forty-five minutes later we're back in the VIP area for round two.

All the water I had consumed was finally starting to catch up with me, so I stand up and walk over to the waitress asking directions to the bathroom. When she informed me that our section had its own private bathroom, I headed there with Julio in tow.

After taking care of business and washing my hands, I exit the bathroom, crashing straight into Matt's chest. I look into his gorgeous eyes as they are staring right back at me with a hunger that I recognize. It's the same one I feel at this very moment. The one that wants to strip him of every stitch of clothing so I can run my hands over every inch of his naked body. The naked body that he has been teasing me with for months now.

I'm at the limit of denying myself since I've now discovered how close I've come to getting it. The hunger is burning through the blood in my veins and the only way to extinguish it is to finally give into that hunger.

He grabs my hand, enveloping it tightly into his as he pulls me a couple feet down the hallway into a darkened corner. I'm confused, but I don't question him. When it comes to Matt I already know he always has a motive for what he's going to do, and I've learned to go along for the ride.

He pushes me against the wall, trapping me against it with his body, grabbing onto my waist with his hands right before he lowers his lips to connect with mine. My lips instantly give in to his request, starving for the taste, opening to allow him to explore my mouth. He entangles his tongue with mine and I can taste the alcohol he's been drinking tonight, mixed with his own flavor. His taste is so intoxicating that I immediately get drunk from it, wanting more. I'm like an addict when it comes to his kiss, craving my next fix against his mouth. I reach for his neck pulling him tighter against my body, not wanting to give him a chance to escape.

His hands begin to slowly explore my body, his left creeping up my body to grab my breast, gripping as he massages it. His other hand quickly makes its way down to my leg, hooking it under my knee, pulling it up to wrap around his hip. He grinds his cock against my center, and I feel him come alive against it. His hand starts to travel back up the same leg, making its way up my ass, gripping it with demand. I react by trying to pull him tight with my leg, hating that we have clothing to impede the contact.

I grip his head tightly within my hands, needing something to help support my now weakened body. I want him to know how badly I need him as we're still intensely kissing. I can barely breathe at this point. He's stealing every ounce of breath from me, drowning me of air. The loss makes me lightheaded, but the desire to taste him overpowers my need to breath.

We finally come up for air and I stare into his eyes, seeing how hungry he is for me. If I didn't want him just as badly I would be terrified. He slowly begins to trail his lips down my chin to my ear, sensitizing my skin with every kiss he leaves behind. He finally reaches my earlobe and I can hear his heavy breathing against it, matching my own.

"Matt, you're drunk. You don't know what you're doing right now," I say to him, trying to reassure myself that we should stop, but in reality I don't want to.

"I know exactly what I'm doing right now. I'm going to prove to you, beautiful, that I'm not teasing you," he growls into my ear right before he takes it into his mouth to bite it. He moves his mouth right below my ear to my sensitive spot and does the same, sending my body spiraling into weakness. If he wasn't holding me up against the wall with his body my legs would have given out and my whole body would have dropped to the floor.

How is it that he's able to bring my walls down in one kiss? This is exactly the reason why I was trying to keep him at a distance. I was trying to avoid his touch because I knew the minute he did it I would become weak and give in. I knew that my body would succumb to him and it's finally happening as I grip his shoulders with the only strength I have left.

He pushes himself harder into my body. Grinding his hips up against my wetted core, he starts kissing me again, and I moan into his mouth from the pleasure rising in my body. I want him inside me so badly right now; I know I would let him take me right here on the dirty floor if he were to ask. I don't care anymore.

He suddenly stops kissing me, and I whimper from the loss of his lips. He drops down to his knees, his head disappearing under my ruffled skirt. I'm so dazed from his kiss that I can't even comprehend what he's doing until I feel him hook the same leg that was around his hip, up onto his shoulder. I feel him rip my thong with his hands and his mouth connects with my core. The contact burns from the tip of my toes all the way up my body as he slowly licks his way up my clit.

I quickly grab onto his shoulders for support, throwing my head back. I close my eyes, letting out a loud moan that vibrates in my neck as I'm standing there digging my fingernails into Matt's shoulders for support. He's torturing me with his tongue, licking his way up and down my clit, twirling it around in his mouth, slowly prolonging my climax. I knew his mouth would be sinful, but fuck, I never expected it to torture me with pleasure.

I feel him start to slow down, giving me a chance to catch my breath, before he kisses his way to the inside of my thigh. First, he nips the skin lightly with his teeth, and then he starts sucking it with his mouth. If I wasn't so turned on right now, I would be questioning why he was doing this, but I can only stand there, letting him.

After a couple of seconds I feel his tongue once again begin to work its way back up to explore me, licking and sucking at my clit. It makes me weak and prolongs my pleasure again. He's tormenting me by not allowing me to surrender to orgasm, but my body is persistent and the tension of my impending climax takes over. I explode into his mouth, the fireworks of stars lighting up behind my closed lids as I scream from the pleasure.

If it weren't for the pounding of the music throughout the club, I am sure that everyone in there would have heard my screams. As I'm coming into his mouth, I'm thinking that he's going to stop, but he doesn't. He continues, lapping up my juices with his long licks and makes me come all over again. I can't take it anymore and my only standing leg buckles from the weakness. He instantly catches me, standing up quickly, hooking his arm around my waist, and holding me against his body as I catch my breath.

As I'm leaning my head against his shoulder, holding on for dear life from being so weak, panting for air, he says to me, "I'm not done yet. I'm going to fuck you so hard, beautiful, you're going to be feeling me when you run on Sunday."

Wanting him to keep his word, I begin to unbutton his pants with my fingers, digging into his pants, grabbing for his cock. Pulling it out for better access, I tightly wrap my hands around the silky smoothness of his skin. His cock jumps, as it grows larger in my hand. I stroke it up and down, from the base to the tip of the head. He grabs for my hand pulling it off him, making me whimper from the loss. But just as fast he groans loud enough for me to hear and he hoists me up wrapping my legs around his waist. I can feel his cock against my core, as I'm coating him with my juices.

I... want... more... and I want it now.

Using the strength in my legs and arms, I lift myself up

higher so I can position him right at the tip of my entrance. I feel the tip of the head about to enter me, when we hear Kelly slur, "Hey big guy, if you're up here that means your boss lady is too."

Both our bodies freeze, not wanting to move or lose contact, but obviously we are not going to finish what we just started now. I turn my head to see exactly where Kelly is, and when I look in her direction, I notice that Julio is standing near the bathroom door with his back to us. Shit. This whole time he was standing there while I was letting Matt eat me out.

Crap, how much did he see? He obviously knew something was happening, or else he wouldn't have his back to us. This is why Matt is every kind of dangerous for me. All he has to do is kiss me and I totally lose myself, forgetting about the world around me.

Kelly is looking at us, and my legs still wrapped around Matt's waist, while he's holding me tight at my hips. Knowing that our wanted sex session is over, I unhook my legs, forcing them to fall to the ground. Matt turns away, adjusting his pants in a hurry.

She stands there, swaying, smiling from ear to ear. "Are you guys finally hooking up? 'Cause if you are, it's about damn time. I'm tired of seeing how much she wants you, but you won't take a Goddamn hint and screw her already. You're too busy fucking other people on tables," she slurs, pointing at Matt.

Matt's turns around quickly. My eyes go wide in embarrassment, and Matt looks down at me just as shocked. That's when I notice that Kelly doesn't look too good and she begins to gag. I immediately run over to her, pushing her into the bathroom, having her barely make it to the toilet before she lets it all come out. I kneel there next to her holding her hair while she throws up, thinking about what she just said.

The harsh reality of what she said is a reminder of Matt's past. It leaves me wondering if it was the alcohol that was responsible for what he did, was it allowing him to think clearly? He's used to using girls. He takes what he needs from them without any strings attached, and then throws them aside. Would he have done the same to me after to-night?

A couple of minutes later a very drunk David shows up at the door. From looking at him, I know he's in no condition to take care of Kelly, so I wave him off and stay there until she's finally done.

After cleaning her up and with Julio carrying her, we head back to our little section. Kelly is passed out in Julio's arms by the time we get there and everyone else is looking three sheets to the wind. I decide to call it a night. I close out the tab with the waitress by handing her a couple of hundred dollar bills for putting up with us and she ushers us to the exit.

As we are leaving the crowd outside has increased and although the party bus is waiting for us, the crowd starts noticing I'm exiting and begins to try to hound me. Great, my hired muscle is too busy carrying my passed out friend to protect me. Right when I think I'm screwed, I feel Trey come up with Matt and they both flank me as we walk onto the bus, passing a screaming group of people taking picture after picture of us leaving.

After taking a seat, my exhaustion from the whole night finally catches up to me and I fall asleep against Matt's chest, not caring what message it's sending to him. I wake up as the bus pulls into our driveway and I feel Matt's body against mine as he picks me up and carries me into the house. I wrap my arms around his neck for support and bury my face into his neck taking in his scent as I usually do, closing my eyes again. The next thing I know I feel my dress coming off and I start to panic thinking that Matt wants to finish what we didn't get to at the club.

"Matt, I don't think this is a good idea," I say to him, trying to sound calm.

I feel him climb up into bed with me, pulling my body against his chest. "Don't worry beautiful, it's late, and we only have a couple of hours left to sleep. You need your rest for the race," he says before placing a soft kiss on my lips and holding me tightly with his arms, sending me into a blissful sleep.

# Chapter 31

AS WE CLIMB out of the SUV that took us to the airport to board the charter plane that Paul had provided for us, I see a lot of unhappy faces around me. I am the only one who didn't consume alcohol, besides Julio, since he was working, so I feel better than ever. Except for the lack of sleep that is still dragging my body around, I am the only coherent one to make decisions that morning.

Julio showed up bright and early, with Carne Asada burritos for everyone, stating that greasy foods always helped with a hangover. Since I knew it wasn't going to help with my diet, I had passed and opted for my usual light carb load, but everyone ate those burritos like they were candy. How Julio knew the answers to everything still amazed me, but I was very grateful.

Upon boarding the plane, I go to the rear of it, wanting to be away from the grumpy grunts and faces that I was receiving for being the only one not ready to spill my cookies. Matt follows, taking the seat next to me, reaching for my phone that is in my hand. Although I try taking it from him, he holds it up and out of my reach making me mad about it. He opens the screen and I see him head straight into the settings app. I'm about to lecture him about messing with my phone and he can see it in my face, but he puts his hand up to silence me, making me scowl at him.

I want to piss him off just as badly as I feel right now. "So sunshine, how do you feel?"

He looks up at me after a couple of seconds, tilting his head, with his eyes looking up into the ceiling. "Better than I thought I would." Then he goes back to messing with my phone, my comment not even fazing him. He hands the phone back to me. He grabs his own out of his back pocket and proceeds to punch at the screen until I hear my phone start to sing. It is blaring *Teenage Dream* and I can't control the smile that plasters across my face as I remember the music video.

I look over at him blown away by the ring tone that's he's chosen. Oh yeah, two can play that game. I yank his phone out of his hand with my right one, and hold up my left hand at him, stopping his protest.

Matt tries to lean over and look at what I'm doing, but I shove his face with my hand a couple of times and he gets the point, finally giving up. After a couple of minutes I've finally made my selection. I push at my screen to call him back and his phone begins to sing the chorus to *Sex on Fire*. We might not have had sex yet, but every time I think about how close we've come to it, my body turns to fire.

Matt looks up from his phone and at me. "Oh really, beautiful, I can't wait to find out."

I smile, and look away from him, with my cheeks burning. In the corner of my eye I see Julio smiling from ear to ear, while acting like he's reading a magazine. I'm pretty sure he knew what was going on with the ring tones. I look to the front of the plane to see if anyone else noticed, but they are all close to passing out from still being hungover.

"So how soon can I discover how bad you can be?" he whispers into my ear, the heat of his breath sending shivers throughout my body.

I roll my eyes as I turn to look out the window. "I liked the ringtone I originally had. At least it didn't give me any false hopes when it came to you." I'm not able to keep out the disappointment lacing my voice.

"What are you talking about?"

I bring my attention back to Matt. "So does this little trip qualify as us running away together and never looking back?" I refer to my designated ring tone as I twirl my finger around in the air.

Matt's face grows serious and he reaches for my hand, entwining the fingers of our hand, making them tingle from his touch. "I don't want to look back at the mistakes I made with you Abigail, ever again. Can we do that?" he says with a worried look on his face.

I think about what he's said. "What happened last night Matt? Was I another mark you're going to add to the list of girls you have? I'm pretty sure you laid it clear on the table that you didn't do relationships from the beginning." I feel torn as I say it.

He drops his shoulders and sighs, turning to face his body more into mine. "I know what I said beautiful, but for you I'll be willing to risk starting a relationship. You're worth changing my mind for."

My heart gets excited and starts rapidly beating. His response makes me smile and gives me hope, knowing that he's finally put his ex-girlfriend in the past. He brings his left hand to my neck, pulling me to him, giving me an intense kiss. I keep kissing him, not even letting the moving plane distract me as it begins to taxi for take-off. I feel like I need him closer to me right now more than ever, so I grab his waist practically trying to pull him into my seat on top of me.

This makes him laugh into my mouth. "Calm down beautiful, as much as I want you, I don't want to have an audience, and I really doubt there's a comfortable way of joining the mile high club on this plane," he huskily says to me.

Dammit, why does something always end up being a cock blocker for me when it comes to Matt? "Are we ever going to be able to finish what we keep starting?" I whine into his mouth.

He laughs and kisses me again, bringing my body up and onto his lap as the seat belt sign turns off. I sit there in his embrace, getting into my treasured spot of my face into his neck, taking in his scent, and easily fall asleep. With Matt rubbing my thigh, like he does so well, letting me know he has to touch me just as badly.

It feels like I've been asleep for only a couple of minutes, when I feel lips lightly nipping at my neck. Then I feel my shirt near my shoulder being pulled to the side, giving Matt access to nip and kiss there as well. His sinful mouth only makes me wet and I squirm in his lap.

I feel him groan into my shoulder, and then hear him say, "I can't wait until we get back home. I'm going to fuck you so hard, so long, and in so many different ways you won't be able to walk for days."

I laugh into the crook of his neck, and then pull my

head back to look into his eyes, challenging him. "Don't make promises you can't keep, Matthew Garcia."

He reaches with his hand in between my legs to squeeze my pussy through my pants, making me yelp. As I'm about to give him the same treatment, the stewardess shows up, telling me to move into my own seat and buckle up since we'll be landing soon.

With the glare I give her, I'm surprised she's still smiling at me. Being that I have to listen to her, I do as I'm told. I'm not happy about it and you can tell by the look on my face, which causes Matt to laugh at me, making me feel like a child. Once I'm done buckling up, Matt reaches for my hand again, entwining our fingers together, and holding my hand tightly.

The plane finally lands and we load up into another black SUV that will take us straight to the expo. Since we decided to wait to come on Saturday morning, instead of Friday, like Paul had wanted us to do, I was on a very tight schedule for the weekend. I hated being rushed, but that was no one's fault but my own for wanting to spend it with Matt.

We arrive at the expo and I head inside, leading the way straight to the pick-up tables for my packet. Once I've picked up my race packet and goodies, I do what I love doing at these expos, shop.

I'm like a kid in a candy store, a running candy store, and I've got no limit. Actually I do, which Matt reminds me of at every booth. If it weren't for him, I would have bought one of everything there. Which made it the disappointment of the morning. At least I thought it was, until something replaced it.

As we are walking I hear someone shout, "Matt, is that you?" from the side of us.

Matt's drops my hand as if I've burned him and I see his body tense up. He turns towards the voice and a petite girl throws herself at him, causing him to catch her as she's hanging herself from his neck.

"Oh shit, this isn't good," I hear Kelly say, along with Trey's, "Oh fuck," as his mouth falls open with a wide O.

By the look on David's face, he knows her as well. But nobody wants to say anything, which is not a good sign. Who the hell is this girl and why is she hanging all over Matt? I keep getting bumped from all directions, as I stand there shocked about the whole situation.

Julio comes up close to my side pushing me against a wall, out of the middle of the line of people that we were trying to press me to keep moving. Trey decides to wander off, his face giving away that he doesn't want to be any-where near us at the moment.

I watch Matt make friendly conversation with her, not caring about the people around them and then they start laughing together. I'm standing there wondering what the hell is going on. All of a sudden I see this girl pull Matt down by the neck and give him a kiss on the mouth. Not just a peck, a full-blown take me right here, right now kiss. The kind I've been giving him lately.

Matt stands there holding her, and then he must have woken up a second later, because he pushes her away and looks around searching for something or someone. Then he sees me and smiles awkwardly.

I'm left shocked. Is he really trying to brush off what just happened by smiling at me? He grabs her hand with his and leads her over in my direction. Kelly instantly grabs for my hand and gives it a light squeeze, almost as if reassuring me that everything will be ok. Why?

Matt comes up to us and stops right in front of me. "Abigail, this is Laura. Laura, this is my friend Abigail," he happily says, swaying his hand back and forth in our directions.

Her eyes go wide. "Matt, you know Abigail Adams!" she shouts at him, lightly jumping in place, while grabbing at Matt's arm.

He laughs, like this is usual for her and it amuses him. "Yeah, I'm her assistant," he says, shrugging his shoulder, while he smiles down at her, as he goes back to making conversation with her about what she's doing at the expo.

Oh, so now he's back to being my assistant? I know this is what we use when we're out in public, but if he knows this girl, which he obviously does, since she's kissing him on the lips, I would at least think he would have dropped the whole assistant thing, and declared me his roommate.

I tune out their conversation so I can really take in this girl. She has black hair, brown eyes, and the top of her head only comes up to Matt's chest. I'd tower over her like a giraffe in my heels if I were wearing any. She's wearing a yellow dress, almost like she's still stuck in the summer, instead of the cold of winter. That's when I notice that she also has a race packet in her hand. So she's running as well? Well I know for sure with my long legs that I'll be leaving her in the dust and I'll be happy to do it. I can't help but smile to myself from the thought.

Then I hear Matt speak again, looking directly at me, and the gloom on his face begins to worry me once again. "Abigail, this is the girl I was telling you about," he says cautiously, as if to clarify what he's saying, "the one who is going to Berkley." He says the last bit, with his body going tense, like he's waiting for a blow to come straight at him.

I realize that he's never once mentioned his ex-girlfriend's name when he spoke about her. No wonder I didn't know who she was right away. But, it does explain why everyone else knew who she was. Laura is the one. The one he's been holding out for. Right now I want nothing better than to beat the shit out of him, since his body is ready for it. I simply force myself to breathe and control my temper. It's not like he came looking for her. Right?

I extend my hand to her. "Nice to meet you Laura," I say with a wide and friendly smile. "Matt has told me so much about you; it's finally nice to meet you." She reaches out pleasantly to shake my hand.

As my hand touches hers, my mind disappears into the blackness that takes me to somewhere else.

*I'm sitting in a kitchen. It's not the one where we currently live. This one is white, with a French themed décor. I'm sitting at the breakfast nook, with a cup of coffee in my hands, trying to decide what we should do today. As I take a sip from my cup, the object of my affection walks into the kitchen to join me.*

*I laugh at his lack of clothing. "Matt, why is it you always choose to join me like you're ready to do a Calvin Klein shoot?" I lightly tease him.*

*He's wearing nothing but black boxer briefs and every single one of his defined muscles is glistening from the sun shining in from the French doors to my right. He scratches his chest with his right arm, yawning, and starts stretching his left arm into the air as he's walking in my direction.*

*Once he's finally reached me, he gives me a light affectionate peck on the cheek, "Good morning, Em." Then he sits in the chair next to me.*

*He folds his arms on top of the counter in front of him, and then lays his head on them, facing in my direction. He still has sleepy eyes and is constantly blinking himself awake. It's hysterical to me that no matter how tired he is, he'll still wake up early in the morning to spend time with me.*

*Beaming with pride, I proceed to make small talk, "So, how are things with you and your girl?" I curiously want to know.*

*He sits there, quiet, without an answer, but his frown is obviously answering the question for him.*

*I reach over to touch his shoulder. "Did you guys break up again?" I know that their relationship could be compared to a Ping-Pong game. They were always breaking up, and then making up.*

*He takes in a very deep breath before saying, "Yup, we decided that maybe this time we should take a long enough break to let ourselves see other people." He ends the last of the sentence in a low whisper.*

*I sympathetically sigh, "Well, maybe this is a good thing. I do think you guys should see other people. You never know, you might end up finding the girl you really want to marry," I plead.*

*He lifts up his head while shaking it. "No Em, she's the one I plan to marry. I love her, she owns my heart and no matter how hard someone else tries, they'll never get it. I promise you Em, she's the one, and if it takes me giving her time to realize it then I'll just have my fun while I wait," he says, shrugging his shoulder.*

*My heart sinks a little knowing he's jumping to conclusions about the whole situation, but not wanting to be judgmental. "Are you sure that's what you want?"*

*He nods his head. "Yeah. I've already decided that's what I want to do." He finally perks up, "Don't worry Em,*

*I'll be careful. You're not going to unexpectedly become an aunt. She's the only one who is going to be popping out your nieces or nephews when the time comes." He smiles.*

*I hold out my arms to embrace him and upon wrapping himself to my body I say, "Whatever makes you happy Matt, just remember that I'm always here for you no matter what." I squeeze him harder to emphasize my meaning.*

I feel someone place a hand on my shoulder and it draws me from the memory. I don't know how long I was blacked out, but as I take in everyone's expressions they don't seem to realize that I was somewhere else. I let go of Laura's hand and fold my hands in front of my waist.

I see Trey finally make his way over to us saying. "Oh good, Matt's girlfriends are playing nice with each other. I thought I was going to need Julio's help in keeping super-model here from pounding the lights out of Laura." He hooks his thumb in my direction.

All our heads snap to Trey's and I give him my signature "I'm going to kick your ass" look before Kelly whacks him on the arm.

"What did I say?" he asks totally confused and rubs his shoulder.

"I'm sorry but I really have to go," I say, looking down at my phone to emphasize my point. "I have a meeting upstairs with Paul in 15 minutes."

Matt looks torn between Laura and me. "Oh yeah. Is it okay if you go alone to the meeting, Abigail? I want to catch up with Laura." He gives me a pleading look.

Even though I feel hurt right now with his plea, I know I have to ignore my jealousy and trust Matt. "Sure, I'll catch up with you later," I say to him, before turning to Laura to say, "It was a pleasure finally meeting you." I wave bye to her as I walk away.

She waves back, then turns to Matt and begins cheerfully speaking to him. I hate the feeling that is boiling inside me as I'm walking away from them. I have to force myself since I know that I'm leaving Matt with the only girl he's still harboring feelings for.

After my meeting with Paul to go over the security clearances for Matt and Julio, and going over all the details needed about when to arrive and how the race is run, I leave for my own hotel room taking time to try to relax.

It's been two hours since I left Matt and he still hasn't texted or called me and I'm starting to freak out. I kept checking my phone during the meeting in hopes that Matt would have changed his mind, but I was disappointed. Not knowing what the hell is going on, I finally force myself to push the negative feelings aside, and we start planning where we are going for dinner.

Finally choosing a restaurant on Fisherman's Wharf, Trey sends a text off to Matt to meet us there, but when we arrive he has a guest in tow. Great, she's even having dinner with us tonight. I tell myself to put my big girl panties on and play nice. The last thing I need is to go ape shit on her in the middle of a restaurant.

Kelly and Julio see the tension that is coursing through my body and between the two of them they try to lighten me up. But seeing her sitting next to Matt at our table drives me crazy. I want to know what is really going on between them.

They look like old friends just catching up, but knowing that this girl is the reason why Matt fought so hard to avoid another serious relationship, only fuels my anger.

I try to carb load for my race the next day, but my appetite was shot the minute I saw them walk in together. I want to go back to the hotel already. I end up having two glasses of red wine that I know I shouldn't have had, but I desperately needed them. As I ordered the first glass in hopes that it would help relax me, Matt tried reminding me that I had a race the next day, but I ended up snapping at him to shove it. After the look I gave him, he backed off, turning back to Laura to make conversation with her. Even the rest of the table didn't challenge me after that little scenario.

I ordered the second glass when I overheard Laura make a comment to Matt that since I was a supermodel it must be normal for me to always be so high strung. She even added that I must have been paying him really well for him to put up with my attitude. It only pissed me off even more when Matt didn't defend me.

If it weren't for Kelly grabbing my hand under the table reassuring me of her support, I would have walked away from the table. I was surprised with how well I was behaving about the situation. We finally wrapped up dinner and I couldn't get out of there fast enough. It looked like the hounds of hell were trailing me. At this point, I was proving just how high strung I could be, and I didn't give a shit anymore. To say I was jealous of this girl was a major understatement. I envied her. She owned something that I had wanted since the day I met Matt. His heart. With all the attention he was giving her, it was written all over his face how much she still had control over it.

We finally made it back to the hotel, minus Laura, thankfully, because even *I* wouldn't be able to control myself if she would have followed. Once inside the hotel room I couldn't control my temper anymore, especially with the wine coursing through me, giving me the courage I needed.

As I hear the door click behind the last person, I turn

around to face Matt. "So what the fuck is she to you now Matt? Are you guys back together?" I shout at him.

Everyone freezes up with a look of shock and awkwardness, not knowing whether to stick around for the show or walk away. But of course they choose to stay and take in the show. At this point I don't care if we have the whole city watching us. I wanted an answer for him... right now... right at this moment.

Matt's eyebrows draw in and you can tell he's trying really hard to control his temper. "I don't know what you're talking about *Abigail*," he claims, standing his ground in front of me.

"Oh, so now we're back to using *Abigail* again, are we? Fine, I know where I stand when it comes to that shit, but I'm telling you right now... *Matthew*. You better make up your fucking mind before you board that plane tomorrow, because I'm keeping my part of the deal. I refuse to become one of your fuck buddies, so... help... me... if you screw me over, I will walk out of your life, and never look back," I say as I stomp away from him, into my chosen room. I slam the door behind me with all the force that I can muster.

I lock the door right away and go straight to the bathroom so I can take a shower. It'll give me a reason to ignore anyone who tries to knock on the door.

I stand under the streaming hot water for a very long time, letting the heat of the water beating down on me take the tension away from my body, wishing it would take me down the drain with it.

After a while I finally start washing up, knowing that I have to get to bed. As I'm shaving my legs for the next day I notice something on my inner left thigh, up very close to my vagina. It's a reddish-purple mark.

My eyes go wide in shock when I realize what it is. It's a huge fucking hickey.

I groan in irritation, leaning against the cool tile of the shower for support. I realize no matter how much I try to push him away, my body will always have a way of knowing that it belongs to Matt. I'm fucking screwed.

# Chapter 32

I WAKE UP the day of the race, feeling physically and mentally like shit. I hadn't gotten much sleep, both from nerves and from thinking about the night before. I wanted so badly to go to Matt and just curl up next to him, letting his arms take away the pain I was feeling in my heart, but of course I didn't. He was the reason why I was feeling like this.

He didn't try coming into my room either. I would have expected him to try knocking on my door and pleading his case, but it didn't happen. Which worried me more. Instead, the hotel room ended up being very quiet, leaving me to my thoughts for most of the night. The gang decided to go out, where I do not know, I never asked. I did hear them walk back into the room at around two a.m., probably from round two of Matt's birthday weekend.

At around five a.m. I heard a knock at the door and although I was expecting it, my body tensed up in anticipation of Matt.

I was surprised when I opened the door to see a sleep deprived Kelly, who looked like she'd had another bad night. Letting her in, I shut the door behind her.

"Hey sweetie, you ready for your big day?" she says to me almost in a whisper. I know she's doing it more for herself.

I chuckle and respond, "Not really, but I have no choice, right?"

I begin to look for the outfit I had planned on wearing and get dressed, while Kelly walks over to the bed and sits against the headboard. Taking a pillow in her arms, she looks at me with an interested look. "What do you mean you have no choice, I thought you wanted to do this?"

I automatically correct her analysis of my response. "I want to run this race, but my body is not feeling so good right now. It actually feels how you look," I say, giggling at her.

She lets out a small groan. "Trust me, last night didn't help. We ended up going downstairs to the bar. I'm still paying for Friday night, so I should have just stayed away," she says, forcing a smile on her face.

Her smile turns to a frown a couple of seconds later. "David told me you took care of me Friday night. I never got a chance to thank you by the way," she says, tightening her arms around the pillow.

I walk over to the bed and sit in front of her, looking her in the eyes. "You would have done the same thing if it were me, so you don't have to thank me at all."

She looks down at her knees. "But I feel really bad about interrupting what was happening between you and Matt," she whispers. "I finally remembered most of the night yesterday and I'm really sorry."

My eyes go wide, wondering how in the world she remembered what she saw, as wasted as she was. "I'm glad you interrupted us, if not, a lot more would have happened, and I have a feeling I would have a lot more regret than I already do this weekend."

We both sigh and sit there looking at each other sympathetically. I guess more for myself than anyone else.

"How far did it really go?" she asks with her mischievous smile.

This makes me chuckle at her, knowing that she's not going to like my response. "The usual tease and feel," I say to her, watching her face turn to a scowl. "You sort of stopped us right as we were about to start the act. I guess it's not meant to happen if people keep interrupting us."

Kelly throws her hands up in the air in exasperation and groans again. "I swear, you guys dance around having sex like a pair of animals trying to decide if they've found the right mate."

I laugh at her analysis of Matt and me. Although she did have a point about the animal part, every time Matt came near me my body responded like a female in heat. Damn my traitorous body.

We both hear another knock on the door and I know who it is. Since it wasn't him the first time, it definitely has to be him this time, so I get up to go open the door.

The first thing I notice about Matt as he walks in is that he looks worse than Kelly, and I can tell he hasn't had a shower. He's wearing only his basketball shorts and nothing else. That's surprising since his normal choice of sleepwear is usually only his boxer briefs. But as I take in his smell, I scrunch my nose. He reeks of the alcohol leaving his pores. When he sees me, his eyes become hooded as he takes in my body. He eyes me from head to toe with a light smile.

Even in the condition that he's in, my body instantly responds and I want to run my hands all over his body. I tense up and keep my hands on the door. I grip it for dear life, trying to keep myself from reaching out to him. I look over at Kelly trying to distract myself as she's standing up from the bed. Her face lights up and she just smiles at me, as if she is proving her earlier assessment of us.

Dammit.

Pushing my negative thoughts aside, I decide to head into the living room instead, following Kelly. I notice Julio ready and reading the newspaper at the breakfast bar with a cup of coffee and all the usual goodies that I eat before a race.

He hears me walk in and looks up from his newspaper. "Matt arranged for your breakfast to arrive early this morning so you'd have time to digest it," he says in an approving way.

"Of course he would, that's his job, he's my assistant, remember?" I say sarcastically, taking a piece of toast with peanut butter on it.

His face shows concern. "What's really going on with the both of you Abigail?" he bravely asks.

"I don't know. I thought that he was over her and was willing to give us a chance, and bam, she shows up, making him push me aside for her."

Julio tilts his head to the side, while folding the newspaper. "Is that what you think he did? Push you aside?" he curiously asks.

I stop to take in his question. "Well, the kiss she gave him when she saw him proved that she still has something simmering for him. I know I wouldn't go up to Bill and kiss him like that if I saw him again. Then he blew off the meeting with Paul and brought her to dinner with us," I say, stating my case.

I sigh. "I don't know. I just finally grew happy thinking that we were going to take the next step, but I guess I jumped to conclusions."

Julio's face grows serious. "Look Abigail," he begins, "I'm a guy, and so I can at least tell you this. The way that boy is with you, proves that you're more than a casual fling. I think the both of you are too afraid to admit your feelings for each other and it's not helping in this situation."

I think back to the other night. "Julio, how much did you see the other night?" I ask him.

He smiles. "Enough to know that you guys need to take care of that craving soon before it drives you insane," he says chuckling, and then he corrects himself. "Don't worry, I didn't actually see anything, but you are a very vocal girl when it comes to praising him," he says before standing up.

I stand there blushing all over my body, straight down to my toes.

As I'm finishing my breakfast, I notice Matt stepping out of my room with only a towel wrapped around his waist, his body still a bit damp from his shower. He walks over to his bag, picks it up and takes it back into the room with him before he shuts the door again. I swear he must do these things on purpose to torture me.

Great, all I want to do now is stomp my ass over to that room, walk in, lock the door behind me, and prove to Matt that he doesn't need Laura anymore. But instead I sit there trying to calm the inferno of want burning through my veins. No, I don't need this shit today. I need to focus on my run, that's what is important right now.

An hour later, Matt, Julio, and I are piling into the elevator heading downstairs to the start line. I know it's going to be about an hour of waiting around, then no more than another three to finish the race. We leave the rest of the gang to catch up on their sleep. Right now I'm so jealous of them. If it wasn't for all the adrenaline and nerves coursing through my body, I would be falling over next to them from lack of sleep.

As we near the VIP tent at the start line, I begin to get excited and can't wait to start and just get it over with. My nerves are scattered everywhere so I start listening to music, hoping it will help calm and relax me.

Usually I wouldn't listen to music before a race, in fear that I would run the battery down on my phone. Since I refuse to run without music I chose to use a shuffle this time, so I won't have the weight of my phone on my arm. So here I was losing myself to the bass pounding in my ears.

It also helped to distract and shut out the eyes that were staring at me as I waited around. I was standing in a tent with a bunch of elite runners who do this for a living, but the only reason I was getting the same treatment as them was because of my celebrity status. It made me feel like I wasn't worthy to stand here with them, so I needed to find a happy zone and focus on that. I was here for my own purpose. I wanted to beat that three and a half hour mark, and with these hills that San Francisco is famous for, I knew I had a challenge ahead of me.

As it grew near the start time, the elite runners began to exit the tent to go warm up and I followed to watch them line up. On the way, Matt couldn't resist giving me the usual advice for the race.

"Now remember, Abigail, you have to pace yourself. You're starting after the elite runners, in the second corral with very fast runners. Don't try to keep up with the starting racers' pace, they always start off too fast from the adrenaline and then burn out at the wall." The wall being the famous 20-mile mark I was not looking forward to.

"Remember to breathe and keep to yourself. The good thing is since you're starting early there won't be too many people in front of you to make your way around. This is an advantage to your time, which will help once you hit those hills. Just remember, one step at a time when you're taking the hills. Don't push yourself too hard, or you'll burn out. Push your body forward, like you practiced and be careful coming down them, you don't want to injure yourself going too fast."

He looks around at the crowd. "Let yourself get lost in the crowd cheering you on, it will help distract you, since I can't be there with you," he says with a look of disappointment. "But, I'll be waiting for you here at the finish line as you cross it, so remember not to keep me waiting too long," he says with a smile.

I feel Julio touch my arm and begin to push me in the direction of the start line. I give him one last hug, before thanking him for training with him. Then I look over at Matt, and he also gives me a hug, but he doesn't let go of me right away. He just holds me tightly to his body, and says into my ear, "Good luck, beautiful," before kissing me below my ear, sending a jolt through my body.

I hand Matt my phone as they both leave me to walk the rest of the way by myself since they can't actually stand with me in the line. Instead, I see them make their way to the other side of the gates where I can still clearly see them. I adjust my shuffle to my body, plugging in my earphones, and start to lightly bounce in place, pumping myself up to start.

As I hear the first gunshot that signals the start for the elite runners, I begin to get very nervous. After a couple of seconds, they move my corral up and my nerves are streaming rapidly through my blood. Since I've chosen to stay to the outside of the group, I'm closest to the crowd and I begin to hear people saying my name, cheering me on. I can't resist smiling and it takes all my nerves away. I get my body ready and when I hear the gun-shot, I take off with my group.

We leave the start line, running through the streets that are surrounded by the historic buildings of Union Square. We turn the corner of Montgomery and Post, and the excitement of the crowd takes me away to another world. It stays like this and I notice what Matt meant by the other runners starting off fast. I can feel myself trying to push harder to keep up with them, and it's only the beginning.

As we hit mile four, I allow myself to slow down and take in the scenic view of the ocean to my right. Even though they start to pull ahead of me a little, I just keep myself focused on the music entering my ears and distract myself as best as I can with the crowd lining the course.

It isn't until after the fifth mile that I begin to feel the first hill sneaking up on me. I knew it was fairly close to the beginning of the course, but I don't actually see it, so much as feel it under my feet as I climb the elevation. My body starts to slow down from the force that I have to put into placing one foot in front of the other. I simply follow Matt's advice and push my body to lean forward. Those damn training hills he put me through have nothing on this sneaky bastard. At least I saw them up ahead as I was running them and was prepared. This one sneaks up on your ass.

Then just as fast as I feel the pull, I begin to feel the downgrade of the hill and try to slow myself down. It doesn't last too long because as I start enjoying the break, I feel the increase again. I have to keep chanting to myself: Earn the downhill, earn the downhill, it's just up ahead. If you don't get up and over this hill, you won't get to go down. I hope that it will distract me completely.

It continues like this for the next hour and my body starts to feel like it wants to give up. I see more and more mile markers whizz by me, helping me to keep going. I'm more than halfway into the race and I'm keeping a really good pace. I start to feel my infamous wall coming up ahead as I've passed the marker for the 19th mile. But I'm surprised when I see my friends standing in plain view with signs up ahead.

Kelly's sign says, *"Kick this race's ass Abi."*

Trey is holding a sign saying, *"Earn your fucking beer supermodel."*

But, the one that makes me almost stop in my tracks and brings a huge smile across my face is David's. He's holding a sign that says, *"Don't give up beautiful. I'm waiting for you!"*

I just wave to my friends with watery eyes, and push past my wall.

I've timed my playlist to start playing songs that will help push me. *Disturbia* starts to blast into my ears and the beat is what I need right now as I dig deep and push my body. I slowly start to increase my speed and watch the signs go by one by one. I finally reach the 23rd mile and I give it my all, knowing I've only got three more miles to go and I could easily run this with my eyes closed. I turn down my shuffle, allowing the screaming crowd to push me to the end.

As the course starts to become a straight line I dig even deeper, begging my legs to pick up the pace and then I see the crowd start to become fuller. Knowing the finish line is within reaching distance, I start sprinting the last 1.2 miles. At this point my legs are burning, my chest is digging for air, but I ignore the pain and tell myself it will all be worth it when I'm done.

Then I see it, the finish line clock. It reads 3:23:32 and I'm thinking to myself, there is no fucking way I'm letting this race beat me, and try to speed my legs up even faster. As I'm crossing the finish line I see Matt and Julio on the other side and I keep running past the guys in tuxedos and straight into

Matt's body, forcing him to catch me as I jump up on to him. Wrapping my legs around his waist, one arm around his neck, I throw my other fist up into the air in triumph. I'm beaming from ear to ear with my smile, with the crowd cheering loudly around me. I look down at Matt and he's just as proud of me as I am myself. I wrap my other arm around his neck hugging him for dear life, still wrapped around his body. I don't want him to ever let me go.

I finally feel someone tap me on the shoulder and I turn to face one of the guys in the tuxedos, holding a finisher's medal in his hands. I unwrap my legs and arms from around Matt, as he lowers me to stand on the ground. Once the tuxedo guy is done hooking the medal over my neck, he places a kiss on my lips saying, "Congratulations on your race, Abigail."

Matt isn't too happy about this and glares at the guy ready to kill him, making Julio pull him back a little distance. I ignore Matt and say to the guy, "Thank you," as I hug him and give him a big smile.

Take that, Matt. How does it feel to see me kissing someone else? I think to myself as I start to walk away, going to get my well-deserved snacks with the other runners.

As I'm chugging my chocolate milk I see a women walk right up to me.

"Ms. Adams, my name is Rebecca. I'm with Women's Running World magazine and we would love to do an interview of you to feature in an upcoming issue," she says while holding her card out to me.

Matt takes it and looks down at it, concentrating on the card in his hand, but I keep looking at her, considering her offer before saying, "I would love to."

She smiles and says, "Good. I'll keep in touch. I have your assistant's information that I got from Paul," she says looking at Matt, "but if you need to contact me sooner my cell number is also on the card. Thank you, and congratulations on your qualifying time. I can't wait to see you run Boston," she states and shakes my hand before disappearing into the crowd.

This is when it hits me. "I made my time!" I shout at Matt, making him and Julio laugh loudly.

I had totally forgotten about my time as I crossed the finish line. We finally leave the crowd and make our way back to our hotel room where the cheering trio is waiting for me when I walk through the door.

Kelly throws herself at me, giving me a tight hug. Then Trey comes next, picking me up as usual, swinging me around in a circle. I look over at David and smile remembering his sign.

"Thanks for the signs you guys, I really needed them at that moment," I say with a thankful smile.

That must have reminded Trey of my beer because he runs over to the mini fridge pulling out my favorite beer, twists the cap off, and hands me the bottle. I take it from him and instantly take a drink, savoring the taste. Damn right I earned this beer, I think to myself as I groan into the bottle.

Everyone laughs and they start drinking along with me. After finishing my beer and taking my ice bath for my legs, I finally take the nap that my body is so desperately craving. The only thing missing is Matt's body next to mine as I drift into peaceful sleep.

# Chapter 33

I END UP sleeping until early afternoon, my body finally catching up with its much-needed sleep. When I wake up, I take a shower and get ready for our early dinner. As we are heading to the exclusive restaurant where Matt arranged for us to eat, I keep beaming from the excitement of the day. I'm so happy. I feel like nothing in the world could bring me down at this moment. However, that all changes as we enter the restaurant. I see Laura standing near the hostess podium and she lights up when she sees us enter.

I stop walking and Matt crashes into me from behind. I whip my head around to glare at him with a very confused look. He didn't mention inviting her, what is she doing here?

Julio walks past us and up to the hostess to inform her we are ready to be seated, probably trying to get us to our table as fast as possible to avoid a confrontation at the entrance.

Matt sympathetically looks at me. "I'm sorry. I forgot to mention that I invited her yesterday when I had lunch with her," he says, looking frantically from her to me. "If you want, I'll ask her to leave?"

I look back at her and she's still beaming, looking straight at Matt. "No. I'd hate to be a high-strung bitch and ask your guest to leave," I say to him, allowing our little group to be the only ones to hear my response.

Kelly steps up beside me, hooking her arm into mine, tugging me forward to follow the hostess as she leads us to the table. I had requested that Matt reserve a private room for us so we could have enough space for all of us and not draw a crowd if we decided to get loud, as we usually did.

Once we've reached our table, Kelly as usual, takes a seat beside me. But as I'm walking I tug on Trey's arm and pull him to the seat next to me, leaving Matt across from me and confused. It only makes Laura happier since it leaves him to take the seat next to her.

I just sit there, ignoring my menu and stare daggers at Matt. He notices and tries to rub my leg with his. When I feel him, I end up kicking him in the shin causing him to jerk his leg up, hitting his knee against the table. The glasses on the table begin to rattle and everyone is wondering why.

Kelly looks at me curiously and I whisper into her ear about what just happened, causing her to throw her head back, laughing loudly. Matt just glares at Kelly and she sticks her tongue out at him, still leaving everyone else at the table wondering what the heck is going on. I finally allow myself to focus on the menu, feeling better about the situation in front of me.

"So Abigail, I heard about your qualifying time this morning. Congratulations by the way. But I saw the time online and noticed that you only made it by like seven minutes. I thought with all the hype they were giving you,

you'd be a lot faster," she says in a condescending tone, before she takes a sip of water.

I sit there praying she chokes on her water. "I was only aiming to qualify, not run with the elite. All the hype they gave me wasn't as big as I thought. Being that I didn't actually start with the elite, it shouldn't take a brain surgeon to figure out I wasn't one."

Obviously she doesn't like my response. "Yeah, but with the weeks leading up to the race, that's all they kept talking about, you aiming to make the qualifying time. I thought it was kind of unfair how it outshone the important runners."

I want to jump over the table and rip her hair out. Why in the hell am I letting this short little bitch get to me? As I'm about to give her a piece of my mind David speaks up.

"The whole point of Abigail running this race was for her to have a chance to qualify for Boston, which she did," he forcefully states. "If everyone else blew it out of proportion against her will, she has no control over that."

At this moment the waiter shows up to take our order and I'm thankful for it. As we are placing our orders, I'm forced to sit there, ignoring Laura making googly eyes at Matt. Needing to distract myself, I turn to face Kelly to talk about the race. I tell her about the hills and how I kept chanting to myself, and I notice that Laura keeps interrupting us by adding her two cents as well. Like, "Oh yeah, I thought those hills would kill me too." And, "I love how the crowd comes out and cheers everyone on." It's like she was purposely paying attention to my conversation and trying to outdo me.

I look at Matt, wondering why he doesn't tell her to shut the hell up, but he's looking very uncomfortable, almost as if he wants to bolt for the door. Normally I would have felt sorry for him, but being that he's the reason why I'm stuck in this situation I simply sit there glaring at him.

The food finally arrives allowing me to focus on my food and giving me a reason to keep my mouth shut. The guys, including Julio, who I insisted last night start sitting at the table along with us, start talking about football. Since it was something that I hear every day at home, I decided to shut them out.

"Whoa Abigail, that is a lot of food. Aren't you worried about your weight if you eat like that?" Laura asks, eyeing my steak and lobster. "I thought models rarely eat and when they do, they stick to salads?"

Matt finally speaks up to defend me by saying. "Abigail runs a lot, and whatever she eats gets burned off anyways."

Laura frowns at Matt. "Wow, lucky you. I have to constantly watch what I eat, but of course not everyone is as lucky as you to have that body. Are you sure it's only the running that keeps the weight off?" she asks, glancing over at Matt.

I take a deep breath, using every ounce of control, as I grab for my glass of water. Trey snaps at her, "Shut the hell up Laura. Just 'cause you want to get back into Matt's pants doesn't mean Abigail is wanting the same."

I practically choke on my water, making me cough for air. Kelly slaps me on the back to help me catch my breath. The only thing that's been in his pants is my hand. It was nice of Trey to stand up for me, but he knows damn well how badly my body really wanted Matt. By the way he worded it, he made it seem like I had already gotten in.

This obviously upsets Laura and she stands up. "I have to go to the bathroom, I'll be right back," she snaps at us, throwing her napkin on the table.

By the look on her face, I really doubt she has to pee, but I don't blame her for wanting to get away from this table at this moment, that was exactly what I wanted to do, but she beat me to it. What pisses me off is that Matt stands up after her and begins to follow Laura away from the table without saying a word.

We all sit there at the table in silence for a couple of minutes trying to avoid bringing up what just happened. Then I realize that I *really* do have to pee. I had constantly kept drinking water to keep the hurtful words that I wanted to throw at Laura from spewing from my mouth. Plus, the waiter does his job so well. He kept refilling my glass. Great, now it's going to look like I'm purposely trying to follow them.

I give it a couple of more minutes, but after squirming in my seat, I'm about to pee my pants. I inform Julio that I have to go to the bathroom and he nods his head and stands up with me, making our way to the bathroom after asking our waiter in which direction to walk.

As we begin to near the doors I see a small corner leading to what must be a storage room and instantly spot Matt and Laura closely facing each other. They're clearly still speaking, but I see Laura suddenly reach up to wrap her arms around Matt's neck, pulling him down towards her.

As Matt allows himself to be pulled down, my breathing hitches to a stop. My heart feels like it has stopped beating completely and has dropped to the pit of my stomach. I simply stand there, paralyzed, not being able to move at all. When I see their lips meet my body feels like it's been completely drained of life. I gasp without realizing that I had made a sound with it.

I'm quickly pulled back. My body is being forced to move, and the only thing I can do is allow it to be led away. When I'm finally able to bring myself back to reality, I feel Julio's large body next to mine, his arm wrapped around my waist, walking alongside me.

I realize he's leading me away, and the shock has finally abandoned by body. I start to understand that he's leading me back to our table and I already know I don't want to be here any longer.

At this point I forget all about needing to go pee and when we reach our table I start to silently cry, letting the tears trickle down my cheeks. I urgently start looking for my purse under the table, grabbing it, ready to bolt to the door.

Kelly takes one look at me. "What's going on Abigail?"

I shake my head, sniffling my tears up, and turn to head out of the restaurant. We leave them there, wondering what is wrong with me.

As we reach outside, Julio is about to call for the hired car, but I stop him, stating that they're going to need it to get back and I start to flag down a taxi. I'm relieved when one stops right away. We climb in, Julio informs the taxi driver of our hotel and we make our way there.

A minute later I start to hear about a teenage dream singing from my purse and I sit there ignoring it. It stops and then starts up again, this time Julio takes the purse from me, digging around until he finds it. He pushes the ignore button on the top of the phone and then promptly turns it off, before placing it back into my purse. I was so grateful he did. Right now Laura was the one enjoying Matt's teenage dream, and the last thing I wanted was to be reminded of it.

# Chapter 34

I'M IN MY hotel room. I had enclosed myself in my room because I really didn't want to be around anyone right now. I should be out there celebrating with all of them. However, I didn't want to. I had gotten my qualifying time for Boston, but deep down inside my body was numb, and lifeless. I had no reason to smile right now, let alone celebrate. I had no reason to want to drink. I actually didn't have a reason to want to do anything.

So here I am with a box of tissues, squeezing the life out of a pillow, and cried out to a point where my eyes burn.

Seeing Matt kissing Laura this afternoon tore me apart. Like he had reached inside my heart and yanked it out, without any warning, twisting the life out of it until it died. Which is exactly what it felt like happened.

Right when I thought I should finally listen to my heart, he gave me a reason to shut it up all over again. It forced me to rebuild my walls against him. Why was I so stupid? I should have just listened to my gut when it said he was going to use me and throw me aside like he did every other girl who wasn't her. I might not have been thrown aside just yet, but seeing him with her meant just the same. He had made his decision when he'd followed her. I was the ignorant one to think he'd changed.

I hear a knock at my door and I ignore it. I just want to be left alone, in my lonely world of misery. Who knows what they're thinking right now, but I don't care. I hear the knock again, this time the opening of the door follows immediately after it. I stiffen up, hiding my face deeper into the pillow not wanting to see who it is. I had made sure to close the curtains and turn off all the lights when I got back. I enclosed myself in total darkness, the equivalent to my feelings.

"Abi, sweetie. Julio told me what happened," Kelly voices her concern as she walks over to me.

I simply lay there, sniffling into the pillow, refusing to give in. "I'm fine, Kelly. Go back with David and have fun."

I feel her sit on the side of the bed next to me, and then her hand running through my hair. I can feel the comfort radiating from her right now, and it's exactly what I'm craving besides Matt's arms. His arms always have a way of making me feel so much better, no matter what, but being that he is the reason that I'm like this, it's the last thing I'm going to get right now.

Kelly stays quiet, rubbing my hair, then my back, sitting there in silence just letting me cry my silent tears. With the motion of her hand moving up and down, it comforts me, sending me into a deep sleep. Exactly what my body was fighting, but it lost the battle the minute she began to comfort me.

When I wake up again, it must be the next morning because Kelly is once again next to me, but she's in pajamas, and has a tray with breakfast items on it. She places it on the bedside table and looks at me. Her lips are flat and she has a saddened look in her eyes. She doesn't say anything, but she sits next to me, while I force my body to sit up. My body aches and it feels like I have knots all over it. I don't know if it's from me pushing myself yesterday or from all the crying.

"Hey, why don't we try to feed you ok?" she whispers loud enough for me to hear. "You didn't eat anything at lunch after that bitch made her comment, and I'm pretty sure you skipped dinner," she says.

I shake my head. "I'm not hungry right now, just tired," I mumble.

"Sweetie, you have to try to eat. Even a piece of toast, then I'll leave you alone," she begs.

I simply lie back down, turning my back to her, hugging the pillow again.

I hear her sigh, and then feel her get up from the bed and walk out of the room. She quietly closes the door behind her, leaving me to my darkness once again as I fall back to sleep.

A couple of hours later when I awaken, I finally get up off the bed and head for the bathroom. I turn on the light and the brightness makes me flinch. I stand there with my eyes shut, slowly trying to get them to adjust to the light.

When I'm finally able to open them again, I see myself in the mirror and I look like shit. My face is all blotchy, my eyes are swollen, bloodshot red, and my hair is in disarray. I lean on the bathroom counter with both arms and let my head slump forward, not having the fight left inside me to do anything else. Knowing that I have to leave soon, I finally push myself away from the counter and go to turn on the shower.

I manage to get myself in the shower, dressed, and ready very quickly. My body might feel numb, but my mind is still slightly working. Since obviously I'm not in the mood to impress anyone, my hair goes into a ponytail, I've thrown on my hoodie, and dug through my purse for my go-to hide my eyes sunglasses. Once I've packed everything up and double-checked to make sure I haven't forgotten anything, I head to the door of my room.

As I exiting the room, I see everyone's head whip in my direction, and they are all staring at me. They all have a face of wonder and you can tell they desperately want to ask me what the fuck is going on. But I just ignore them, hand my suitcase over to Julio when he grabs for it, and head straight to the door with my head held high refusing to show them my weakness.

I see Matt walking over to me, looking puzzled, like he wants to speak to me, and I hold my hand up to stop him. "No, don't. We're already late and I don't want us to miss our flight," I snap at him, as I keep walking straight out of the door.

I lead my little entourage down the hallway, looking over to Julio. "Do you mind if we take the stairs down? I don't feel like riding in an elevator full of people right now," I say loud enough for them all to hear.

He shrugs his shoulders and nods a yes.

Trey gives me a look like I've lost my mind and hurries over to me before we reach the doors leading to the stairs.

"Abigail, what's going on? You have us all worried. What the fuck happened at the restaurant that has your pant-ies in a twist?" he desperately asks.

Julio steps up in front of Trey and lightly shoves him

back with his arm. "Leave her alone. If she wants to talk to you guys about it she'll talk about it, but right now she needs to be left alone. Got it?" he says, facing everyone behind us, but stopping to stare down Matt.

Knowing that this is the first time Julio has ever butted in when it comes to my personal life, everyone nods their head and I open the door leading the way to the stairs. Julio follows me and grabs my arm, linking it with his. He looks at me with a smile and says, "I read how you ended up in the hospital, and the last thing I need is you tumbling down the stairs on my watch."

This earns him a smile and chuckle. "I'm wearing Chucks not heels this time," I joke but allow him to lead me down the flight of 16 floors. Once we've reached the bottom, he leads me through the lobby, guiding me through the crowd of people.

"I've checked us out and the car is already waiting," I hear Matt say to me as I walk up to stand next to Kelly. I just nod my head and grab Kelly's hand with mine to give it a light squeeze.

"You good now?"

I take a deep breath. "Never better. Let's go, I want to get home already," I say, walking away with Julio.

As soon as we board the plane, I immediately head to the back of the plane again, taking the back corner seat next to the window. Matt tries to follow, but David grabs his arms and shakes his head at him in warning. Matt being still con-founded about the whole situation, heads to the front of the plane, and takes a seat next to Trey, leaving me to wallow in my misery with Julio sitting next to me.

How amusing that the last time I sat in this seat, it was a whole different situation. The way over here was when I had decided that I was going to fight to have something with Matt, now I was fighting to keep him at a distance all over again. As the plane starts to taxi the runway I close my eyes as I lean my head against the window, taking in the noise of the jets.

As soon as I feel the plane climb into the air, I look out the window and allow the clouds to carry me away. Funny how the last time I was sitting in this seat, I was feeling like I was floating alongside these clouds, not flying through them.

Two hours later, we are landing, disembarking the plane, and on our way home. The car ride was just as awkward, nobody really spoke, and I kept silent.

Upon arriving home, I practically jump out of the SUV, running into the house, and headed straight to my room. I stand with my back against the closed door, wondering how in the world my life was able to turn upside down all over again.

I can hear them talking through the door and no matter how badly I wanted to go back outside and lie to them by telling them I was fine, I really couldn't. I just stand there with my ear against the door, thanking whoever built this house for not putting in thicker doors.

"What's wrong with her? Why is she acting like this?" Trey shouts at Matt.

"How the fuck am I supposed to know if she doesn't let me talk to her?"

"Leave her alone, Matt. You've done enough damage to her already," I hear Kelly snarl at him.

"Kelly, maybe we should head home," I hear David say.

"Does this have anything to do with Laura?" I barely hear Matt say, almost as if he is trying to keep his voice down while asking.

There's a silence and I'm frantic for someone to speak again, but they don't.

Instead I hear footsteps in the hallway leading to my room. I immediately tense up and walk away from the door, heading straight into the bathroom instead. As I'm washing my face I see Matt from the corner of my eye standing in the doorframe and he looks as miserable as I feel at this moment.

He's standing there with his hands in the pockets of his jeans, and his head hung, facing the floor. I stand there against the bathroom counter, staring into the air of nothing, refusing to acknowledge him right now.

"It's not what you think, Abigail."

Why is it that line always comes up in the emotional roller coaster of my life? It seems ever since I've woken up from my coma my life has been revolving around those six words. Do they really know what I'm thinking to be able to say that line to me all the time?

"It doesn't matter Matt, I saw you at the restaurant with her. You *chose* her," I say listlessly. "I gave you a choice, and obviously by the way you guys were making up for lost time, you made your decision. You must be really fond of bathroom hallways," I throw at him.

My heart feels like it's shattered into a million pieces as I say it and at this point I really don't want to bend down and pick them up. I'd rather leave them there to be stepped all over. I'm done trying to piece it back together. My heart might have not have been in it with Bill, but knowing what he did hurt just as much. Now, actually seeing Matt with Laura in that hallway, that hurts ten times worse.

I'm still staring at the shower curtain in front of me expecting it to magically do something spectacular, so I don't notice when Matt suddenly moves to stand in front of me. He takes my face into his hands forcing me to look at him. At first I try to yank my face from his hands, but he gently continues to hold it, keeping his eyes on me.

"No beautiful, I never chose her," he angrily conveys to me.

It pisses me off that he would lie to my face. "I know what I saw at the restaurant, Matt. I saw you with her near the bathroom. If you holding her...kissing her, isn't choosing her... then I must be the biggest fucking idiot in the world," I throw at him.

He shakes his head. "I know you saw us, and I'm sorry about that. I promise you Abigail, it's not how you saw. She kissed me, I never kissed her back, and the minute it happened I knew it was wrong. It was wrong because it wasn't you, she can never be you.

"I told right her right there and then that there would never be anything between us ever again. I tried coming after you, but it was too late, you were already gone." His gorgeous eyes are glassy as he's trying to hold back his tears. "I've fucked up one too many times with you, but I wasn't going to fuck up again. When we got back to the hotel room, Julio wouldn't let me anywhere near your door. He was really taking his job seriously last night," he explains to me.

The tears that I thought were all dried up begin to stream down my face once again. "I love you," I say as I drop my head in submission. "I love you so much it hurts, it's tearing my heart apart. I can't keep playing these games with you anymore Matt. I just can't," I desperately cry.

He breathes a sigh of relief, and lifts my head back up so I'm looking directly at him. "Oh, beautiful. I love you too," he whispers emphatically into my face. "I've loved you since that first night you showed up on my doorstep. That night I knew you were mine and I'm never letting you go," he fiercely says.

He kisses me, feeding my body the drug it's been craving. His lips feel so soft and warm as I savor the feeling of his kiss, wanting to hold onto it forever. It's soft at first, it conveys a message, almost as if he's making sure he shows me how he feels. Then he forces my mouth open with his tongue and I meet him with a force of hunger. He tilts our heads, giving me more access and I drown in his kiss. I grab onto his shirt with my hands, pulling myself closer to him.

I can feel his fingers begin to lightly dig into my hair, almost as if he's afraid I would pull away, but right now that's the last thing I want to do. I pull at his waist, proving that I'm not going anywhere. I need to feel him closer to me. I need to feel the warmth of his body next to mine that I've been craving.

As our tongues begin to explore each other, our hands begin to explore each other's bodies. I lift up Matt's shirt, running my hands on his back, feeling the ripples of his muscles and the softness of his skin. His hands begin to lower to my sides, hesitant to touch me. Then he runs one of them on the inside of my shirt, with the other gabbing my ass.

He pulls away from me, intensely looking into my eyes. "I... Choose... You... Beautiful. There will never be anyone else. You are my life, my world, my everything, and you'd have to kill me in order for me to let you go."

I kiss him again, needing to know that he really means it. From the way he's kissing me at this moment I believe every word of what he's just said. Fireworks could have gone off from the force of his kiss. His hands immediately go to my legs, picking me up, and wrapping them around his waist. I feel him begin to carry me out of the bathroom. He walks over to my bed, placing me on it, he looks down at me with desire in his eyes, and I want him just as badly.

"I need you beautiful, I need you so fucking bad," he says to me before lowering himself on me to kiss me again. "Whoever tries to stop me right now will have to pry me off you, because I don't plan on stopping this time."

Between our hungry kisses we somehow manage to remove our clothing, ripping them off, not caring how they end up. As each piece of clothing comes off, the reality of having him next to me, skin on skin, overpowers me. I need him with a passion that overcomes my ability to take things slowly.

When we are both finally naked, I think that things are going to start quickly, but Matt surprises me by saying, "No beautiful, we've both waited so long for this, I'm going to enjoy every inch of your body first."

He begins by kissing me on the ear, taking the lobe, sucking it into his mouth, and sending a wave of pleasure all the way down my body. Then he trails kisses down my neck, lightly nipping at my skin, lowering his mouth to the valley between my breasts. He's torturing me all over again like he did in the hotel room in Chicago, and it's killing me.

After quickly sucking on each one of my nipples, making me almost come from the desire speeding through my veins, he keeps going lower, making sure to remind me just how ticklish I am on my stomach. But what stops my giggling is when he reaches my thighs. He spreads them with his hands, running his hands down my legs, to my ankles.

I look down at him as he's wickedly smiling at me. "I always thought you had the sexiest legs and ass. I could easily stare at them all day. I love how you end up ahead of me in a race, giving me a chance to stare at you from behind. It always gave me a reason to catch up to you when you got too far ahead of me."

I giggle from the sensation his touch is giving me as he runs his palms up my legs. The feeling sends a shiver up and down them as he lowers his head to trail his lips along the path that his hands just took. I close my eyes and delight in the feeling of his mouth along my legs. The heat of his tongue slowly imprints his breath as he makes his way up them.

When he's reached the center of my body, he places both his hands under my ass, giving it a tight squeeze before he lifts it so I can feel his mouth on my core. My breath stops as I feel his tongue on my inner lips taking in his fill, my hands automatically going to my bedsheets, grabbing them by the handful. His tongue is teasing and torturing me, making me want more from him. I throw my head back, lifting my hips to meet his mouth, giving us both more pleasure. My breathing becomes frantic, my moans get louder with every lick he gives me, and my body begins to tighten up.

"Relax beautiful, let it go," I hear Matt say to me, and that's when the dam breaks loose. My body feels like it explodes from the force of me coming into his mouth and I scream his name as I shoot up to the stars. He keeps devouring my pussy, making my body convulse over and over again.

As I finally come down from the blow of the explosion, I feel him crawling slowly up my body, kissing his way up until he's completely covering me with his own. His sexy eyes are looking down into mine and I lose myself all over again. I feel him enter my body, making me gasp from his hard cock entering me, and all I can do is hold onto him with my arms, not wanting to let him go.

He starts moving inside me, taking it slowly at first, then he begins to pick up speed, and I wrap my legs around his thighs holding on for dear life. My nails start digging into his shoulders, urging him on, wanting more of him. I can feel the warmth of his breath on my neck and it feels wonderful.

I lower my hands to dig into his ass wanting him to go faster, to thrust harder. With each thrust forward I can feel him hit me against the heat of my core, and he grips my ass as he lifts it to match each one of his thrusts making me feel him all the way to my cervix. My body begins to feel the build again and this time I can't control it and let go, once again repeatedly screaming Matt's name as fireworks explode behind my eyes.

I feel him thrust a couple more times inside me before throws his head back yelling, "Oh God, Abigail!" He says it so loud that I think even the neighbors might have heard.

We both lay there, trying to catch our breath, and I can feel the sweat all over our bodies, blending together. He lowers his head and kisses me again, before saying, "I told you I keep my promises."

I smile up at him and softly laugh. This is one promise I am glad he kept. With a pleasantly amused look he asks, "Why are you laughing, beautiful?"

I bite my lip not wanting to answer, but he rolls onto his back taking me with him. Our bodies are still connected and Matt holds me to his chest with his arms, keeping them wrapped around my waist. I lower my body to him and lay my head on his shoulder, burying my face against his neck, wanting to prolong this moment.

He kisses my head and we lay in silence for a few minutes just listening to each other breath. I'm scared to speak, from fear of what will come out, but I hear Matt speak first. "I love you beautiful, and I really want to make this work."

I sigh into Matt's neck and then lift my head, staring into his eyes. By the way he's looking at me right now, I know he really means it, and there's no one else in the world I want more than him.

"I love you too, Matt," I say, lowering my head to kiss him, "but how much do you really want?" I desperately ask.

"I want everything. I want to wake up next to you every morning. I want to fall asleep next to you, knowing that I'm going to hold you all night. I want to be there for you whenever you need me, but most of all, I want the whole world to know that you're mine," he declares.

My eyes tear up, but this time, instead of the hurtful tears I'm used to having when it comes to him, they're happy tears. My body starts to slowly float up to the clouds all over again, knowing that Matthew Garcia is finally mine as well. He might not have made it a promise, but I don't care, I'm willing to make the promise for both of us.

I feel him awaken again inside me as he starts to rock my body against his and I eventually take over, once again declaring our love to each other. Promising never to let go.

Are promises always kept?
Find out in the continuation of Matt and Abigail's story in
*Unspoken Promises*.

# Acknowledgments

To my husband and children. Thank you for putting up with my grouchy attitude during this journey, it was a tough one, but I wouldn't change it for the world. You stood by me during the frustration of this journey and I love you so much for that.

To my mom, Rosa, you were the one who opened my eyes to reading and I am forever grateful to you for that. You believed in me from the start, and without your words of encouragement I would have never pushed forward.

To my first official fan Marisol A. Thank you for letting me make a reader out of you, you're one of the reasons why I will keep writing.

To Cassia Leo, for sharing your story to the world for me to read, without it I would have never found the courage to write this book.

To Christa Simpson, for being my second opinion and giving me the advice I always needed.

I have to thank my Crazies…they're too many to name, but they know exactly who they are. You have made me smile when I needed it, laughed harder than I wish to, but most of all, been there with me through this whole process.

Although they were the reasons that I didn't make most of my deadlines on time, I still love every single one of you.

Most importantly, to my fellow Honey Badgers: George, Sarah, Jackie, Susan, and Bert. You guys helped me find my inner Abigail on every single run. You were always there to push me every mile of the way and never let me give up. Those memories will stay in my heart and mind forever.

Last, but not least, to all the betas, readers, and bloggers who took the time to read Unspoken Memories. Without you I wouldn't have a reason to write. Thank you from the bottom of my heart.

For more information about Gabbie
and her books, visit:

## GOODREADS

www.goodreads.com/author/show/7093957.Gabbie_S_Duran

## FACEBOOK

www.facebook.com/authorgabbiesduran

## TWITTER

https://twitter.com/gabbiesduran